THE KITCHEN BOY

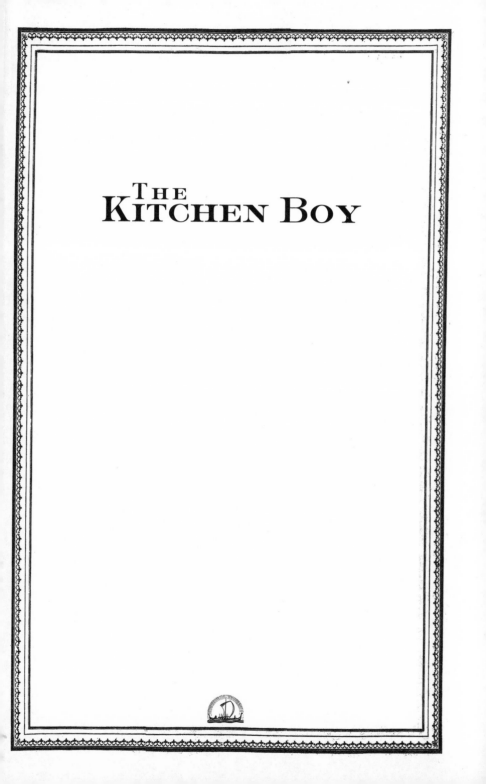

The
KITCHEN BOY

Robert Alexander

viking

VIKING
Published by the Penguin Group
Penguin Putnam Inc., 375 Hudson Street,
New York, New York 10014, U.S.A.
Penguin Books Ltd, 80 Strand,
London WC2R 0RL, England
Penguin Books Australia Ltd, 250 Camberwell Road, Camberwell,
Victoria 3124, Australia
Penguin Books Canada Ltd, 10 Alcorn Avenue,
Toronto, Ontario, Canada M4V 3B2
Penguin Books India (P) Ltd, 11 Community Centre, Panchsheel Park,
New Delhi–110 017, India
Penguin Books (N.Z.) Ltd, Cnr Rosedale and Airborne Roads, Albany,
Auckland, New Zealand
Penguin Books (South Africa) (Pty) Ltd, 24 Sturdee Avenue,
Rosebank, Johannesburg 2196, South Africa

Penguin Books Ltd, Registered Offices:
Harmondsworth, Middlesex, England

First published in 2003 by Viking Penguin,
a member of Penguin Putnam, Inc.

3   5   7   9   10   8   6   4   2

Publisher's Note
This is a work of fiction. Names, characters, places, and incidents either are the product
of the author's imagination or are used fictitiously, and any resemblance to actual persons,
living or dead, business establishments, events, or locales is entirely coincidental.

Library of Congress Cataloging-in-Publication Data

Alexander, Robert, 1952–
The kitchen boy / Robert Alexander.
p.   cm.
ISBN 0-670-03178-X
1. Nicholas II, Emperor of Russia, 1868–1918—Assassination—Fiction.
2. Nicholas II, Emperor of Russia, 1868–1918—Family—Assassination—
Fiction.   3. Russia—History—Revolution, 1917–1921—Fiction.
4. Assassination—Fiction.   5. Witnesses—Fiction.   I. Title.

PS3601.L355 K47 2003
813'6—dc21   2002066383

This book is printed on acid-free paper. ♾

Printed in the United States of America
Set in AGaramond
Designed by Erin Benach

In memory of my mother,
Elizabeth Cottrell

Acknowledgments

Many thanks to many people, particularly to:

Lars, who's been by my side since the start of all things Russian. Meri and Sasha, the dearest of friends who by chance and good fortune happen to be the best business partners. My writing pal, Ellen Hart, with whom I talk all the time but never enough. Katie Solomonson, my favorite reader. Dr. Don Houge and his vision. Susan Moody for her constant support. Olga for her help. James Rea for his innovative book trailer, www.thekitchenboy.com. Leslie Schnur and her brilliant insights. Jane von Mehren and Stephen Morrison at Viking for restoring my faith. And my particular gratitude to my agent, Marly Rusoff, who not only steered a steady course but made it wonderful.

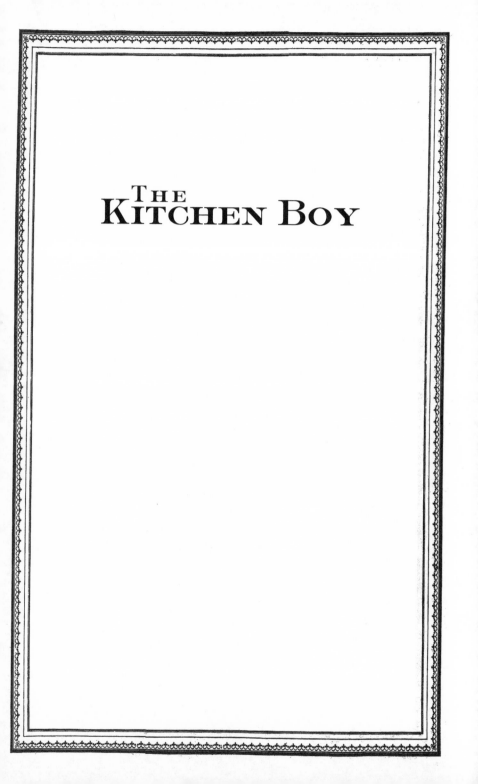

THE
KITCHEN BOY

Prologue

Saint Petersburg, Russia
Summer 2001

Peering through the peephole of her apartment door, the old woman didn't know what to do. Finally, she cleared her throat and called out in a voice as frail as an October leaf.

"Kto tam?" Who's there?

On the other side of the thick, padded door, the young stranger, tall and striking, her hair brown and thick, replied not in Russian, but English, saying, "A friend from America."

Instantly, the babushka's weary eyes blossomed with tears. It could be no one else. It had to be the girl from Chicago. And realizing it was the moment she had both feared and prayed for, the aged Russian beat her chest in a frantic cross. Next, almost without thinking, her hands worked the crude Soviet lock and she heaved back the door. Fully aware of their miraculous collision of fate, the two women stood in quiet awe.

The American, her eyes shimmering with tears of relief and grief, broke the awkward silence. "Perhaps you don't realize who I am, but—"

In a language she had barely spoken since before the times of

Stalin, the woman strained for the English words, and in a hushed, careful voice said, "I know who you are, dear Katya. Of course I do, and not just from what they write of you in these newspaper stories, either. *Konechno, nyet.*" Of course not. "No, you should not have come . . . but I prayed with all my heart that you would, which of course, was so very selfish of me." She reached out, touching Kate first on the shoulder, then her soft cheek. "Yes, it's really you, and yet . . . yet how did you even think to come looking for me?"

Hiding her pain behind a pathetic smile, the young woman pulled a cassette tape from her black leather purse. "My grandfather left this for me."

"I see," muttered the babushka with a wise cluck of her tongue. "Now come in, my child. Come in quickly. We have much to discuss and you can't be seen standing out here."

1

America
Summer 1998

"My name is Mikhail Semyonov. I live in Lake Forest village, Illinois state, the United States of America. I am ninety-four years old. I was born in Russia before the revolution. I was born in Tula province and my name then was not Mikhail or even Misha, as I am known here in America. No, my real name—the one given to me at birth—was Leonid Sednyov, and I was known as Leonka. Please forgive my years of lies, but now I tell you the truth. What I wish to confess is that I was the kitchen boy in the Ipatiev House where the Tsar and Tsaritsa, Nikolai and Aleksandra, were imprisoned. This was in Siberia. And . . . and the night they were executed I was sent away. They sent me away, but I snuck back, and that night, the moonless night of July 16–17, 1918, I saw the Tsar and his family come down the back twenty-three steps of the Ipatiev House, I saw them go into that cellar room . . . and I saw them shot. Trust me, believe me, when I say this: I am the last living witness and I alone know what really happened that awful night . . . just as I alone know where the bodies of the two missing children are to be found. You see, I took care of them with my own hands."

Misha took a deep breath, tried to push himself on, but couldn't. Panicking, he hit the *stop* button on his tape recorder, and just sat there on the flagstone terrace of his home, his eyes fixed straight ahead on the curling waters of Lake Michigan. Despite his determination, he'd faltered, been unable to proceed.

Over the many years since the Russian Revolution, Misha had come to realize that on a single night in 1918 he had witnessed far too much for an entire lifetime, particularly in the tortured silence he had so sternly observed in the ensuing decades. But such was his punishment. He was an old man, certain that this long life and clear memory were the torture he deserved. Yes, there was a God, for if there were not he would have been spared this suffering. Instead he kept on living. And remembering. True, he had gained some wisdom, for over the course of all this time he had come to look at that night as the start of everything horrible that had since befallen his poor Rossiya. As he looked back from these United States and through the distance of the decades, it was all so clear. A great curse was unleashed that night, inundating every corner of his vast homeland. If his comrades could commit such an act, was it any wonder that Stalin could kill upward of twenty million of his own people? No, of course not. On a hot night in the Siberian city of Yekaterinburg the individual had become expendable.

Misha was a tall man who walked with the slightest of limps, but over the last fifteen years, of course, he had grown smaller and his gait more halting as his body had settled and lost muscle mass. He'd always been trim, and it was this leanness that had undoubtedly contributed to his longevity and his lack of major illness. His hair, which he had always combed straight back in an elegant manner, had been snow white for more than thirty years, and while it had receded only slightly, it had definitely thinned. His face was narrow and long, his nose simply narrow, while his upper lip was straight and noticeably, almost oddly, small. Since his fifties, the tone of his skin had gone from robust to ruddy to its present parchment color, skin that now hung loosely from his sharp cheekbones. Always a dapper dresser, he wore lightweight gray wool pants and a yellow cashmere sweater over a pressed and starched blue shirt from Brooks Brothers.

Seated in a wrought iron chair on the raised terrace behind his grand, twenty-room house, he stared out over the bluff and at the lake, himself the very image of old Chicago money. Nothing, however, could have been further from the truth, for when he'd arrived in the United States in 1920 he'd had but a rucksack, one suitcase, and the clothes he was wearing. And while everyone believed that he'd made his millions on the stock market down at the Chicago Board of Trade, that too was a lie, albeit one that he had carefully cultivated.

Staring out at Lake Michigan, Misha was transfixed by the flashes of light upon the blue water, flashes that sparkled like diamonds. He'd been tormented his entire life because of that night more than eighty years ago, a night which until now he'd never spoken of to anyone except May, his beloved wife. But now he must, now he had no choice. May was already two weeks in the grave, and he was determined to follow her as soon as possible. Before he left this world, however, he had certain obligations, namely, to reveal a kind of truth to their only heir, their lovely granddaughter, Kate. May, who'd also fled Russia after the revolution, fully understood the delicacy of the matter, and even though she'd helped Misha decide just how it might be done, he'd put it off. Now, however, the time had come, he could wait no more: he must give the young woman not simply a way to understand, but a reason to fulfill a pledge he had made so long ago. No, he thought, he had to give her more than a reason. He had to set her on a mission, his mission, otherwise he feared she might flounder in confusion, even despair, and perhaps thereby stumble upon . . . upon . . . No, thought Misha, he couldn't let that happen.

He raised his wrist and checked his thick, gold watch, which these days hung so loosely on his thin wrist. It was teatime. And if May were still alive, he would be joining her upstairs. Their maid would bring up a pot of tea, Misha and May would each have exactly two cups, a biscuit or two, and May, who'd been bedridden for the past three years, would reminisce about Russia, as she had done so frequently in her last

5

years, chatting about this and that, but . . . but . . . well, she was gone. All that was over. And now Misha needed to take care of this as soon as possible.

Clutching the tape recorder in one of his thin hands, with the other he grabbed the arm of the wrought iron chair and pulled himself forward. With no small amount of effort, he pushed himself to his feet. And then he simply stood there, swaying like a flag in a gentle breeze. Once he'd gained his balance, he started across the flagstones, one hesitant step at a time. At the house, he pulled open one of the French doors, lifted up his foot, focused all his attention on the effort, then stepped into the grand central hallway, a gallery of sorts, that ran from the front to the back of the house. The living room lay immediately to his right, and he carefully made his way into this grand room with its dark-beamed ceiling and matching woodwork. At the far end stood the focal point, the large, stone fireplace amputated from some French château, while a palace-sized Oriental carpet in deep reds and blues ran from one end to the other.

As he moved slowly through the room, Misha wondered what his granddaughter was going to do with it all, these antiques, the oil paintings, the Tiffany sterling and Steuben crystal bric-a-brac that May and he had collected over the decades. Perhaps she and her husband would keep everything, perhaps they would sell it all. He didn't much care, these common things didn't matter. However, the numerous Fabergé items—including the little jade bulldog with the diamond eyes that sat on the coffee table and the cobalt blue enamel opera glasses of the Tsaritsa's sister perched over there on the piano—were an entirely different matter. He'd left detailed instructions in his will, and he prayed Kate would follow his precise instructions. If only his story would induce her to do just that.

On the far side of the living room Misha moved through an arched opening and into his library that was filled with two red leather chairs, a large desk, and a massive built-in walnut bookcase that held his entire collection of books on the Russian royal family. Focused on the task at hand, he went directly to his desk and put down the small black tape recorder, laying it next to a manila folder—his dossier—which contained a variety of historical documents. Sure, a thousand truths, that was what it was going to take to convince his Katya, daughter of his son, which was precisely why he'd carefully collected copies of letters and diary entries and telegrams from that time. And he would not only read from these, but leave the complete dossier for her to peruse, even scrutinize.

Wasting no time, he sat down, opened the top desk drawer, and withdrew a sheet of letterhead. He then took a gold ink pen, and wrote:

August 27, 1998

My Dearest Katya,

    This tape and these documents are for you. Perhaps together they will help you understand the complete picture. Please forgive me. Yours forever with love and devotion,

Dyedushka Misha

Satisfied, he laid aside the pen and paper. And now he had no choice but to continue, to press on to the end. He reached for the small tape recorder, held the microphone to his dry lips, turned the machine back on, and slid into the past.

"Yes, so as I was saying, my sweet one, I know what happened that horrible night the Romanovs were murdered. But the truth of the matter is that the beginning of the end of my Nikolai and Aleksandra commenced a few weeks earlier, which is to say I'll never forget the twentieth of June, 1918, the day we received the first of the secret notes."

2

It was as warm as only Siberia could be in the summer—humid, buggy, stifling. You'd never expect such a warmth in Siberia, but the northern sun, which had only set for a few brief hours, was already rising high, and in a couple of hours it would be hot, so very hot, in the Ipatiev House. To make matters worse, all the windows on the main floor had been painted over with lime and we hadn't been allowed to open a single one, which greatly irritated Tsar Nikolai. In the past few days it had been like an oven, really, all of us crammed in there without any fresh air blowing through. And it smelled so . . . so stuffy. That wasn't just from the samovar or from our cooking, either. No, it was the guards who roamed our rooms at will, the guards who perhaps bathed only at Easter and on their birthdays. They were so stinky, I say kindly. Greasy and filthy. For two weeks the former Emperor had been asking—just a single window, just a little fresh air, that was all the former Tsar wanted for his family, but the *Bolsheviki* have always proved inept at making the simplest of decisions, except of course when it comes to purges and murder. I can't imagine what it must have been like for him, for Nikolai Aleksandrovich. One day he commands one-sixth of the world, the next he isn't even in charge of a single pane of glass. Plus the Tsar had been suffering from hemorrhoids—he'd been in bed one whole day earlier that week. I've been told it was hereditary.

Sure, my sweet Katya, we know many intimate things of those last weeks. In the dossier—the one I've made for you—I have part of his diary, in which Tsar Nikolai himself wrote:

> Thursday, June sixth. My hemorrhoids gave me terrible pain all day, so I lay down on the bed because it is more comfortable to apply compresses that way. Alix and Aleksei spent half an hour in the fresh air, and after they returned we went out for an hour.

Aleksandra—his Alix—was more circumspect, less trusting, but not Nikolai. He wrote everything in his diary, including their plans to escape.

So that was the way it was when the first of the four notes came, all of us stuck there in that stuffy house that smelled of unwashed guards and soup that had been reheated too many times. And that was how I became involved. After all, the Tsar of all the Russias—even if there'd been a revolution—never opened his own milk bottle. *Konechno, nyet.* Of course not. That was my job, me, Leonka, the kitchen boy. Sure, and my morning duties also included getting the samovar going and greeting the nuns who brought us additional foodstuffs. For a long while no sisters had been permitted into The House of Special Purpose, which was how the *Bolsheviki* had rechristened the Ipatiev House, but then all of a sudden they were bringing us milk and eggs and bread a few times a week. Komendant Avdeyev, who was in charge before Yurovksy took over, changed his mind out of the blue. I think he was bribed. I think Rasputin's daughter, who lived in a village not far away, gave him money.

The Ipatiev House was fairly new, but constructed in the style of old Muscovy with an elaborate facade and exaggerated cornices. It sat on the side of a small hill, with the main living quarters on the upper floor facing Ascension Square in the front, and the service rooms in the lower level opening onto the garden in the rear. Built of brick and big stone that was whitewashed, the house was topped with a low, green metal roof. It wasn't like the governor's house in Tobolsk town, where the Romanovs and all of us had first been kept in Siberia. That was more like a summer palace, while this, the Ipatiev House, was more like the home of a well-to-do merchant. Yet even though it was supposed to look like the home of a boyar—an old nobleman—it was in fact a modern house with indoor plumbing and even electricity, including electric glass chandeliers that came to life with the turn of a switch. This house stood, as a matter of fact, all the way until the 1960s, when a young Boris Yeltsin ordered it demolished because it was becoming a secret shrine for monarchists.

And so, early that morning of the twentieth I was going about my duties not in the main kitchen down below, but in the makeshift kitchen that had recently been set up for our use on the main level. I was as thin as a reed and fairly tall for a fourteen-year-old, and yet I was still not big enough for my large feet, which caused me no end of awkwardness. My cheeks were large and rosy with youth, and after I had stuffed the center chimney of the brass samovar with charcoal and pinecones and bits of straw I huffed and puffed on a glimmer of fire. I was just getting it lit, just attaching the vent to the outside, when in walked our Sister Antonina and her young novice, both of them dressed in a waterfall of black. A good share of the nun's face was swathed—the black head cloth covered her forehead, went around her eyes, and the folds of her wimple came up just under her mouth, so that even her chin was covered. A pink, plump windshield of a face— that was all you could see of our sister, a dumpling of a nun who was not only a good deal shorter than me, but who seemed so terribly ancient. The novice, on the other hand, was not so severely dressed; she wore a black gown and black head cloth, but her face was not covered.

"Good morning, my son," said the nun, coming in with her usual basket.

With my right hand I tamed my brown hair. "Good morning to you, Sister Antonina."

"I believe you know my charge, Marina."

Of course I did, and I bowed my head slightly to the girl. She blossomed the color of a soft rose petal, which in turn caused my cheeks to flush with warmth. She was about my age, the daughter of a local Russian woman and an Englishman who had worked for years at the English consulate there in Yekaterinburg. They said the girl was very well educated, that she spoke both perfect English and perfect Russian, even some French, though she hardly ever said anything to me.

Sister Antonina said, "We have brought more fresh goods for . . ."

She glanced out the door and down the hall, spying a guard, a young fellow with a blond beard, who had been recruited from the local Zlokazov Factory, where not long ago the workers, infected by the Reds, had revolted and killed their bosses. This young man carried his rifle over his right shoulder—not his left, of course, for that was the rule of the evil "formers"—and had a hand grenade hanging from his belt, and Sister Antonina, taking note of him, dared not finish the sentence. *Nyet, nyet.* As far as she was concerned, Nikolai Aleksandrovich was still her Tsar, but she dared not refer to him as *Y'evo Velichestvo*— His Greatness—for she'd be thrown in jail for that. Nor could she bring herself to call him something ridiculous like *Tovarish* or *Grazhdanin*—Comrade or Citizen—Romanov.

Setting the basket on a small table, Sister Antonina said, "The milk is still warm from the cow. The eggs are just as fresh too—Marina herself gathered them only an hour ago."

"*Spacibo bolshoye, sestra.*" Thank you very much, sister, I replied.

"The butter is very good. You must try some butter on the bread. It's so nice and sweet."

"*Da, da, da.*"

It was then that I noticed that Sister Antonina was still leaning against the edge of the table, her eyes fixed on me, her body not moving a centimeter. I stared back. What, had I done something wrong?

Again I said, "*Spacibo bolshoye, sestra.* I'll take care of everything."

"The eggs are for The Little One," she said, referring to Aleksei Nikolaevich, the Tsar's son, who suffered so terribly from what we called the English disease, hemophilia.

"Certainly."

Turning around, Sister Antonina nodded ever so slightly to Novice Marina. The girl edged slightly out into the hall, looked one way, the other, then offered a small nod in return. Sister Antonina, satisfied that the guard with the blond beard was no longer nearby, reached into her basket and lifted the glass bottle of milk.

"Take this, *molodoi chelovek.*" Young man.

Her eyes were fixed on mine, and I stepped over and took the bottle from her, which contained a *chetvert* of milk, something like two liters. And just like she said, it was still warm from the cow.

She whispered, "Open this bottle at once. God willing, we will be back in a few days."

I was young and clumsy in many ways, but I understood. Since the ancient Time of Troubles, which preceded Tsar Mikhail, the very first of the many Romanovs, we Russians have used our eyes to say what our mouths cannot speak. And Sister Antonina did this, staring at me and then blinking both of her eyes. I dared not move. Rather, I just stood there, clutching the warm *chetvert* as the sister moved into the hallway, the antechamber that separated the kitchen from the dining room. There she said a few kindly words to one of the guards, who in turn gruffly escorted her to the front of the house and out. Later on, of course, the Reds killed her for that, for being part of the plan to save the Romanovs.

Well, so, once the *sestra* and novice were gone, I turned my back to the hallway and stared down at the bottle of milk. There was something special about it, of that I had no doubt, but just what I certainly couldn't tell. I stood there in my worn, brown pants and white shirt of coarse cotton, then swirled the milk around in its container. Everything, however, looked, well, *normalno.* I decided to take a whiff of it, perhaps even taste it, so I tugged at the cork stopper, pulled it out, and smelled the rich, creamy milk. And that was when I saw it. Rather, I felt it first—the slip of paper. A tiny pocket had been cut into the side of the cork and a small piece of paper had been tucked in, which is what I felt—the sharp edge of the paper. Knowing the danger, I glanced over my shoulder and saw no one. There were some noises in the house as the Tsar and his family started to get up from bed, but I was alone there in the kitchen, just me and the samovar, which was starting to rattle as it warmed. I tugged at the paper, pulled it out, and unfolded it. Although I could read and write back then, I couldn't make out a single word, for it wasn't in Russian. Rather, I recognized the letters of the Latin alphabet, but just what language I couldn't tell—French, German, English, they were all the same to me.

Only much, much later did I learn that it said: *"Les amis ne dorment plus et espèrent que l'heure si longtemps attendue est arrivée . . ."*

All the notes, even the replies from the Romanovs, were to be in the French. I didn't memorize any of them back then. And of course I thought them lost forever, so I was greatly surprised when a few years ago I opened up a book and there they all were, every single one of the secret notes, completely reprinted. All this time, all these years, the original note that I had pulled from that cork—as well as the next three—had been carefully stored in the Gosudarstvenyi Arkhiv Rossiskoi Federatsii in Moscow. Sure, as incredible as it may seem, these notes are still there in the State Archive of the Russian Federation, proving beyond a doubt that there'd been a plot to save the Imperial Family.

Da, da, Katya, *vnoochka moya*—granddaughter of mine—for a brief while there'd been a candle of hope in the note that read:

> Friends are no longer sleeping and hope that the hour so long awaited has come. The revolt of the Czechoslovaks threatens the Bolsheviks ever more seriously. Samara, Cheliabinsk, and all of eastern and western Siberia are in the hands of the provisional national government. The army of Slavic friends is eighty kilometers from Yekaterinburg. The soldiers of

the Red Army cannot effectively resist. Be attentive
to any movement from the outside; wait and hope.
But at the same time, I beg you, be careful, because
the Bolsheviks, before being <u>vanquished, represent
real and serious danger for you</u>. Be ready at every
hour, day and night. Make a drawing of your ~~two~~
three bedrooms showing the position of the furniture, the beds. Write the hour that you all go to bed.
One of you must not sleep between 2:00 and 3:00 on
all the following nights. Answer with a few words,
but, please, give all the useful information for your
friends from the outside. You must give your answer
<u>in writing</u> to the same soldier who transmits this note
to you, <u>but do not say a single word</u>.

From someone who is ready to die for you,
An Officer of the Russian Army

Ever fearful, I carefully folded up the small note and slipped it in
my pocket. This was something important, something dangerous,
something for the Tsar, but I just went about my business, unloading
the basket. I took out the eight eggs—brown and not so terribly big—
and the pale butter, which was in a little billycan covered with a torn
piece of oil cloth. And as I waited for the large brass samovar to boil,
my face beaded with sweat, my heart raced, and my mind struggled for
a course of action. I couldn't just barge into the Tsar's bedroom while
he and Aleksandra Fyodorovna were getting up.

Suddenly a voice behind me boomed, "Well, Leonka, so the fire's
lit and the water is heating? *Ochen xoroshow.*" Very good.

It was cook Kharitonov, all groggy and yawning, his shirt a mess,
his oily hair sticking up. He hadn't shaved in almost a week, but then
I hadn't had a bath in almost a month. Komendant Avdeyev didn't allow us to make that much hot water, although Nikolai Aleksandrovich
had been granted a bath of nine liters just the day before.

I thought I should tell him, but I remained quiet, for even then I understood the importance of the note.

And so I lied, "Yevgeny Sergeevich has asked for a glass of water." I was referring to Dr. Botkin of course. Dr. Yevgeny Sergeevich Botkin, the Tsar's personal physician, who had voluntarily followed the family into exile and imprisonment.

Kharitonov puffed out his lower lip. "So do as the good doctor requests, lad, and take him his glass of water."

The drinking water was in a large crock covered with a cloth, and I took a dipper and ladled water into a thin glass with a chipped rim. Saying nothing more, I headed out, clutching the glass in both hands because I was shaking so. As I skirted the dining room, I saw one of the *Bolsheviki* leading the Tsar's second daughter, Tatyana Nikolaevna, to the water closet on the far side of the house, because that was the way it was, none of the Romanovs could use the facilities without being escorted by an armed guard. Tatyana Nikolaevna, so thin, so pretty, her light brown hair put up, glanced briefly at me, smiled slightly, and hurried on as a guard with a rifle and hand grenade followed immediately after her. She had turned twenty-one just the previous month.

Walking so very carefully lest I spill a drop, I passed from the dining room into the drawing room, where the manservant, Trupp, was putting away his bed things. I proceeded quickly past him to the alcove at the far end, where Dr. Botkin slept on a cot next to a wooden desk. When I walked in, the doctor was standing next to a large potted palm and fastening his suspenders.

I was almost too afraid to speak, but in case there were any guards nearby, I forced myself to loudly say, "I brought the water you requested, Yevgeny Sergeevich."

He was a tall man, a big fellow with a goatee, small gold specs, and little eyes, whose granddaughter, by the way, still lives in Virginia. Well, this Dr. Botkin just stared at me, surprised at my impudence. Without hesitation, I went up to the wooden desk and set down the glass of water, managing of course to spill a bit in the process. As I frantically mopped aside the water with my hand, I glanced about the drawing room. There were no soldiers, so I jabbed my hand in my pocket, pulled out the small folded piece of paper, and dropped it on the desk next to the glass.

"This was hidden in the milk stopper," I whispered, my voice trembling.

Studying me, he screwed up his eyes and then quickly snatched the note from the desktop. I know he wanted to ask me what in the devil's name I was talking about, but only his eyes dared question. I turned and scurried out, just like that, and returned to the kitchen where cook Kharitonov was preparing the tiny pot of concentrated tea and slicing black bread, yesterday's of course, which was no longer so moist but still nice and sour.

Despite my worries, I was exactly right in what I did, in how I handled the note. Going that early into Nikolai Aleksandrovich's bed-chamber might have attracted attention. However, directly approaching Yevgeny Sergeevich did not. And I trusted the doctor would know exactly how to handle the situation, for he was not only the Tsar's personal physician, not only his close adviser, but at this point in their captivity also his dear friend.

I didn't know then if Dr. Botkin could read the letter since it was written in a foreigner's tongue, but he immediately passed it on to the Tsar and his wife. Aleksandra Fyodorovna, a woman of tightly strung nerves, never slept well, and hence was always loath to rise in the morning, particularly by eight-fifteen for the morning inspections. Such were the rules, however, and in the twenty or thirty minutes that passed between the time I gave Dr. Botkin the note and when the *komendant* viewed the household, Dr. Botkin must have entered the Tsar's personal room. The Emperor and Empress shared the corner room with their ailing son, the Heir. And Dr. Botkin must have gone there under the pretext of checking Aleksei or perhaps the Empress herself—she had a bad heart, not to mention bad legs—and then slipped them the piece of paper.

By the time we were gathered for inspection it was obvious the Romanovs had read the note. Ever since the Heir's lackey, Nagorny, had been hauled off to prison, we had been using the Empress's rolling chaise, a large wicker device on wheels, to carry the Heir, for Aleksei was still recovering from a recent bleeding episode. And as I pushed Aleksei into the dining room and around the end of the table, I burned red with embarrassment akin to fear as the Tsar and Tsaritsa stared upon me, Leonka, the kitchen boy. Had I done wrong? Was I in trouble?

Even though Aleksei Nikolaevich was ill, even though he had lost so much weight, everyone kept saying he was growing as fast as a mushroom after a spring rain, and it was true. Tsar Nikolai, who took after his diminutive mother, was the exception in the family, for he was no taller than five feet six or seven inches. On the other hand, the Heir Aleksei, had he not been murdered, would have been a real Romanov, tall as a tree and big as a bear. And that summer the two of us were nearly the same height. He had dark hair, bright, sharp eyes that seemed to drink in everything, and as usual he wore a white bed shirt and his legs were covered with a blanket. That day, though, he told me he'd slept poorly—truly, this handsome lad was as pale as the moon, his skin almost translucent—because hours ago he had been woken by Red troops marching past the house.

"The Whites are on the way!" he whispered with excitement as I positioned him next to his mother.

So there we all were, gathered in the dining room, the seven Romanovs, Botkin, maid Demidova, cook Kharitonov, valet Trupp, and me. Lining up behind the heavy oak table, we automatically assumed our positions, first the Tsar, the Tsaritsa, the Heir Tsarevich, the four daughters from oldest to youngest, and then the five of us, from Dr. Botkin down to me, the last. That was the way it always had been at court before the revolution and still was in this house, everyone perfectly aware of their rank and automatically assuming their preordained position. And what a handsome family they were. As always Nikolai wore a khaki field shirt with the epaulets ripped off—cut away by order of the *Bolsheviki*—khaki pants of coarse cotton, worn brown leather boots, and of course that cross of Saint George on his chest.

Sure, he was short, sure his nose was a bit stubby and his neck not too long, but he was trim, his arms surprisingly strong, his beard so beautiful, his eyes so sweet, his voice deep and rich. And Aleksandra? She was quite tall, quite imposing and regal, and that morning she wore little jeweled ornamentation and the same loose, dark blue cotton dress she had been wearing for many days. Though she was by then painfully thin, in her youth she had been a true beauty, her hair light, her complexion pure and white. It was no wonder their girls were so beautiful, their son such a treasure.

Waiting for the Bolshevik leader, all of us stood silent except Anastasiya Nikolaevna, the youngest daughter. In her arms she held her little black and tan dog, Jimmy, the tiniest of King Charles spaniels, and the young Grand Duchess kept saying little bits of nothing into the creature's ears as she rocked him back and forth.

Finally Komendant Avdeyev came in—a fat man with a greasy beard and dirty shirt—who always went beltless. He suffered from the Russian disease, which perturbed the Tsar, because he couldn't abide that, such inveterate drinking. Or disorder for that matter. Nikolai Aleksandrovich was a tidy man by nature, and he hated Avdeyev, particularly since Avdeyev had been allowing the other guards to slowly loot the shed where the Romanovs had their trunks stored. The *komendant* said they needed to examine everything, but in reality they were pilfering linens and table services and selling these fine goods in the town market. When this was later discovered, Avdeyev was rightly sent to the front.

As ever, the *komendant* was a mess, an awful sight. More than likely he'd polished off an entire bottle of vodka the night before, and that morning he must have just gotten up because his hair went every which way, his eyes were all swollen, and even his shirt was unbuttoned. I glanced at the Empress, who was glaring at him with disdain. Anastasiya started to giggle, but then her mother gave her the eye.

Avdeyev, who could barely focus, rubbed his eyes, and grumbled, "So, Nikolashka, are all of you here?"

All of us flinched—using that form of Nikolai's name was incredibly rude, especially for the country's number one person—but the Tsar, good soldier that he was, not to mention former commander in chief of the world's largest army, calmly replied, *"Da-s,* all of us are present."

I thought that would be it, that we would be dismissed, but then this slob of a man leaned on the table with both hands, cocked one of his fat eyes, and turned to me and said, "Tell me, Leonka, no one plans to secretly escape, now do they?"

Suddenly I had to pee just terribly. It flashed through my mind that they'd caught Sister Antonina and tortured her. Was this a trap? Did they know about the note?

"Speak up, Leonka," commanded Avdeyev. "You're young, but I'm sure you have big eyes. You haven't seen anything suspicious going on, have you? Hey?"

"Well, I . . ."

Everyone in the room, from the Tsar on down, turned and stared at me, the little kitchen boy with the big feet. I thought the Empress was going to faint right there. The first serious attempt to save them, and she thought I was going to blow it.

"Nyet-s," I replied, which was short for *"nyet-soodar"*—no, monsignor—for that was how proper people of that day spoke.

He eyed me, studied me for the longest moment. I swear he was going to ask me more questions when all of a sudden Aleksei's dog, Joy, a black and white English spaniel, came bolting into the room with a squealing animal in its mouth.

Demidova, the Empress's maid, tall and chubby, screamed, "Oi, the dog has a rat!"

"Bozhe moi," my God, "it's alive!" exclaimed Botkin.

Well, you should have heard the girls scream. Those grand duchesses had lived an extraordinarily sheltered life. Sure, the entire family had been imprisoned ever since their father's abdication eighteen months earlier, but they'd all been more or less imprisoned in the Alexander Palace in Tsarskoye their entire lives. Rarely had they been exposed to the world beyond the golden walls of their nursery, which is to say I'm sure that no daughter of *Evo Imperatorskoye Velichestvo Nikolai V'toroi*—His Imperial Greatness Nikolai the Second—Tsar of All the Russias, Poland, Finland, and so on and so forth had ever seen a big fat dirty rat before that moment. And all hell broke loose. No Bolshevik guard could control those white princesses, and they went running and screaming out of there so very fast. That in turn scared the dog, who had simply brought to his masters a wonderful trophy, this big fat rat with a long, skinny, pink tail. And when the girls screamed, Joy dropped the rat, and Aleksei . . . Aleksei . . .

Well, the *Naslednik*, the Heir, seeing the rat scamper in terror around the dining room of The House of Special Purpose, suddenly came to life, and he led the charge, sounding like his mightiest ancestor, the terrible Ivan, as he shouted, "After it, Leonka!"

He was a rascal, that boy. A real imp. He'd been deathly ill, but he'd also been deathly bored, just lying around in a hot, stuffy house in Siberia, the windows painted over with lime so that he couldn't even look out. What could be worse for a child? And this rat was surely the most exciting thing Aleksei had come across in months.

Following my orders, I shoved the wheeled chaise along, charging around the heavy oak dining room table. Everyone was yelling, the dog was barking, the girls screaming, and this rat . . . well, I drove the chaise as if it were the wildest of troikas, dashing this way and that, following each and every order of my young master—turn to the left, the right, there over by the sideboard, Leonka! Wait, no, next to the fireplace, go! Charge! The Empress didn't budge—she wasn't terrified of the rat, she just stood there, hands clasped to her cheeks, terrified lest anything happen to her beloved son, that I might crash him and an entirely new bleeding episode would begin.

After a few short moments we had this fat, juicy rat cornered, Aleksei and I did. The dog was ready to bolt forward, but Aleksei leaned from his vehicle and grabbed Joy by the scruff of its neck, and we all stood staring at the big rat, and it curled back its teeny lips, exposed its little teeth, and snarled back at us.

And then Aleksei, *Naslednik* to the House of Romanov and the throne of imperial Russia, released his dog, screaming, "Get him, Joy!" And what did the rat do? Well, it took off not toward the Tsar and Tsaritsa, but toward Komendant Avdeyev, who stood on the other side of the room. Avdeyev—big, old, fat, sleepy, hungover Avdeyev— yelped like a pig and turned and bolted into the hall, the rat chasing after him, the dog chasing after them both, all the way down those twenty-three steps and into the courtyard out back.

Aleksei burst into hysterics—can you imagine, a rat chasing away the Bolshevik pig? It was too perfect. In fact, I had never seen the Heir laugh so long, so carelessly, and that in turn started a chain reaction. The Empress was only somewhat amused by the scene, but she was overjoyed at seeing her sickly son so . . . so *vivant*. And then the Tsar started laughing, as did Botkin and the others. We all started and then we just couldn't stop.

"Bravo, Aleksei Nikolaevich!" called Botkin in a hushed voice so that the guards in the hall wouldn't hear.

It was the one and only time that I ever saw the Empress just let loose and laugh and laugh. And when she did she was so beautiful— that pure skin, those radiant blue-gray eyes. Before the war, all the best society and almost everyone at court had grown to disdain Aleksandra, calling her haughty and aloof. But that just wasn't so, that wasn't the Empress I knew. Instead, from what I saw back then and from my readings since, I've come to understand not only how nervous Aleksandra became in public, but how shy and reticent she was with anyone except her immediate family. In truth, I think, she was horribly depressed and insecure, for her soul was damaged, having lost her parents at a young age, and she was ever fearful of losing her son from a bleeding attack or her husband from an assassin's gun. But right then she clasped one hand over her mouth, one around her waist, and she rocked back and forth with such mirth. It's my guess that that was the last true laugh of her life.

"Nicky, can you believe it?" she managed to say in Russian, because of course those were the *komendant*'s orders, that they speak in the language understood by the guards.

Almost always the Tsar called her "Alix" but right then he said, "*Solnyshko*," Sunny, he said, using his pet name for his wife, "I . . . I . . ."

But lacking words, he came over and bussed her. He wrapped his strong arms around her and kissed her ever so passionately.

And even though there were others present, she spoke her heart, saying, "I love you. Those three words have my life in them."

Yes, this I know without a doubt: never have a king and queen loved each other more than Nikolai and Aleksandra.

3

Katya, do you know what is as asinine as *kommunizm*? Autocracy. One man, one person, cannot rule the hearts and minds of millions. Liberty, freedom, truth—this America can be such a silly place, so fickle and naive—sometimes so childish!—but it saves itself because of those first three things.

If only Nikolai hadn't so ardently believed in divine rule. If only he'd loosened the reigns. If only Aleksandra's first child had been a healthy boy. The whole country was waiting for an heir, and when she finally gave birth to a boy, her fifth child, and he turned out to be so sickly, it all but killed her, it truly did. You know, it's really so odd they called her *nemka*, the German. True, she was born a minor German princess, but after her young mother's death Aleksandra was raised primarily by her "darling Granny," as she called her beloved grandmother, Queen Victoria. So she was essentially English. And then during the Great War there was so much gossip and slander against the Tsaritsa. The newspapers printed such terrible things, they threw so much gas on the flames of discontent. Why, they wrote that she, the most prudish of all tsaritsas, slept with Rasputin, that mystical monk from Siberia whose hypnotic eyes alone eased the pain of Aleksandra's sickly son. Yes, Rasputin was a scoundrel of the first degree—his debauchery ruined the reputation of the Imperial Family and, no doubt about it, his horrendous advice to the Tsaritsa hastened the revolution—but did she ever have sexual relations with that tall, brutish man with the animalistic stare? Absolutely not. The papers also wrote that Aleksandra kept the Tsar perpetually drunk and had a direct telegraph cable line from her mauve boudoir to her relations in Berlin. And the Russian people—both the nobility and the masses—came to believe it all, that not only was she Rasputin's mistress, but that she was a traitor to the war and the fatherland. In fact, nothing could have been further from the truth. Why, after her husband's abdication they dug up her rooms, searched for that cable, and what did they find? Nothing! Aleksandra hated the Prussians, thought her cousin, the Kaiser, a fool, which he was. Her truth is revealed in a letter to her dearest confidant, Anna Vyrubova:

> What a nightmare, that the Germans are supposed to save everyone and establish order. What could be worse and more degrading than that? . . . God save and help Russia!

Actually, it wasn't Aleksandra but Lenin himself who dealt secretly with the Kaiser. It was the Germans who secretly smuggled Lenin back into Russia in a sealed train car, it was Lenin who signed away all of Poland and a third of European Russia in the treaty of Brest-Litovsk, it was . . .

Ouf, what's been spilled by buckets cannot be retrieved by droplets. Now where was I? Ah, *da,* the rat and the *komendant.* The gray rat was chasing the red pig, and the black and white dog was . . . was . . .

What a delicious scene!

Well, soon thereafter cook Kharitonov, the maid, Demidova, and I put out the tea. Kharitonov had made the tea concentrate, which he poured into each cup, then added the hot water from the spout of the samovar itself.

"Nice, hot, black *chai.*" Tea. "Again, no sugar. Again, no *limon.* But the children will love this!" said cook Kharitonov, reaching for a small bowl of fruit preserves.

"Strawberry jam—what a delight," exclaimed the maid, a woman with a round face and big body who was most devoted to her mistress. "Wherever did you get it?"

"Sister Antonina brought a jar a few days ago and I've been saving it as a surprise. One of the sisters made it from their own fruit. Now, go on you two. On your way."

Demidova carried a tray with the teacups, while I followed behind with the small bowl. Once she served the tea, she took the jam from my hands and placed it on the table with great flourish.

"What a nice treat we have for you this morning!" she said.

"Sweet preserves! Me first!" pleaded Anastasiya.

Aleksandra issued her dictum: "That will be fine, dear, but you must wait until everyone is seated."

As we took our places, we were overcome with awkwardness, for the *komendant* had ordered that we must all sit at one table, master and servant alike. The family and Dr. Botkin were already seated at the large, oak table, and one by one we sat, Demidova, Trupp, me, and cook Kharitonov, who came in bearing eggs for the Heir. The Romanovs accepted the brutal affront to rank more quickly than we, the last of the thousands upon thousands of attendants who had formerly waited upon them hand and foot. And even though we'd been doing this for weeks, it didn't feel right, the likes of me sitting right across the table from Nikolai Aleksandrovich, even if he was now the former Tsar.

Once we were all at the table, we waited for *Batyushka,* the Dear Father, to make the first move, signaling the start of our meal. When Nikolai Aleksandrovich reached for his spoon, however, he found nothing.

"Here, Papa," said Olga, the eldest daughter, unable to hide a smile.

But that's the way it always was. We were always a spoon, two forks, or a few knives short, because in addition to banishing silver and linen from the table as too decadent, the *komendant* had purposely ordered a deficit of cutlery.

"Thank you, my dear," said the Tsar to his daughter.

I thought the shortage of utensils very mean, very humiliating, but Nikolai and Aleksandra dealt with such rudeness without complaint, they did. Nikolai simply accepted it as his fate, for his saint's day was the day of Job, the long suffering, while Aleksandra found it her duty to follow her husband's example. And those five royal children likewise complied, never once complaining.

After the Tsar stirred his tea, we all began. That morning we were minus not only one spoon, but one knife as well, and soon the cutlery and the bread and the bowl of jam were going this way and that among us.

"Tatyana," commanded the royal mother, "make sure that Leonka gets some of the jam as well."

"Yes, Mama."

It was only for us children, that sweet heavenly mixture of fruit, and I was not to be excluded, nor was I ever, even though I was born of such lower state. They treated me with fairness and kindness at every turn that morning and every other.

Hardly a word was spoken during breakfast, and after we finished and were excused, I as usual assisted in the cleaning up. I was just wiping the crumbs from the table when Dr. Botkin appeared on the edge of the dining room.

"Leonka," he said, beckoning me with a slight tilt of his head.

Once I was sure no guards were watching, I headed after the doctor, and was led into the drawing room, a long spacious room with heavy furniture. The Emperor and Empress were seated by the two windows, and as soon as I approached they turned their attention upon me. The Empress even stood, rising from her chair.

By then Nikolai's beard was speckled with gray, and yet there was still a hint of blond or red around his mustache. He had recently turned fifty, and he was unusually fit, a firm believer in exercise, which

I hasten to add had been curtailed. I mean, their walks and wood sawing and such. And while he had terrible teeth, all crooked and tobacco-stained, it was the eyes that I remember the most. The Emperor had the most amazing bluish eyes, and when he held you in his gaze he gave you the feeling that there was nothing more important than his conversation with you. And at that moment, right then and there, I suppose nothing was.

"*Izvolite-li vyui, molodoi chelovek*, Would you be so kind, young man," said the Tsar, his voice hushed, "as to tell me the entire story of how you came upon this note? Only keep your voice low so as not to be overheard. Agreed?"

"Absolutely, Nikolai Aleksandrovich," I replied, my voice faint and trembling.

Nikolai was very good at that, at making his subjects feel comfortable and not the least bit threatened. So I told them how Sister Antonina and the Novice Marina had come and had brought the milk and things.

As soon as I finished my story, the Emperor asked, "And do you know, Leonka, what it says, this note?"

"*Nyet-s.*" So that he wouldn't think me ignorant, I quickly added, "I can read, Nikolai Aleksandrovich, but that is a foreigner's language."

"Exactly."

Aleksandra, her hands grasped nervously together, stepped closer, and eagerly, rather desperately, said, "Nicky, it's from her, it has to be."

Of course Aleksandra was supposing that the letters were the doings of Rasputin's daughter, the one who eventually left Siberia and became a lion tamer in California, the very one who lived out her final years in a little house beneath the Hollywood Freeway. And it was under this belief—that the daughter of their sacred monk was organizing a group of soldiers to rescue them—that the Empress grew so excited, so hopeful.

"We must respond at once," she said. "But who knows if we'll ever see any of the nuns again?"

"Leonka," said Dr. Botkin, who towered over me, "who was this soldier? The note says something about a soldier that we may trust, yet you say the note came in the stopper of the milk bottle from Sister Antonina?"

"*Da-s, da-s,* Yevgeny Sergeevich," I replied. "Sister Antonina brought the milk and eggs. As usual, she was accompanied by Novice Marina. There was a guard in the hall, but that was the only one I saw."

"And which guard would that be?"

"The one with the blond beard."

Of course there were many guards in and around The House of Special Purpose, but they all knew who I meant, for there was one guard whose beard in particular was very light in color. He was also the youngest, twenty at most. Just last week he'd made Tatyana Nikolaevna sit down and play revolutionary songs at the piano.

"*Nyet-s,*" said Nikolai Aleksandrovich, brushing at his mustache. "Trusting one of them—it's too dangerous. We simply can't."

"But—" the Tsaritsa began, her skin turning red and somewhat blotchy, because she was very strong willed, very determined.

"Absolutely not. I forbid it. What if it's a trap of some sort?"

This didn't please Aleksandra Fyodorovna much, for she was quite eager to make contact with the letter writer, and she said, "But, Nicky, if you don't think we can trust any of the guards, then surely we must find someone else to take our reply to them."

There's been much speculation as to how these replies were smuggled out of The House of Special Purpose. Some have suggested that there was in fact a guard loyal to the Tsar working in the house—some have suggested it was indeed him, the young one with the blond beard—but they've never been able to identify him by name. And that doesn't make any sense, because if there'd been such a hero wouldn't he have presented himself to the Whites once they took over Yekaterinburg? Of course! Others have suggested that it might have been the Heir's doctor, Dr. Vladimir Derevenko, who took these notes out. After all, Derevenko was virtually the only person authorized to come and go at the Ipatiev House, which he did—he came every day to check on Aleksei. You see, there wasn't enough room in the house for all of us, so Dr. Derevenko and his young son, Kolya, lived across the street. So since Derevenko could come and go, many have assumed it was he who carried the secret notes, that it could have been no other. But this too is false. One hundred percent false.

At first Botkin did in fact suggest, "What about Doctor Derevenko?"

"*Nyet-s,*" replied Nikolai Aleksandrovich. "That wouldn't be wise. Derevenko is our friend and is therefore always suspect to them. Two days ago the guards at the gate even searched his medical bag and the pockets of his coat. Furthermore, he is always accompanied by the *komendant* when he visits our rooms, so it's impossible to say anything to him. We must find someone . . . someone totally innocent, some-one they wouldn't even think of searching."

To me it was instantly obvious. In any history book, I, Leonid Sednyov, am nothing but the smallest footnote in the remarkable story of the murder of the Romanovs. There have been some absurd specu-lations, but to serious historians I am still to this day nothing more than the "little kitchen boy." Even to Nikolai Sokolov, the investigator the Whites brought in to try to determine what happened—they couldn't find the bodies, so no one was really sure if the Tsar was truly dead or if perhaps the entire family had been smuggled away. But even this Investigator Sokolov fellow didn't bother to search me out for an interview. Can you imagine anything so stupid? Such an idiot. He should have tracked me down, for I was with the Romanovs right up until a few hours before their end, so as far as the world knows I am the only survivor of The House of Special Purpose. In Investigator Sokolov's book, however, I was just the kitchen boy, as I have been all these years to the historians. The insignificant kitchen boy. And that is exactly how the *Bolsheviki* saw me as well—harmless!—which is why they decided to move me to the Popov House just hours before the Tsar and his family were killed.

Of course it's true that the Heir's doctor, Dr. Derevenko, was the only one to come and go, but that's not to say others weren't allowed out of The House of Special Purpose for specific tasks. Namely, me.

On the main floor of the house we only had a makeshift kitchen where a few things were prepared. Everything else was prepared for us a few blocks away at the local Soviet of Workers' Deputies. And who did they send once or twice every single day to pick up the *solyanka* and *kotletti,* their soup and meat cutlets? The *komendant* himself? *Konechno, nyet!* Of course not. They sent me, the kitchen boy, that's who! They sent little Leonka, they did!

So I said to the Tsar, I said, "Nikolai Aleksandrovich, once or twice a day I am allowed to go to the soviet for your food. And once or twice a day I pass the church there. Perhaps . . ."

The Tsar, the Tsaritsa, and the doctor each saw the simple logic of it all. They knew me, they trusted me. To them it was a beautiful plan—that their kitchen boy, who the whole world would forever overlook, should be their secret courier. And I think we would have succeeded. We nearly did, actually, we very nearly did. Over the next few weeks we received a total of three additional secret notes, and I carried a total of three replies. The replies to three of the four notes. We very nearly succeeded in saving the Romanovs, and we would have, I truly believe we would have, if only . . .

Oh, I was so young. And they were such awful times. In short, I must confess that I did something very foolish. Would that I could change one thing . . . just that one small thing. Oh, such a mistake I made!

Gospodi Pomilooi—the Lord have mercy—the Romanovs all died because of me.

4

But again, I anticipate. Forgive me, my dear granddaughter, there's simply so much I wish to tell you.

Back then, during the horrible times of the revolution, Yekaterinburg and the Ural Mountains were a real hotbed of Red activity. The Red Urals, that was how it was known, and this was the worst place for Nikolai and his family. Nikolashka, that was how the *Bolsheviki* so disrespectfully called him. The Blood Drinker. The Blood Sucker. The Number One Capitalist.

And there we were in that fateful house.

"Crammed in like herring in a barrel," laughed the Tsar one evening.

The *Bolsheviki* were constantly afraid that the Tsar would try to signal someone on the outside, which is why the windows were painted over with lime and we weren't allowed to open a single one of them. It was like being surrounded by thick fog. Only the very top pane was left untouched, and through that you could see daylight. As a matter of fact, you could also see a bit of the Church of the Ascension across the square.

"At least we can see the top of the church tower," the Empress said any number of times. "At least they haven't taken that away from us."

What still surprises me most was how well the Tsar and his family coped, how easily they accepted their imprisonment. Maybe Nikolai understood that his fate was to be a martyr tsar. Perhaps. But toward the end, during those last few weeks, he grew terribly depressed, for he saw how much worse things had become. I think he was beginning to realize his mistakes, that all of this could have been avoided if he'd only made a few simple concessions.

And yet they were a kindly family, those royals. During those last months and even last weeks I recall no outbursts among the family members, no screaming or tantrums. There was no fighting, not even among the children. And never once did I hear a raised voice between Nikolai and Aleksandra. No, never. How do I explain this? Nikolai— well, he found his wisdom too late to save his family and the House of Romanov, but all along he was a tender man. Really, I must say he was much too nice to be a Tsar of All the Russias. And Aleksandra—how could such a caring person have alienated so many? How ever you choose to fault Nikolai and Aleksandra—and they had many faults, to be sure—the most honest thing one can say about them was that they had a warm, devoted family. And the truest thing one can say about them was that nothing was more important to them than the well-being of their Mother Russia. That these two things ended in utter disaster is their tragedy, to be sure.

So perhaps in the end that is how they will be judged, on their love of family and country. Yes, perhaps . . .

Frankly, from the one side that seems as it should be, but on the other it seems too generous, too simplistic, for they lost Russia, and I for one, no matter how badly I feel about what took place, no matter how terrible I feel for what I did, can never forgive them for that. One must understand that they lost her because they never truly realized that Russia was not a seventeenth-century empire, but a twentieth-century industrial power and society, which meant that every step they took to help their country was in fact a misstep. Simply, Nikolai and Aleksandra were desperately out of touch with the modern world, they just couldn't comprehend that he wasn't semidivine, they couldn't separate the problems of their family from those of the country. Perhaps they would have survived if Aleksandra hadn't meddled so terribly in the affairs of government. And Nikolai, well, he made an enormous mistake by taking control of the armies during the Great War. You see, he went to the front, which in turn left the Tsaritsa in complete control of the government, and then things went to hell in a handbasket, they did. But . . . but it is always easy to judge, harder yet to comprehend.

So, yes, the notes . . .

All the rest of that morning I heard nothing more about any plans. It must have been close to noon when cook Kharitonov exploded.

"Radi boga," for the Lord's sake, he shouted. "Those idiots have been at it again!"

I hurried in from the hallway. "What is it? What's happened?"

"Those stupid Reds!" he cursed, though not too loudly. "They come in here and help themselves to anything they want. What pigs! Just look, they've eaten all the cutlets we were to have for dinner."

"Now what will you prepare?"

"I don't know. There's nothing . . . nothing! I'm going to have to request permission for you to go again to the Soviet."

And with that I shrank away, leaving cook Kharitonov to rant and rave. Wanting to alert the Tsar that I might be sent out of the house, I snuck from the kitchen in search of Botkin. Entering the drawing room, however, it was very quiet, meaning that the Emperor, his four daughters, and the doctor were still outside in the scruffy garden, where today they'd been allowed thirty minutes to pace in the fresh air. But what about Aleksandra Fyodorovna, who so seldomly went out? Not too long ago I'd seen the maid, Demidova, straightening up the dining room, but where was she, the Empress?

I passed from the living room, through the dining room, and di-

33

rectly into the room shared by all four girls, my eyes glancing over the nickel-plated cots they had brought with them from their palace in Tsarskoye. I'd heard Demidova say they were exactly the same kind of camp beds their great-grandfather, Aleksander II, had used in the warring he had done against the Turks, and that's what they looked like too. Army cots. Each bed was perfectly made by the grand duchesses each morning, yet each bed was slightly different, one with a flowered shawl placed squarely in the middle, another with a red and white Ukrainian coverlet neatly arranged. The metal footboard of each cot was carefully covered with a striped slipcloth, and at the foot of each bed stood a simple chair on the back of which was carefully draped a light blouse. The blouses were identical, I noticed, because the girls so often wore identical clothing. Though their clothes had more than likely come from the fashionable dressmaker, Lamanova of Moscow, nothing they ever wore was very racy, never for a daughter of Aleksandra.

Losing my nerve, I hesitated, for I had not been invited into these rooms. As I stood there, my eyes glanced over their things—next to each cot stood a small bedside table on which sat books and Bibles, an assortment of icons, and a few glass bottles filled with, I assumed, perfumed waters. The orderliness of the room ceased at the walls, however, for on the wall above their beds each great princess had tacked a jumble of mementos, primarily photographs. The snapshots were mostly of their mama and papa, their dogs, a favorite soldier or two, the Livadia Palace—a large white palace overlooking the Crimean Sea, which Anastasiya Nikolaevna had told me was their favorite home—but there was also a handful of sketches and watercolors the girls themselves had done. Sure, the *komendant* had recently eliminated their favorite pastime, photography, by confiscating the girls' square, wooden Kodaks, but they were still drawing, and they were all reasonably capable at this.

An attractive electric chandelier hung from the ceiling—it looked like a bouquet of flowers hung upside down, with the blooms fashioned in colored glass. That was where the electric bulbs were, in those glass blooms, and I passed beneath this fixture. Even though I was being extremely bold, even brazen, by entering these rooms uninvited, I pressed on, my feet shuffling across the brown linoleum that covered the floor.

"Aleksandra Fyodorovna?" I called, my voice quivering with nervousness.

This next chamber—their room, where the Emperor, the Empress, and the Heir Tsarevich slept—occupied the front of the house, with two windows facing Voznesensky Prospekt and Ascension Square, and two windows on the side facing the lane. It was a fairly good-sized room, certainly befitting a well-to-do merchant, and it was filled with some polished wooden desks and tables, a wardrobe, a few chairs, one of them soft and upholstered. The walls were covered in pale yellow striped wallpaper, with a frieze of flowers at the top. There was one larger bed, and there to my right—

"Zdravstvoojte." Hello, he said in a sheepish voice.

I was as surprised to catch him as he was to be discovered, for Aleksei Nikloaevich was not only out of bed, he was standing on his own and holding a small wooden box. We'd all been told that he couldn't walk, that if he went anywhere he either had to be carried or taken in the rolling chair, yet . . .

"You won't tell anyone that I'm up, will you, Leonka?" he pleaded. "Especially Mama—she would be very angry."

Before I could say anything the pallid boy aimed the wooden box at me, looked down into it, and pushed a button.

I said, "I thought the komendant took away all the cameras."

"All except mine. I have a secret place where I keep it hidden."

To be sure, he didn't walk well, and the Heir quickly hobbled over to his bed and jumped in. He wore a white nightshirt, and when he pulled a white blanket over his legs he was like a ghost disappearing into a cloud. Working as quickly as a thief, he took hold of a wooden table that stradled his bed and brought it closer to himself. He pushed aside a couple of books and some paper that lay on the table, and then removed the glass plate from the camera and put in a fresh one.

"Now you take my picture," he said, handing the apparatus to me.

"But . . ."

"Don't worry. It's easy."

As he sat there in bed, propped up by several pillows, he quickly told me how to do it, take a photograph, which I had never done before. Photography was still very much a folly of the nobility, and I'd rarely seen a camera, let alone held one. The Romanovs, on the other hand, were fanatics. They'd all had cameras. They'd always been snapping away. Because of this and their extensive diaries and letters, the Tsar and his family were better documented than any of today's most famous people. And these things—their writings and something like one hundred and fifty thousand family snapshots—are still kept not only in the archives in Moscow, but also at the libraries of Harvard and Yale.

Once the young Tsarevich explained, I stepped back several feet, aimed the thing, and repeated what a photographer had told me when he'd taken my one and only portrait, "Now say *eezyoom.*"

Rather than saying "raisin," Aleksei Nikolaevich remained silent, staring oddly at me and raising both hands, palms out. I operated the shutter, made it open and close, and then just stood there, afraid to move.

"It's done. You took the picture," advised the Heir. "Here, now give me the camera."

I did as the Heir asked, of course, passing him the wooden Kodak. Wasting no time, Aleksei Nikolaevich took it, turned, and reached around the white, metal railings of his bed's headboard. I moved forward, watched as he leaned over and plied away a piece of the tall mopboard, revealing a secret hiding place. Inside the dark wooden compartment sat the Heir's treasures, pieces of wire, some rocks, coins, a few nails, and a few folded pieces of paper.

"This is where I keep my special things," whispered the Heir as he pushed his camera into its hiding place. "You never know when we might need some of them."

Aleksei Nikolaevich had to give the Kodak a good shove, but it fit, just barely, and then he set the mopboard back in place, tapping it with his hand. He loved collecting little pieces of things, small bits of tin, rusty nails, wine corks, rocks. And in that regard he was just like any other little boy, curious, energetic, always fiddling. Of course, in every other respect he was entirely different. Before his father's abdication lackeys were always falling over him because he was the Heir Tsarevich, and his family, too, was loath to deny him because he was so sickly. So he was indulged, rather spoiled, and also not as well educated as he should have been because he'd lost years of study due to his bouts of bleeding. On the other hand, he was compassionate because he knew pain, real pain, and real suffering too. Yet even in those bouts when it looked for sure as if he would die, he was never given morphine, not even as his screams of pain rattled the palace windows. That poor child had traveled to the bottom of life and back again, and naturally that had had a profound effect on him. I liked him. In another world, in another time, we would have been true friends. Rasputin had predicted that if Aleksei lived to age seventeen he would outgrow his hemophilia, a brilliant dream the Empress lived for and perhaps the only one that kept her alive. Had this happened, had he matured into a healthy young man and become tsar, he would have been one of the greatest, for while his father found his wisdom too late, Aleksei Nikolaevich had found his much too early.

"You can't tell anyone about our hiding place. It's our secret. Agreed?" said the Heir, studying me with a naughty grin.

"Agreed."

From the side of his bed he grabbed a game board. "Do you want to play *shahmaty?*"

I shrugged, a bit ashamed to admit, "I don't know how."

"I could teach you."

"Well . . ."

"It would be fun, I promise. Really, it's not too hard. It just takes some practice, that's all."

Staring down at him, I couldn't help but pity this sickly boy whose empire stretched barely beyond the limits of his bed.

"Everyone should know how to play *shahmaty,*" pleaded the boy, desperate for any kind of diversion.

"Perhaps, but . . ."

Just then I heard heavy, firm steps. Boots. It was one of the guards heading this way.

"I can't, not right now," I said.

"Please . . . don't say anything."

"I won't."

Even as I ducked out of the room, the boy was deflating, falling back onto his bed, where he all but disappeared beneath his sheets and into his despair. *Shahmaty*—the shah is dead. How prophetic it now seems. I should have let him teach me. Instead I was perhaps the only Russian who didn't learn to play chess until he was an adult.

As it turned out I wasn't sent out after more food. Had we any force meat, cook Kharitonov would have prepared *makarony po-flotsky*—macaroni navy-style—but instead he made a simple macaroni tart sprinkled with dillweed.

We served lunch at one, just as we always did; life for the royals had always been and was still terribly regimented. I must say that no one starved, not by any means, but toward the end the food was very plain. That day we had watery bouillon first and then the macaroni tart. Bread, butter, and tea as well. Actually, vermicelli and macaroni were nearly all that the former Empress could or would eat, and honestly, she partook of so little that I don't know how she managed to stay alive. Toward the end she had grown so terribly thin that even her tea gowns hung like sacks on her. Yet neither she nor any of the others ever complained. They suffered well, those Romanovs, they truly did. They read their Bibles and their religious works, they prayed to their icons, and they suffered very well indeed. As Aleksandra wrote to her friend Anna:

> The spirits of the whole family are good. God is very
> near us, we feel His support, and are often amazed
> that we can endure events and separations which
> once might have killed us. Although we suffer horri-
> bly still there is peace in our souls. I suffer most for

Russia . . . but ultimately all will be for the best. Only
I don't understand anything any longer. Everyone
seems to have gone mad. I think of you daily and love
you dearly.

It was that day too that Kharitonov made a compote for lunch, a
stew of dried fruits—apples and raisins—which greatly pleased the Tsar.

"Just delicious. There's nothing better than honest Russian food—
so wholesome. Honestly, I tell you, people always used to serve me
fancy French food with rich creams and sauces, and I don't miss any of
it at all. Give me good, solid Russian food any day!"

I heard nothing more about the note the rest of that afternoon, nor
the rest of the evening, as Nikolai deliberated what to do. On the one
hand, a response to the letter meant taking a large risk—what if they
were caught? Would that give the *Bolsheviki* perhaps what they were
looking for, an excuse either to throw them all in a real prison or the
unthinkable, grounds to shoot the Tsar himself? On the other hand, if
the Romanovs didn't reply did that mean they would lose their only
chance at being rescued?

As it turned out, no action was taken until the afternoon of the following day, the twenty-first. As usual I assisted cook Kharitonov in
cleaning up after lunch, and no sooner was I was done than the woman
servant, Anna Stepanovna Demidova—Nyuta, we called her—came to
me in the kitchen.

"Leonka," she said, staring at me as if she were peering into my very
soul, "would you be so kind as to help me? I need some assistance."

"He's finished here!" bellowed Kharitonov.

That's the way it was. Any time anyone needed to take care of a
lowly task, they called me. "Leonka, help us wheel Aleksei Nikolaevich
into the other room, please." "Leonka, be so kind as to bring some
water." "Leonka, fetch some wood." "Get this . . . get that . . ." "Start
the samovar."

So none of the others thought anything of it, not cook, nor even
the guard who was lingering in the room just beyond. And yet I knew

something was up, for again it was the look, the way Demidova spoke to me more with her eyes than her voice, and I quickly followed her through the service hall where I slept every night across two chairs. Entering the dining room, we found the youngest daughter, Grand Duchess Anastasiya, known simply to her family as Nasten'ka, sometimes Shvybz. At seventeen she was such a cute girl, always a twinkle in her eye. It's no wonder, either, that it was she who spawned that cottage industry of silly speculation—did she really escape?!—for if any of the Romanovs had wanted to hoodwink the *Bolsheviki* it would have been her. Oh, how she would have loved to outfox them and escape to Europe! Of her, Grand Duchess Olga Alexandrovna—the Tsar's sister who fled as far as she could from the Reds, finally dying in 1960 in an apartment over a Toronto barbershop—said, "What a bundle of mischief." Yes, the girl was a royal rascal, rather like you, Katya, when you were so young and given to playing in the woods and on the beach. That's right, she was a real tomboy, infecting her family with her joie de vivre, again so like you, my granddaughter, who have been such a star of happiness to us. And this energetic Anastasiya often wrote to her father, always beginning with "My darling sweet dear Papa!!!" and always ending with "A big squeeze to your hand and face. Thinking of you. Love you always, everywhere!" And in those letters she told her father, Tsar of All the Russias, about the worms she was trying to breed or the problems she was having with her big sister, very unroyal problems like, "I am sitting picking my nose with my left hand. Olga wanted to biff me one, but I escaped her swinish hand."

Anyway, that day young Anastasiya sat at the dining room table, dressed in the same light blouse and dark skirt that she'd been wearing for days. With a book open before her, she sat there pretending, rather poorly, to read. Her eyes darted over at me, and she grinned ever so slightly in conspiracy. I understood, but didn't smile back.

In silence I continued behind Demidova, who led the way into the doorless room of the grand duchesses. One of them was in there too, Maria Nikolaevna. "Mashka," that was her nickname, though sometimes in English they called her "Little Bow-Wow," because she had the blind devotion of a dog. She liked so to please everyone, to take care of everyone, to do exactly as everyone wished. She wanted nothing more in life but children, scores of them.

Maria Nikolaevna was sitting on one of the metal cots, a Bible perched on her lap, but I could tell she wasn't reading either. She looked briefly at us and then stared into the dining room. It was then that everything was perfectly clear: the girls had been set up like a warning system. I doubt it was Nikolai who had thought of something like this. He just wasn't cunning enough, not the former Tsar. But she, on the other hand, well, surely this was the doing of Aleksandra Fyodorovna. I couldn't tell for sure, but I had little doubt that Olga and Tatyana were stationed elsewhere in the house, ready to drop a book or cough or somehow telegraph the approach of one of the guards. And when I followed Demidova into the next chamber we found the former Empress standing right by the door, awaiting not only our arrival, but any signals as well.

"*Spacibo,* Nyuta," thank you, said Aleksandra Fyodorovna to her maid, "that will be all."

"*Da-s,*" replied Demidova who bowed her head slightly and retreated.

The Empress ushered me in, resting a hand on my back and gently steering me toward her husband, who sat at a desk. I glanced to my immediate right, saw the boy, Aleskei Nikolaevich, staring at me from his bed. In front of him was the same table, covered with various distractions, including some needlework, which the Empress had taught him, for she firmly believed that idleness was illness's sister. That was the English side of her, I'm sure. Something she got from the old Queen.

So upon my entry the Tsar rose from his small wooden desk, where I might add not a single item was out of place. During his reign he never had a personal secretary, which was a point of pride to him, but to me now seems absolutely foolish. After all, the Tsar's duties concerned one-sixth of the earth's surface, not filing, not addressing envelopes.

The Tsar stood and pulled me into his sphere with those remarkable eyes. He cleared his throat, stroked once the trademark of his face, his beard.

"Your idea turns out to be quite a good one, *molodoi chelovek*," young man, said the Emperor. "Are you still willing to act as our courier?"

An odd noise came from the girls' room and Alekesandra Fyodorovna hurried back to the doorway. A moment later, she turned to her husband and nodded the all-clear. For the rest of my audience, however, she remained thus positioned.

He repeated, "Are you willing to act as our courier?"

There really wasn't any question in my mind simply because of what the Reds had done to my Uncle Vanya just a month earlier. My dear uncle, of course, had served the Imperial Family for years, and it was in fact he who had brought me to work for the Romanovs that previous year. He was deeply devoted to the Tsar, so that previous month when the soldiers' committee decided that Aleksei didn't need two pairs of shoes, just one, my uncle and Nagorny, the mansvervant who watched over the boy, loudly protested. And for this they were taken to the city prison. Right up until the end we thought the two of them had been dumped in a cell with Prince Lvov, the first minister president of the Provisional Government, who'd already been arrested for some other silly reason. It was only years later that I learned that my dear uncle and Nagorny hadn't been sitting in jail all along, but had instead been shot just a few days after they were first taken. The prince, on the other hand, later escaped to France, where he wrote his memoirs.

As I look back through all these decades it now seems obvious that the *Bolsheviki* knew all along what they were doing. So intent were they on liquidating the entire House of Romanov that they had started whittling away at our little group, getting rid of those who might be trouble, specifically the strongest among us. They'd already separated away Mr. Gibbes, the English tutor of the children, Pierre Gilliard, their French tutor, Baroness Buksgevden, a lady-in-waiting, all of whom survived, very likely because of their foreign-sounding names.

Many other attendants were not so lucky. Countess Gendrikova, another lady-in-waiting, and Yekaterina Shneider, the children's *lectrice*—reader—were shot in the city of Perm that September.

So in response to the Tsar's request, I bowed my head and said, *"Da, soodar."* Yes, monsignor.

He said, "Now, Leonka, you understand the seriousness of this, do you not? You understand that I am entrusting to you the safety of my wife and children? Do you realize how dangerous this is not only for us, but for you and everyone else as well?"

"Da-s."

"Xhorosho." Good. "I know we can depend on you."

And how I wish they could have. How I wish they could have depended upon me to . . . to . . . ensure their rescue.

The Tsar then asked, "When are you next scheduled to go to the Soviet for food?"

"I am to go within the hour, Nikolai Aleksandrovich, to fetch more food for this evening's supper."

"Excellent." He turned to his desk and pulled two pieces of paper hidden beneath a book. "Here is the note which you brought us yesterday morning. On it we have written our reply. I am sending that along with this."

He held up a sheet of lined paper on which was drawn a map. Or more precisely, a floor plan. Nikolai Aleksandrovich then folded it into three, took an envelope from the drawer of his wooden desk, and carefully placed the two pieces of paper in that very envelope.

"You must hide this on your body, Leonka," he instructed.

Of course I had to. I hadn't ever been searched leaving The House of Special Purpose, not ever, but I still had to be careful. So I started pulling up my shirt, then stopped. The Empress, who'd been watching me from her post in the doorway, quickly turned away. I glanced briefly at Aleksei Nikolaevich, who was playing with a toy boat with a little wire chain, and then I lowered my pants and stuck the envelope into my undergarments.

"Molodets," good lad, Nikolai Aleksandrovich said, brushing at his mustaches and looking at me with those generous eyes of his.

No sooner had I buttoned my pants than Nikolai Aleksandrovich handed me a second sheet of paper, this one folded simply in two with no envelope. He said, "Now, Leonka, I want you to carry this letter in your hand, and I want you to show it to the guards should they ask. Open it up, go ahead, read it."

"Now?" I asked.

"Da, konyechno." Yes, of course.

Although I had received very little formal education, I was able to read, unlike most of the people in Russia at that time.

> Dear Sisters,
>
> Thank you for the *chetvert* of milk and the fresh eggs, which The Little One greatly enjoyed. We are in need of some thread and Nikolai Aleksandrovich would be grateful for some tobacco, if this would not be too difficult.
>
> May God be with you, A.F.

Nikolai was a terrible smoker, he was. Always smoking. Frankly if the *Bolsheviki* hadn't killed him he probably would have soon died of lung cancer. And Aleksandra Fyodorovna and her girls did in fact need thread. They had consumed great quantities of it, not merely because the Empress was now darning the Emperor's socks and pants, not simply because she and the girls were mending all of their own clothes, but because right up to the end they were secretly stitching all of their "medicines," as they called their secret cache of diamonds, into their undergarments. I still don't understand how they'd kept nineteen pounds of gems secret up to that point—perhaps hidden in the corners of their suitcases?—but in the end they stashed over 42,000 carats of diamonds into the girls' corsets. Other gems, such as rubies and emeralds, disappeared into their buttons and the men's forage caps, while whole ropes of the most astounding pearls vanished into the waist and sleeves of Aleksandra Fyodorovna's dress. Later, when the *Bolsheviki* were hacking apart the Empress, they found those pearls too. Entire ropes made of hundreds of pearls, just one of which was valuable enough to feed a family of peasants for a year.

Oh, what a mistake, how they suffered because of Aleksandra's devious needle . . .

And the Tsar said to me, "On your way to the Soviet, I want you to stop by the Church of the Ascension. You might even tell the guards that you are taking this note there. Go right ahead and show it to them. Tell them that you are dropping this note off at the church so that one of the deacons will take it to the sisters at the monastery. When you reach the church, however, I want you to ask for Father Storozhev. You must speak to him and no one else but him, Leonka. And when you are alone with the Father you give him this note and also the envelope. He will make sure it is delivered to the correct people."

For a while, then, I was no longer Leonka, the kitchen boy, but the Tsar's spy. And what did the note say? And the map, what did it show? Those have been preserved as well. They too have been kept all these years in the *arkhivy* in Moscow. All the notes to the Romanovs were in French, as were all the replies from the royal captives. Nikolai himself always passed the letters to me, but they were not his handwriting. It is the florid hand of a girl, that of Olga, the oldest grand duchess, for she was the most capable in French.

And the first reply reads:

> From the corner up to the balcony there are 5 windows on the street side, 2 on the square. All of the windows are glued shut and painted white. The Little One is still sick and in bed and cannot walk at all— every jolt causes him pain. A week ago, because of the anarchists we were supposed to leave for Moscow

at night. No risk whatsoever must be taken without being <u>absolutely</u> certain of the result. We are almost always under close observation.

As for the map, it was a penciled floor plan of the dwelling, done by none other than Aleksandra Fyodorovna who, like all women of the nobility, had received not a formal education, but the proper instruction in drawing, watercolors, piano, literature, foreign tongues, and, of course, needlework.

Within the hour Komendant Avdeyev himself led me out the front door and through the two palisades surrounding the house. I crossed the muddy square, just as Nikolai Aleksandrovich asked, and I went directly to the Church of the Ascenscion, a big white brick structure. Only one small door was open, and I entered and was struck with the scent of the heavens, frankincense and beeswax candles. Searching the hazy church, I spied a nun on her knees in front of a golden icon of Saint Nicholas. Crossing herself over and over again, she dipped repeatedly, bowing her forehead against the cold, stone floor.

As I approached, the prostrated woman paused in her prayers and stared up at me with sunken eyes. "What is it, my son?"

"I come from The House of Special Purpose to see Papa Storozhev."

The nun quickly crossed herself in the Orthodox manner—using three fingers to represent the Trinity, she dotted her forehead, stomach, right shoulder, left—pushed herself to her feet and hurried away. Disappearing into a forest of icon-covered pillars, she slipped into the dark corners of the church. Within seconds Father Storozhev himself came out, his head and hair covered with a tall, black hat, his flowing, black gown dragging behind him. His eyes as dark as ink pots, he stared down upon me as if I were a Red infidel.

I boldly said, "Aleksandra Fyodorovna herself asked me to deliver this note, with the request that you pass it on to the sisters at the monastery."

I handed him the note requesting thread and tobacco, and Father Storozhev screwed up his eyes, studied the paper. I started to speak yet again, but then hesitated and checked to make sure we were not being observed. Only when I was certain we were alone did I unfasten my garments and withdraw the envelope containing the map and the response to the officer's letter.

"Papa, this is from *Batyushka*. Please deliver it to the proper people."

And then, of course, began our long wait in The House of Special Purpose.

5

There are so many things, Katya, that I have never told you nor even my very own son—your father—but I had been with the Romanovs since shortly before they were exiled to Siberia. My own father—your great-grandfather—was off to war, and the food situation at home in the Tula province was difficult, so when my Uncle Vanya wrote to my mother and suggested I come to work at the Aleksander Palace in July of 1917, I was sent right away. We were a poor family, and my mother was only too glad to have one less mouth to feed, particularly during such horrible times.

I arrived by the end of the month, a fortnight before the Romanovs were sent from their home in Tsarskoye Selo, a suburb of Sankt-Peterburg. The Tsar and his consort had many years earlier decided to make this their principal home, for there the air was clean and fresh, the gardens lush, and of course they were far away from the capital and decadent society. In essence, overwhelmed with the poor health of the Heir Tsarevich, they withdrew, which in the end actually precipitated their fall.

Of course, another reason they withdrew from Peterburg was fear for their safety. Since the uprisings of 1905, political assassinations had been all too common. Indeed, during those times the whole of the House of Romanov feared for its life, realizing that the anarchists were intent on exterminating the dynasty. In retrospect, I often wonder how Nikolai could not have foreseen so dark a storm as 1918—almost everyone else did—but again I'm sure he was blinded by religion.

For as rich and all-powerful as they were, the Emperor and Empress decided not to make their home in the Great Palace of Tsarskoye, an enormous palace built by Catherine the Great herself. That one had hundreds upon hundreds of grandiose rooms all decorated with gold and marble and crystal chandeliers. Instead, Nikolai and Aleksandra wanted a family home, so they chose the nearby and substantially more modest Aleksander Palace, which Catherine had built for her favorite grandson, the future Aleksander I, the one who trounced Napoleon. Nikolai II himself was born there, and the last Tsar and Tsaritsa chose not the entire palace, but only one wing for their apartments. Sure, they still had many rooms, and spectacular they were, for they gutted the left wing and redecorated a number of rooms in the *stijl moderne,* otherwise known in the West as Art Nouveau. It was there too, in a vitrine in her mauve boudoir that Aleksandra kept her Fabergé eggs, which along with all her pearl necklaces and diamond tiaras and her bejeweled this and that totaled so many millions upon millions of dollars. In today's dollars a billion, I think. Perhaps a bit more, perhaps a bit less. I should add that when they were exiled to Siberia, the Provisional Government, which ruled for eight months before being toppled by the Reds, allowed Nikolai and Aleksandra to take everything but the Fabergé *objets* with them. They took two suitcases full of gems, to be exact. And it all disappeared, all of the jewels except the nineteen pounds of diamonds and things found hidden on their bodies when they were killed. While the Romanovs were under arrest in Tobolsk—months before they were brought to Yekaterinburg—many nuns visited them, and these sisters of God smuggled everything else away. Stalin initiated a big search in the 1930s, and after torturing a few nuns and such the Reds found one of these suitcases buried beneath a hut. It contained one hundred and fifty gems, including a 100-carat diamond brooch and a 70-carat diamond crescent. Alas, the second suitcase has never been located. It's supposed to contain one pood— about thirty-six pounds—of diamonds and rubies and emeralds. As far as anyone knows, it's still buried somewhere in the taiga of Siberia.

It was during my short time at the Aleksander Palace that I came to understand several fundamental things about Tsaritsa Aleksandra Fyodorovna.

My work was in the kitchens, and I was never allowed close to the Imperial Family until the night before we departed the Aleksander Palace, when so much was being packed up for the long train ride—to where, no one at that time knew. Because their English cousins proved to be nothing but ninnies by withdrawing their offer of asylum— which would have saved the Romanovs—we knew we weren't being sent abroad. In truth, actually, that was a relief to the family, all of whom hoped and prayed that we were being exiled to their favorite palace, Livadia, in the Crimea. But that was not to happen, of course, because between Peterburg and the Black Sea stood the raging mobs of Moscow. As it was, we didn't realize we were being sent to Siberia until the train was hours underway.

In any case, I was enlisted to help carry the luggage and trunks and crates, a parade of things that went on through the night. It was only then that I entered the Emperor and Empress's private bedchamber. It was a large room with soaring ceilings, white wallpaper covered with pink garlands of the Empress's favorite flower, hydrangea, the design of which was carried onto the curtains and the chintz fabric covering all the painted furniture. Very bright. Very *elegantno.* I didn't know it then, for I was so young and unworldly—a mere lad from the provinces—but this was pure English style, the Empress's favorite, a taste acquired, of course, at the court of her granny. Yet all of this beauty was not what impressed me so. What first astounded me was the number of photographs, pictures of aunts and uncles and cousins and children that covered the walls and virtually every tabletop. Such was the importance of family to her. But then I saw her obsession, her sickness—all the icons. The walls of their sleeping alcove were covered from floor to ceiling with hundreds of religious pictures. Pictures of the Virgin Mary. Saint George the Dragon Slayer. Saint Nicholas. Saint Michael. Big, silver-covered icons. Little jewel-encrusted portraits of every saint imaginable. On and on. There was not a square inch that was not covered with an icon through which God was supposed to work, a window for him to reach from the high heavens to the lowly earth. Aleksandra was continually arranging and rearranging them too, as if she only had to get the order correct for God to hear her fervent prayers. *Nyet, nyet,* not *normalno.* Not at all. Even I recognized this, young as I was. She was more than a fool for God. She was a fanatic. Why, after giving birth to four daughters she was desperate to bear a boy, an heir, and to achieve this she had the monk Serafim of Sarov canonized. And after that grand ceremony Nikolai and Aleksandra crept down to the spring where the monk was known to have worked miracles hundreds of years earlier. And there, in the dead of night, they bathed naked, just the two of them. The next day there were a number of known miracles—children healed of terrible maladies, a blind woman who regained her sight, an invalid who walked for the first time in ten years—and soon thereafter Aleksandra became pregnant with Aleksei. Some say it was an act of God Himself, but why would he do such a dark thing, give Russia such a troubled heir? Rather, I think it was this inescapable Russian fate.

But, sure, while our Empress was cold on the outside, she was at the same time wildly passionate on the inside, and in this way so very, very Russian. In the carnal sense, she and the Emperor were the most loving of couples; in their early letters to one another there is even mention of their pet names for their genitalia. And this, from a granddaughter of that tight Victoria! *Radi boga*—Dear Lord—Aleksandra must be rolling in death, knowing that those pet names for their privates have been published around the globe!

Late that very same night my uncle and I were carrying a trunk marked N.A. NO. 12—ALBUMS, meaning it was Nikolai Aleksandrovich's twelfth trunk, the one filled with photo albums. We proceeded from the maple living room, a very attractive, two-story room covered with bear rugs and filled with mementos—it was here the family often lunched together in private—and passed into what was known as the corner living room. It had not been redone in the *stijl moderne,* but rather left in the older classical style. And as Uncle Vanya and I carried the trunk around a small gilt table and two chairs, I looked over and saw Aleksandra Fyodorovna herself staring up at a large tapestry of a woman, her three young children gathered around her. It was after midnight, and despite the chaos swirling around the Imperial Family, the Empress just stood there, not so much as flinching.

"Why does the Empress stare at that rug on the wall?" I asked my uncle as we passed through the main doors from their apartments, the very doors once guarded by their faithful Negroes, the huge men dressed in turbans and colorful dress. "Who is the woman pictured?"

"Marie Antoinette," he replied in his deep voice, leaving it at that, as if I should know.

Of course I didn't have the faintest idea. We continued down the long hall to the rotunda, where all was gathered, but later, as I carried baggage from Aleksandra's infamous mauve boudoir I saw a painting of the same woman hanging on the wall. As it turns out, this was the second thing I learned that night about the Tsaritsa, her obsession with violent death, which took the form of her fascination with Marie Antoinette. It seems that the Empress, so mystical, so fatalistic, had suspected for years what awaited her own family, though never in all of history has an imperial brood, the symbol of a nation, been so crudely butchered, children and servants and pets, all liquidated, all except a young kitchen boy. To hell with the *kommunisty!*

How strange is history. The Aleksander Palace was preserved as such, just the way the Emperor and Empress left it when they walked out the door. It was kept that way until World War Two, when the Nazis used it for their headquarters and the nearby Great Palace for a stable and garage. This was during the nine-hundred-day siege of

Leningrad, as Peter—Sankt-Peterburg—had been renamed by the *Bolsheviki,* and those were the days of utter hell on earth. It was during this time that the Gestapo assumed the basement beneath the Tsar's wing as a place of torture, and to this day the gardens of that stately palace are filled with an untold number of bodies. At the end of the war the palace and its rooms were damaged, but not horribly so—the German booby traps were found and defused just five hours before they were to blow—and Nikolai and Aleksandra's apartments could have been easily restored. Instead, some Soviet general decided to wipe away any memory of Nikolai the Bloody and Aleksandra the *nemka,* the German. And so today, only two of Nikolai's rooms remain, his gorgeous, *stijl moderne* office and his cozy, warm reception room, which the hypocritical Red general kept for his own personal use.

One other odd thing, and this concerns Rasputin. Late in the fall of 1916, before my time with the Romanovs, that mysterious monk with the long, greasy hair and sharp nose finally began to understand the hatred against him, that many powerful princes and grand dukes believed he was leading the dynasty and country to ruin. In fact, he correctly supposed that he would soon be dead, or more precisely murdered. With this in mind, Rasputin wrote a note to his Tsar and Tsaritsa, which was only delivered to them after he was killed by young Prince Felix Yusopov, who was married to the Tsar's own niece, a pretty young thing who died just a short while ago, actually, in '67.

In his prophetic letter, Rasputin wrote:

> Tsar of the land of Russia . . . If it was your relations who have wrought my death, then no one of your family, that is to say, none of your children or relations will remain alive for more than two years. They will be killed by the Russian people.

Strange, is it not? Rasputin was murdered in December of 1916—poisoned, stabbed, shot, and finally drowned. It took all of that to kill that powerful peasant, and he was right. Nikolai and Aleksandra, their children, and many other Romanovs—in total almost twenty—would be dead within the predicted time. How in the name of God did Rasputin, the holy mad monk, know this? It's almost enough to make one a Believer.

So Aleksandra knew well what had happened to Marie Antoinette, just as Rasputin's words reverberated in her chest with each beat of her weak heart. But let me make one thing very clear, the Romanovs never gave up hope. To the very end itself—even as they descended those twenty-three steps in the depth of that night—they never stopped praying, hoping, believing that they would be rescued by a storm of three hundred officers. Yes, there were many depressing hours in each one of those days, but Nikolai and Aleksandra kept praying to their God, kept hoping for dear friends to save them . . . friends, who in the end never appeared, which is perhaps not that surprising. After all, while 90 percent of the Russian people did not want them dead, the same 90 percent did not want them back on the throne either. Such was the horrible paradox—saving them would have meant restoring the autocracy, which was at that point untenable to almost all of Russia.

And so the long wait for the second note . . .

I found the first note to the Tsar and his family on the morning of the twentieth, and then carried a reply to Father Storozhev on the afternoon of the twenty-first. I think all of us were expecting, or at least hoping, that Sister Antonina would bring a reply on the twenty-second. Instead, she failed to appear, leaving us awash in anxiety.

How did the time pass?

Well, for starters, that morning of the twenty-second the weather on the street was glorious, sunny and pleasant, about sixteen degrees of warmth, but soon it was more than twenty Celsius inside.

"Dear Lord in Heaven," moaned Nikolai Aleksandrovich, sweat beading on his brow, "it's been two weeks now—two solid weeks—and they still haven't decided whether or not we can open a window. It's absolutely inhumane!"

"Of course it is, my sweetheart," said Aleksandra Fyodorovna, standing behind him, a pair of scissors in her hands. "Now be still before I do you serious damage."

"Better you than them."

"I'll hear no such thing."

She'd cut his hair for the first time ever a month earlier; this was the second attempt. Just fifteen minutes earlier, Nyuta, the Tsaritsa's maid, had laid a sheet in a corner of the dining room, then placed a chair atop that. And now Nikolai Aleksandrovich sat there trying to be still, which wasn't his nature. Already he had paced for an hour around the dining table. He needed more time outside; a half hour once in the morning and once in the afternoon just wasn't enough.

While the Empress was trimming his hair, my duty was to entertain the Tsarevich, and as such we were playing troika. He sat in the wheeled chaise, and I pushed, obeying his every command.

"Off into the woods—faster!" ordered Aleksei Nikolaevich.

"Alyosha!" beckoned his father. "Alyosha, I want you two to be careful. Am I clear?"

"Of course, Papa."

As I slowed the vehicle of Aleksei's imaginary escape, one of the girls appeared, the front of her frock all dusted white.

"Look at me, look at your Nasten'ka!" proclaimed Anastasiya Nikolaevna.

"What ever have you gotten into, *dorogaya*?" asked her father, entirely amused.

"Cook Kharitonov is teaching us how to bake bread."

"Really?" said her mother, unable to hide her surprise.

"Yes, he showed us how to knead it, and it's rising right now. I'm sure it's going to be delicious."

Nikolai Aleksandrovich smiled and said, "I have no doubt about that. Pretty soon you girls will know how to do everything in the kitchen."

"I love you all and kiss you a thousand times!" she said with her usual flare as she spun and hurried off.

Aleksandra Fyodorovna smiled after her, and said, "In spite of everything, they're growing up."

"I suppose they are," agreed her husband.

"I do hope Anya keeps growing, though. Her legs are too short, her waist is too thick."

"That's the least of our worries."

"Yes, of course . . ."

Again the Heir ordered me off into the woods, and I turned the troika and started our pursuit of wild Siberian tigers and bears. Suddenly, however, a real monster appeared in the form of a guard, who blocked our route into the living room. He was tall, big-shouldered, had a long greasy mustache, and he wore a filthy tunic and rumpled, baggy pants. From his shoulder hung a long rifle with a rusty bayonet on the end, and hanging from his belt, of course, was a hand grenade.

"Get back," he ordered.

I halted the chair and looked from the guard to the Tsar, then back to the guard.

"The women are here," said the guard, his voice as deep as it was abrupt. "You must return to your rooms. They will wash the floors."

"But can't you see I'm cutting my husband's hair?" protested Aleksandra Fyodorovna, glaring imperiously at him.

"By order of the *komendant* all of you must return to the far room."

"Just five more minutes," she said, not as question, not as a request, but as a statement of fact.

"Now!"

"But—"

Nikolai Aleksandrovich, brushing off his shoulders as he rose from his chair, calmly said, "Actually, Alix, I think you're finished. If you take any more off I'll be bald."

I watched as she looked momentarily into the soft eyes of her husband, then, her eyes burning, turned her attention on the guard. Her lips trembled as if she wanted to lash out at him, her skin got all blotchy and red. And then in one quick swoop, the Empress threw her cutting shears on the dinner table, gathered up her long skirt, and stormed out of the dining room.

"You must forgive my wife—she slept poorly last night," said Nikolai Aleksandrovich, starting after. "Come, Alyosha. Let's get out of here so the charwomen can clean."

I followed after my master, pushing the wheeling chaise and Heir out of the dining room, into the girls' room, to the left, and into their bedchamber, where Aleksandra Fyodorovna stood, her face bowed into both hands. Weeping quietly, she shook, and I witnessed the Tsar go up and embrace her from behind. In the flash of a second, she spun around, throwing herself into his arms.

"There, there, my Sunshine," he said, kissing the top of her head.

"Forgive me, Nicky. Forgive me, please, my darling. I know my greatest sin is my irritability. You know how hot-tempered I am. I want to be a better woman, and I try, I really do. For long periods I am really patient, and then out breaks my bad temper. It is not so difficult to bear great trials, but these little buzzing mosquitoes are so trying."

"Of course they are, my dearest."

"I long to warm and comfort others—you know I do—but I don't feel drawn to those around me here. I am cold toward them, and this too is wrong of me."

"All that matters is that we seven are together and safe."

"Yes, yes, of course, my love. You're right. Always right. Oh, how I love you, my treasure, my life. What bliss you have given me." She sighed, pressed her cheek against his, and keeping her voice low, said, "But where is the sister today? Why didn't she come with another letter? Oh, Nicky, I'm so scared. We will hear more, won't we? Promise we will!"

"I swear with my heart, all my heart."

I stood silent and still behind the wheeling chaise, and both Aleksei and I, as if staring upon a silent film, didn't flinch, only stared on as the Tsar whispered something in her ear, and she half laughed and half cried, her polished nails digging into his muscular back. A few moments later I heard the rustle of clothing and turned to the open doorway. All four grand duchesses, their hands and long skirts powdered with flour for the first time in their lives, were looking upon their parents as well.

Hearing them, the Tsar turned, his face reddening. "Well, so, all of us are here, are we?"

Tatyana Nikolaevna, the second daughter and the most responsible of them all, softly said by way of explanation, "The floors are to be cleaned."

"So they are," replied her father as he tugged at his collar. *"Gospodi,"* dear Lord, "but it's hot in here, isn't it, children? So . . . who'd like to play a game of bezique?"

Thus, for the next two hours, we passed the time playing a type of pinochle, not just the seven Romanovs and me in the bedchamber, but Dr. Botkin, Demidova, and the footman, Trupp, all of us day by day compressing into one unit. Only cook Kharitonov was allowed to carry on as before, and his meager cooking filled the whole of the closed-up house with its smells. Potatoes, beetroot, and more compote. That was the lunch we later took at one o'clock, though by that time it was so stuffy, the heat so intense, that no one much felt like eating. Really, it was broiling in there, not a movement of air. On the street it was thirty degrees, so God only knew how hot it was inside.

The Reds had evicted the Ipatiev family with barely any notice, and after lunch the Emperor found one of Mr. Ipatiev's own books, *Sea Stories* by Belamor, which the engineer had left behind as he fled. Choosing a passage, the Tsar read aloud to his son until close to two-thirty when we were allowed into the garden for an entire hour on account of the intensity of the heat. All of us went out, including the Empress. As innocent, as unsuspecting as they would be on the night of July 16–17, the Romanovs descended those twenty-three steps, passed out the door, and into that untidy little garden. Dr. Botkin and Trupp managed the rolling chaise, and Nikolai Aleksandrovich himself carried his son down the steps. I followed the girls who followed their father as he paced a circle, while the Heir and his mother took refuge from the fearful heat beneath the branches of a lilac bush.

There was nothing to cling to in our lives but our regimen, and at four-thirty, just as punctual as ever, I helped serve tea in the drawing room, where all seven Romanovs and Dr. Botkin were gathered. Cook Kharitonov sliced some of the fresh bread, which was still hot, and I carried it out on a plate along with a bit of butter, handed it to Demidova, who in turn placed it on the tea table. This produced no end of delight for the grand duchesses, who were quite proud of their creation. It wasn't white bread, the preferred sort of the nobility, for both Aleksandra and Kharitonov had been carefully hoarding what little white flour we had for Aleksei, thinking it more healthy, more digestible. Rather these princesses had made real Russian *chyorny khleb*, black bread that was dark and earthy and so deliciously sour. An endless stream of questions and comments and praise followed.

I was just returning to the kitchen when the door burst open and six unknown men stomped into the room, led by none other than the *komendant* himself. A flash of unspoken terror shot through us all: Had Sister Antonina been found out? Was the rescue plot so quickly dashed?

His voice trembling like a schoolboy's, Nikolai Aleksandrovich quickly pushed himself to his feet, and said, "Good afternoon, gentlemen. May I—"

Avdeyev looked in Nikolashka's direction, and muttered, *"S'yad!"* Sit!

"But—"

"Sit down and be quiet!"

Good soldier that he was, the Tsar sank back down, and all of us watched in terror as this group of thugs moved from the drawing room, into the dining room, and then proceeded into the bedchambers. Maria Nikolaevna and I, peering through the open doorways, watched and tried to discern what they were saying, but of course it was impossible. Their voices were low and deep, a lot of grumbling went on. For what purpose had they come? I looked over at the Tsaritsa, who was clutching the Tsar's hand, her eyes clenched shut in fright. Would they search the rooms, tear apart their things in search of evidence against them? Might the "medicines" be discovered?

But then . . . then . . .

The group of men was going from one whitewashed window to the next, and I whispered to Maria, "It looks like they're checking out which windows can be opened."

"They must be from the regional soviet."

And so it became evident that they were in fact a soviet—a council, a committee—that had been formed to decide which, if any, windows might be unglued. For more than twenty minutes these Reds went from room to room, from window to window, discussing all this with the utmost intensity. They must have been terribly afraid of anarchists or conspirators—that is, worried that one group might take a shot at the Tsar through that open window, or fearful that another bunch might try to rescue their monarch via an opening. Finally, in the end they seemed to agree not to agree. Perhaps they had a report to make. Perhaps they were afraid of answering with their lives. In any case, this group of six men emerged from the bedchambers, staring at the Imperial Family as if they were circus freaks.

As they headed out, Nikolai Aleksandrovich rose again to his feet, pleading yet once more, "We would be most obliged for a single window to be opened. You can see for yourselves not only how hot it is in here, but how unhealthy it is. Please, I ask you to consider the health of my wife and children, all of whom are suffering."

Komendant Avdeyev glared at his Nikolashka.

And the Tsar continued, saying, "On another matter, we would also be happy to be given any work. For example, we would appreciate the opportunity to clear the garden in the rear, which is quite a mess. I myself would greatly like to saw more wood—to cut and stack it."

"At this point, nothing of that sort is permitted," snapped Avdeyev as he and the others departed.

Depressed, forlorn, the Romanovs melted back into the heat, which could only be described as colossal. The family sipped at their tea and nibbled at the bread, which only minutes earlier had provided such joy, such pride, but was now only so much of nothing. After a few minutes Nikolai Aleksandrovich began to read aloud to his son, while

Aleksandra Fyodorovna took out some cards and began to lay patience. Two of the girls played dominoes, but of course not for money, which Aleksandra, with her grandmother's tight Victorian morals, would never allow.

Very little happened during the rest of the day, at least not until Vladimir Nikolaevich—Dr. Derevenko—came to check on the health of the Heir. By that time of day, nearly six, I was back in the kitchen helping Kharitonov with the preparations for the meager dinner that would be served at eight. Cutlets and leftover macaroni tart. It was Demidova herself, her face forlorn, who came into the kitchen.

"Vladimir Nikolaevich has arrived." She tried not to say it, but could not restrain herself from whispering, *"Neechevo."* Nothing.

So there was no news, no reply to our reply. Sure, even the Tsaritsa's maid knew we were awaiting more news from the outside, for that was how the Tsar and Tsaritsa handled this. No one was excluded, which was very democratic of them.

"Leonka, the doctor requests hot water," said Demidova.

"Da-s," I replied.

A few minutes later, bearing a bowl of hot water, I walked into the bedchamber and found not just the doctor, but also Komendant Avdeyev himself seated at the foot of the Heir's bed.

"Ah, thank you, Leonka," said Vladimir Nikolaevich.

The doctor, who'd been using his special device to electrify Aleksei's knee—and thereby stimulate circulation—placed the mechanism and tangle of wires aside. He then beckoned me forward.

"Come here, boy."

And so I stepped toward him and held the bowl as he dipped in a cloth and wrung it out. For the next ten minutes, I didn't move as the doctor applied warm compresses to the boy's left arm. And during that entire time, Avdeyev just sat there, yawning, scratching his nose, not doing anything but making it impossible for the Emperor or Empress to pose a single question to Derevenko. Most disturbing, though, was that the doctor simply went about his usual business without any pretense that he knew something was going on. Not one of us spoke during his treatment of the Heir, and fifteen minutes later Vladimir Nikolaevich simply packed up his medical kit and departed without so much as raising an eyebrow. Or our hopes, for that matter.

Shortly before dinner the girls washed their parents' pocket handkerchiefs. And later, after dinner, all of us gathered in the drawing room and listened to Nikolai Aleksandrovich read aloud. The heat and the lack of air continued to be intense, and I went to bed soon after Aleksei Nikolaevich. Sometime toward midnight a huge storm came upon us, the wind ferocious, the rain strong. The first crashes of lightning and thunder woke me, and then I lay awake for a long time, listening to the heavy drops beat against the metal roof of The House of Special Purpose.

Thus ended our first long day of waiting, which seemed extraordinarily calm in comparison to the next.

6

June 23, 1918, started out to be a lovely day. A Sunday it was, and the heavy rains of the night had washed away the heat. Weeks earlier the *Bolsheviki* had painted the thermometer with lime as well, but even they realized the cruelty—not to mention the senselessness—of depriving the Romanovs their only divertissement. That little glass thermometer that hung outside the girls' room was the family's only contact with the outer world, the only vehicle of news from their lost beyond. And so after much protest from Nikolai Aleksandrovich, the whitewash was scratched from a tiny corner of the window pane and from the thermometer itself, and in this way were we able to note the dramatic moods of the Siberian day. Without fail, master and servant alike followed the fluctuating mercury with the utmost interest. One of the girls would pause in her reading, jump off her bed, check the measuring device. The Emperor would slow in his pacing of the rooms, bend over, see what God had decided for the day. Demidova would steal a glance as she straightened things. Even the guards posted inside found it a welcome distraction.

When the household awoke for the new day, it was thirteen degrees of warmth on the street. Inside it was nearly as cool, for the powerful winds of the night had not only swayed the trees, but poured through every crack of the Ipatiev House. For the first time in days the stale air had been forced away, and in the rooms it was pleasant, refreshing, almost delightful. It gave us hope, truly it did, and early that morning Aleksandra Fyodorovna sat in bed writing to the mother of a wounded soldier about how one shouldn't lose faith, that God would bring better days. Yes, sure, her belief in the Almighty gave her remarkable inner strength, and she often said, "Don't worry. The deadly illness must be borne, then the organism becomes stronger and life becomes easier and lighter."

Unfortunately, the day's events soon took a turn for the worse. I was just stuffing bits of charcoal into the samovar when I heard short, heavy steps. Turning, I saw Nyuta standing there, her face flushed red, her breathing quick and short.

"Leonka, quickly—water for Yevgeny Sergeevich!"

I was constantly carrying water this way and that, but my first thought, my automatic one, was of course that something horrible had happened to the Heir Tsarevich, for all of us knew that death forever lingered in his shadow. Had Aleksei Nikolaevich fallen from his bed? Bumped his toe? Sneezed too hard? So casual an event could easily prove a mortal catastrophe for the boy, and those were the darkest of our days, actually, when the Tsarevich suffered, when we feared his end was imminent. When the blood flooded his joints, swelled his skin, twisted his limbs, the boy's screams of pain—against which medicine was then helpless—were as piercing as a bullet. There was no escape, not for him, not for any of us, least of all the Empress, who would sit by The Little One for days on end without sleeping, without eating. She couldn't hold her child, no, that would be too painful for him. All that she could do was kiss his brow, his cheeks, and listen in guilt as he moaned an occasional "Mummy." Only when he was back on our side, clinging to life again, would Aleksandra Fyodorovna retire, collapsing in her own bed, from which she wouldn't emerge for days upon end.

And that was when we were called in to entertain him—the sisters, both pairs, big and little, and eventually me, of course, for only I took equal delight in the Heir's treasures, his bits of wire, the rusty nails, as well as his prized coins, the very ones he had positioned on the train tracks back in Tsarskoye.

"Look at what Papa's locomotive did to this kopek!" he would exclaim to me, showing the flattest of them all.

Fearing the worst for the Heir, I poured a large bowl of water, grabbed a small cloth, which I threw over my shoulder, and started quickly out. Passing through the hall in which I slept, I headed into the dining room and began to circle the large, dark oak table.

"Nyet, nyet, molodoi chelovek!" No, no, young man, called Nyuta from the doorway into the main parlor. "This way! In here!"

Confused, I came to a halt, sloshing the water from my bowl. But . . . ? Was it not Aleksei Nikolaevich who was in need?

"Come on, Leonka! Hurry!"

I changed my direction, circled back around, and followed Demidova into the parlor, whereupon the commotion led me to the front of the room. Heading around the large, potted palm, I entered the alcove, where I saw the Empress, her second daughter, Tatyana Nikolaevna, and not Aleksei, but Dr. Botkin, who lay moaning on the reed settee that served as his bed.

"Yevgeny Sergeevich has had an attack of the kidneys," whispered the Tsaritsa's maid to me.

I don't know what it says about the Empress, a woman of extraordinary complexity, but the suffering of others always brought out the best in her. From all the books I've read, I've come to understand she was horrendously insecure, pathologically so. Her friends were either totally hers and under her complete domination—for make no doubt about it, she was amazingly strong-willed—or they were simply her enemies. There existed for her nothing between those extremes of devotion and rejection. And yet when someone was in need, friend or foe, this shy woman, whose mother had perished when she was six, rallied with amazing inner strength and determination. More than anything

65

else, she could identify with pain and suffering. In this century, however, there has been no woman more maligned or misunderstood than the Empress Aleksandra Fyodorovna, consort to the Tsar of All the Russias, just as there has been no woman whose gross mistakes—no matter how inadvertent—have hurt, even killed, so many millions. A wise woman she was not. Passionate, loving, beautiful, sure, but worldly ignorant. More damage she could not have done to her beloved adopted Russia. This scandal she caused by inviting Rasputin into the royal palace was outrageous. Imagine, while the Tsar was off fighting the Germans that stupid *yurodstvo,* holy fool, was all but signing imperial decrees.

Well, Aleksandra Fyodorovna placed a glass thermometer between Dr. Botkin's lips, then turned to me and beckoned, "Leonka—the water, please."

And then as I stood there the Tsaritsa bathed the doctor's big, red face, wiping it gently, even professionally, you might say. After all, Aleksandra Fyodorovna and her older daughters, the big pair, Olga Nikolaevna and Tatyana Nikolaevna, became nurses soon after the outbreak of the Great War. Daily they went to the wards and the surgery theaters. Many noble women of Peterburg thought it outrageous that an Empress would bloody her hands, quite literally. Many gossiped that their Tsaritsa was wasting her efforts on a few soldiers, many of whom she befriended, many of whom died, when she should be sweeping through as many hospitals as possible, making herself seen as widely as she could. But my mistress was of the strongest conviction otherwise. She was *Matushka,* the Dear Mother. There were those in dire need. She had to do whatever it took, even the lowliest work, and she was often seen carrying away amputated arms and legs and worse.

Aleksandra Fyodorovna checked the thermometer, and said, "Thirty-eight point eight. Not good. The pain persists, Yevgeny Sergeevich?"

"Da-s," weakly replied the doctor.

"Then I believe an injection is called for. Am I right?"

He nodded. "Would you . . . would you be so kind?"

The Tsaritsa turned to her number two daughter. "Tanechka, prepare me a syringe of morphia."

"Certainly, Mama."

"Nyuta, Leonka—you are excused."

"Da-s," replied Demidova, backing away.

I likewise muttered, bowed my head, and retreated. Glancing back once, I witnessed Tatyana Nikolaevna confidently pulling a glass syringe from the doctor's brown leather bag.

Breakfast that morning was served not too terribly late. We had our morning inspection and then we served the morning tea and bread. Everyone was gathered there in the dining room except Dr. Botkin, who was resting more comfortably, and Aleksandra Fyodorovna, who remained by his side for the rest of the morning.

The early drama thus melted into our routine. The Tsar paced the dining room. The girls made their beds, then the older pair started reading, while the younger girls came and sat at the dinner table and began to draw. I wheeled about the Heir. Cook Kharitonov fussed in the kitchen over our meager provisions, and Demidova and Trupp emptied the enamel chamber pots employed for night use. Our morning walk in the garden was scheduled for half-past ten, and we all anticipated this silently but with great urgency.

Just as the day before, however, the doors were suddenly and unexpectedly thrown open. It happened at ten precisely, and this time it was but two men, neither of whom we had ever seen, who marched into our world. I was just wheeling the Heir around the dinner table when they stormed in, proceeding directly past their former master as if he were a stupid dog. I pulled the wheeling chair to a quick stop, and both Aleksei Nikolaevich and I watched as they continued through the room. They carried not guns or grenades, but tools, entering the girls' room in utter silence, for all visitors to The House of Special Purpose were under strict Red orders not to speak with us.

Raising his right hand, the Heir bid me forward, and I rolled him thus, creeping around the table, past the chairs. And then, like the Tsar himself, who came up behind us, we cautiously peered through the doorless opening. Several of the grand duchesses sat on their beds, and we were all transfixed as the men quietly but surely set to work on one of the windows. It took but moments, and as we witnessed the seemingly unbelievable, I saw the Tsar's brow rise in surprise, witnessed the dumbfounded shake of his head, received the thrilled wink of his eye. *Da, da,* the two workmen did the impossible: they unglued a single, wonderful, beautiful window.

"*Oi,*" softly muttered the Heir in joy.

Just as quickly as they had come, so the men left, their heads hung, their eyes cast to the floor, their lips sealed. At first none of us moved. I think we were expecting the fat, Red pig, Komendant Avdeyev, to come marching in. Instead, the workmen departed, closing the outer doors, and then . . . then . . . we poured toward the open window.

"Papa!" called Olga Nikolaevna, leaping from her bed.

"*Oi, kakaya prelyest!*" Oh, what a joy, shouted Tatyana Nikolaevna.

"*Hourahh!*" shouted the Heir as I wheeled him to the window that overlooked his former empire.

"Thank the Lord!" proclaimed the Tsar, sucking the air as deeply as he could.

Huge billowing gusts of air swarmed upon us, and we all gathered around, held our arms out, felt the breeze swirl around and lift our hearts like kites into the boundless sky.

"Isn't the fragrance tasty?" said Nikolai Aleksandrovich.

"I can smell every garden in town!" proclaimed Anastasiya Nikolaevna, squinching up her shoulders and her nose and drinking it all in. "This is heaven!"

We heard her steps, heard her voice scared and worried as she called out, "What is it, Nicky? What's happened? What—"

"Look, Mama!" exclaimed the Heir. "They opened a window!"

She froze at the threshold, clasped both hands over her mouth. The Tsar, laughing, turned to his consort and held out his arms. The next moment they were embracing. I rolled Aleksei Nikolaevich right up to the edge of the sill, and he grabbed on to it, clutching to all that might yet be. That was all. It only took that little bit, a single open window, to feed the royal family with delightful hope.

"Oh, Nicky, *dusha moya*!" My soul, said the Empress, clasping her husband.

"You see, my love. As you've always said, after the rain—"

"Sun."

"After the darkness—"

"Light."

"And after the illness—"

"Health."

"Exactly," said the Tsar. "We mustn't give up faith."

"No, my love. Never."

But the luck of Nikolai and his brood was like an ocean liner, very difficult to turn around. At that particular moment Anastasiya Nikolaevna took it upon herself not simply to poke her head out the window, not simply to stretch outside as far as she could, but to actually climb up on the windowsill. A character, she was. Full of energy and mischief. One of her royal cousins had long ago taught her to climb trees, a habit that she could never be broken of, no matter her rank or gender.

"Careful, Nasten'ka!" chided number three sister, Maria Nikolaevna.

"*Oi,* Mashka, stop your worrying! I just want the air all around me. I want it to lift me up, to carry me away, far away!"

Her father, the Tsar, turned from his wife, saw his daughter perched on the ledge two floors above ground, and shouted, *"Bozhe moi!"* My God! "Anastasiya Nikolaevna, you get down right this moment!"

"But, Papa—"

"Now!"

"Oh, all right. I—"

But just as she turned her back to the endless world beyond, just as she readied herself to jump back into the hole of our existence, a blast rang out. More specifically, a shot. The next instant the wall of the house, not but a few centimeters from Anastasiya's head, was struck by a bullet, and bits of stucco and brick exploded into the air. As much by fear as anything else, the poor child was thrown into the room, where she landed upon two of her sisters. They all screamed and came crashing down onto the floor, collapsing in a terrible heap of arms and legs. Before I knew it, before I could even think what to do, the Tsar grabbed the wheeling chaise from me, jerking his son from the environs of the window and pulling him back against the far wall.

Terrified, Aleksandra Fyodorovna cried out and threw herself forward, grabbing for her youngest daughter, screaming, "Anya!"

All of a sudden a huge wail rose above everything else, a terrified cry as the girl replied, "Mama!"

I stumbled back, plastering myself against the wall. Before my eyes Aleksandra made a frantic examination of her youngest daughter—limbs, head, torso—but, no, Anastasiya was not wounded, she was unscathed, merely terrified. As the girl broke into a flow of tears, Aleksandra clutched her daughter to her chest, cradling her and sobbing as well. A moment later the three other grand duchesses fell upon them, and this heap of womanhood shook like a volcano until finally, for the first time, they erupted. All this time, all these months, not one of them had broken down, not one of them had let go, and now . . . now they bellowed forth.

"My babies!" cried Alix, poring over her three other daughters—Olya's hand, Tanechka's head, Mashka's cheek. "My precious babies!"

The Tsar turned the wheeling chaise around, pushed his son to this mass of family, and they all melded into a heap, mother and daughters on the floor, son slightly higher on his chaise, and father standing firmly above them. They all clutched and grabbed for one another, Alix hanging onto her Nicky's leg. For the first time, the only time, I saw amazing pain boil in the Tsar's body. He closed his eyes, bit his bottom lip. Strong, he had to be strong for family, for Russia, for God. But he couldn't. No more. He had reached his limit, and for fear of totally falling apart, he dared not move; he simply let his terrified family drape from him like a defeated flag. With every bit of courage he had left, he pinched his lips lest he cry out, clenched his eyes shut lest he spill his fear, and his face passed from white to crimson. And yet there was only so much he could control. A tear emerged in his right eye. Two tears. They were huge and round, and slowly, quite slowly, they began to travel down his cheek and into his beard.

Everyone came flooding into the room, Demidova, Trupp, Kharitonov, the guards, and, of course, finally the *komendant* himself.

"What have you idiots done!" Avdeyev yelled at the family. "You, Citizen Romanov, were you trying to escape? We open a window, and what do you do a minute later, try to run away? Is that it, hey, Nikolashka, you coward, trying to get away from us?"

I thought the Tsar was going to rip off the man's head. I saw his body quiver, his fists curl into knots of rock. But Nikolai Aleksandrovich didn't move. No, ever-fatalistic, he silently bore the insult as he had always carried everything, crown and all.

"I . . . I . . ." he said, barely able to speak, let alone control himself, "would never . . . never leave my family."

"Well, that's not what the guard down below said. He said he looked up and saw one of you ready to jump out!"

"That fool nearly killed my daughter!"

"They have strict orders to shoot upon—"

The Emperor flung his arm out, pointing at the doorway as he screamed, "Leave us!"

"Shto?" What? coarsely replied Avdeyev. "Let me remind you that you blood drinkers are the prisoners here! In case you don't yet understand, I am the *komendant* and I give the orders around—"

"Get out!"

"But—"

The Tsar's eyes flared, his entire face flashed red with fury, and, fired with the spirits of his ancestors, he shouted, *"Get out now!"*

Such a moment I will never forget. For the first and only time did Nikolai Aleksandrovich seem like a true Russian tsar, an ironfisted one. He was Ivan and Peter and Catherine all in one, and Avdeyev crumbled in a second. The *komendant* all but started shaking, all but bowed to the ground, for in the end of ends this was his Tsar, and at the very least he would grant him this, the few square meters upon which the august family was now huddled, as their territory and theirs alone. With no further protest, Avdeyev withdrew. And so did we, the rest of their meager attendants. Kharitonov fell away. Demidova. Trupp. Even Botkin, who had come at the last moment, ill though he was. I made my way out of the room as well. I slowly walked to the passage to the dining room, the door of which had been removed, of course. And the last I looked back, Nikolai was dropping to his knees. They were all coming together. All seven of them. Holding hands, they formed a tight circle, bowed their heads in prayer. Aleksandra and Tatyana started chanting a hymn, Nikolai spoke a prayer and . . . and . . .

7

Such a kind man was Nikolai II. So sweet. So tender. And gentle. He loved nothing more than his family and his country. He hated disagreements, either within his vast, squabbling house or among his ministers, both great and small, or anywhere else, for that matter, within his enormous realm. That was the Tsar I knew then, and the Tsar I've since grown to know in my books. Bloodshed was not at all what he wanted . . . and yet any fool would admit that that was his legacy. When *Batyushka,* the Dear Father, departed this world, he left behind a vast sea of blood, his own, his family's, his country's. Up until the ironfisted, totalitarian rule of the Red tsars—the *kommunisty,* who made the terrible Ivan look like a choir boy—his reign was one of the most violent in all the history of Russia. One must not forget that it was during the reign of Nicholas II that two disastrous wars, two bitter revolutions, and countless pogroms befell Holy Mother Russia. And though Tsar Nikolai wanted nothing more than to avoid violence, though many of the disasters were not of his doing, virtually all of them were his fault because he was Tsar, Russian Tsar, absolute Tsar,

Orthodox Tsar. When you look back through the decades, it now seems utterly obvious that there was no way it could be done, no way an autocrat could rule so vast a country, at least not without complete terror and oppression. Why, during his arrest the former Tsar read the anti-Semitic, *Protocols of the Elders of Zion,* which he found "very timely reading matter." He never learned, however, that the book was an entire fabrication, composed by his own tsarist secret police, whose duty it was to maintain order for their master, but who instead incited the hate and riots that toppled him. So in the end this is how Nikolai II must be viewed: a very caring man of moderate abilities who, although utterly devoted to his country, was unable to transform the unworkable autocratic system thrust upon him. Period. That simple.

You know, Tsar Nikolai and Comrade Lenin were like two great trains running toward each other at a colossal speed. The closer they came, the faster they went. They were traveling, however, on two entirely different sets of tracks, and so they should have passed by each other. They should have missed completely and zoomed on, racing toward their remarkable but very different destinations and goals. And yet . . . yet they collided head on with a great, terrible force, killing millions upon millions around them. And do you know why these two trains that were on two different sets of tracks collided so terribly? Because it was their fate, their destiny. And not just theirs alone, but all of Russia's.

Forgive me. It's true. I wander. I wander in my heart and my thoughts. Such is the curse of any emigrant, to abandon one's home and never find another, to always flounder in a sea of remorse. Your dear grandmother handled it much better than I, but then again she was a far superior person in so many ways.

Well, then, fate marched on . . .

Later that day the Romanovs had a real *obednitsa,* a liturgy without communion, their first in three months. Aleksandra arranged a small altar all by herself, draping one of her shawls on a table, setting out her images—her treasured icons—and then surrounding them with birch tree branches. It was lovely in its simplicity. And she and the daughters sang quite nicely. Father Storozhev in fact came, and while we all wondered if he might bring a note or news of some kind, there was nothing. Nor could there have been, because the priest was escorted in by Komendant Avdeyev, who never left his side.

And then?

Well, later in the day the girls darned various linens with Nyuta, then helped their mother arrange their "medicines," for this was an ongoing affair, their hiding of the last of their jewels. While the two suitcases of larger gems had been secretly left with the nuns in Tobolsk, you only have to peruse the last pages of Aleksandra's diary to see evidence of their clandestine stitching of the smaller diamonds. "Arranged things all day, tatted." "Tatyana sowed my j." "Arranged medicines with Yevgeny Sergeevich." "Arranged things, tatted, heart enlarged." "Arranged things." "Arranged things, tatted, read."

Finally, on the morning of July 16, slightly more than twelve hours before they were all slaughtered, the long, secret task was complete. In the final journal entry of her life—the very one where she mentions how I was taken away—Aleksandra simply noted, "Olga & I arranged our medicines." You see, it took the careful hands of all six women—the Tsaritsa, the four grand duchesses, as well as the maid—weeks to finish with the 42,000 carats, and doing so with precious little time to spare. As if they had sensed the hour of death was upon them, by noon of that day all the jewels were wrapped in cotton wadding, then packed and stitched ever so tightly into the double corsets of those beautiful girls, which of course proved such a horrible mistake.

The Tsar spent the rest of the day reading, pacing, and smoking at the open window. Later he had a sitting bath—I, myself, brought him hot water from the kitchen. Later yet he played bridge with his girls and bezique with Yevgeny Sergeevich. And thus, shortly after ten, concluded the twenty-third, a day which ended much more quietly than it had begun.

Did I say it was a Sunday?

I shall pass quickly over the twenty-fourth, which was fraught with tension only insomuch as nothing happened. Yevgeny Sergeevich remained in bed the entire day, as did the Empress, complaining yet again of an enlarged heart and aching eyes. Later, actually, she moved nearby the open window, where she read and played cards with Maria Nikolaevna. About this time, toward one o'clock, the rest of us were allowed into the garden. There we paced for forty minutes. The heat was tropical. Outside, in the full of sun, the temperature rose to thirty-seven and a half degrees, while inside the thick walls of the Ipatiev House it climbed only to a warm twenty-one and a half. Otherwise, we waited and hoped, but once again Sister Antonina and her novice failed to appear. I couldn't help but think that either the nun had been discovered, or the supposed friends of the Tsar and his family had lost their nerve and abandoned us. Although no one else spoke of such doubts, I am sure everyone else felt them, for anxiety hung in the air like thick fog.

Tuesday, the twenty-fifth, began as the other recent days, warm and monotonous. Yevgeny Sergeevich was feeling better from his attack of the kidneys, but he remained in bed nevertheless. After breakfast I wheeled about the Heir, room to room, as was my usual morning duty. We were just passing from the main parlor back into the dining room when both Aleksei Nikolaevich and I heard voices from beyond the double closed doors. The guard room lay there, and I could hear deep, distrustful voices of the men and a single, small one that was full of morning brightness.

Unable to contain his excitement, the Heir twisted in the wheeling chaise, looked up at me, and whispered, "That's Sister Antonina."

"*Da-s!*"

I turned the chair around, aiming it toward the double doors, and the Heir clasped his hands in his lap and eagerly bent forward. I half-expected Jim—the huge Negro from America who'd been a fixture at the Aleksander Palace right up until the first days of the revolution—to swing open the door with his usual great pomp. Instead, however, one of the guards shoved open the door with his foot.

"*Pyat minut.*" Five minutes, one of them ordered. "No more."

"Of course, my son."

Draped from head to foot in folds of black, the sister entered, her head bowed slightly as she tried to conceal a smile. She carried an open, woven basket, in which were nestled brown eggs, a good ten of them, and immediately behind her trailed Novice Marina, who clutched two *chetvert* of milk in her arms.

Upon seeing the Heir, both women stopped still, crossed themselves, and the sister, her head bowed, said, "*Dobroye ootre,* Aleksei Nikolaevich." Good morning.

Until recently, Aleksei had always been greeted so reverently, and he thought nothing of it. With a great deal of enthusiasm and curiosity, he looked upon them and nodded to the basket.

"I see you've brought me more eggs."

Sister Antonina, her eyes fixed firmly on the ground before her young master, gave a polite, "*Da-s.*"

"And milk? Did you bring—"

I heard not a sound from behind, for his worn, brown boots moved with great stealth. Before I knew it, Nikolai Aleksandrovich stepped in, scooted me aside, and took hold of the wheeling chaise. In a single, gentle movement, the Tsar spun it and the Heir around.

"We must not interrupt their work, Alyosha," said father to son.

"But—"

"We'll let Leonka deal with the food. After all, he is the cook's assistant. Now, how about a game of dominoes?"

Only after the Tsar and Tsarevich disappeared into the dining room and beyond did Sister Antonina and the Novice Marina raise their eyes and heads. Looking upon me with a proud, beaming smile, the sister stepped forward and kissed me peasant style, that is to say, three times on my cheeks. As she embraced me so warmly, I glanced over her shoulder, and saw that Marina was looking on, staring at me as if I were some kind of godly hero.

At the tail end of the third kiss, Sister Antonina whispered into my ear, "*Molodets.*" Excellent.

The diminutive sister was musty with the unmistakable perfume of Orthodoxy, so smoky and sweet, and I pulled back, took the basket from her hand. "Here, allow me."

And so it was that the sister and novice followed me out of the parlor, through the dining room, back around, and into the little makeshift kitchen. Cook Kharitonov stood at the counter peeling potatoes, and he eyed us over his shoulder.

"Again we have brought you the freshest of eggs," began Sister Antonina, "as well as milk still warm from the cow. Marina herself helped with the milking."

With that, the young girl stepped forward, handing me one glass bottle in particular and placing the other on the table. She looked at me, blushing as her eyes caught on mine.

"We will be back as soon as possible," said Sister Antonina.

I handed the novice the bottle they'd previously brought, now empty, of course, and escorted them through the dining room and into the parlor. Sister Antonina rapped once on the doors, one of which was opened, and the two women disappeared.

While Kharitonov, potato in hand, kept a seemingly loose eye on the door for a guard, I pulled the stopper from the very bottle Marina had placed in my hands. And that was where the second note from the officer was found, the note that to this day lies with the others in the *arkhivy* of the Russian Federation in Moscow. Later that summer, in an attempt to hide their crimes, the *Bolsheviki* frantically took all such documents—diaries, photo albums, letters, as well as the secret rescue notes—upon their evacuation of Yekaterinburg.

But back then, on the twenty-fifth, the morning thereof, hope seemed to be burning bright yet again. All of the Romanovs likewise supposed that there was a note in that milk bottle, and they were eager to know its contents. Within moments of the departure of the sister and her novice, the Tsaritsa's maid was at the door of the kitchen.

"Would you be so kind," said Demidova, "as to fulfill Aleksandra Fyodorovna's request for a glass of water?"

"Certainly," replied cook Kharitonov.

Of course, I was the one to fulfill the so-called request, because such trivial tasks always fell upon me, little Leonka. And so, clutching the folded note in my hand, I went to the crock of water that we always kept on the wooden counter. I gently pulled off the cloth covering the top and ladled a glass. And then turning to Demidova, I handed her the water. As I did so I slipped the note from my palm into hers. She smiled, her head bobbed in appreciation, and she quickly stuffed the note up the long sleeve of her dress. Immediately she turned to go, but just as quickly Kharitonov spoke out.

"Would you be so kind as to tell the others," said the cook, gazing deep into Demidova's eyes, "that only soup and vermicelli will be served at lunch? There will be no meat until dinner—the *komendant* himself told me that Leonka will not be allowed to go to the Soviet for more cutlets until three."

"I see."

Actually what she said was "*yasno*," which has a very rich meaning in Russian because, of course, Russian is a much richer, not to mention more beautiful, tongue than English, which is so hard-sounding and so rigid in its complex rules. *Yasno* doesn't simply mean "I see," nor does it simply mean, "It's clear," or "I understand." *Nyet, nyet,* that single word says something infinitely more profound. What it implies is that one understands not simply the meaning of the word, but also what lies beneath the surface yet cannot be spoken. It lays out, the true, complex dynamics of a situation. In other words, Demidova understood not the day's menu—for that was not the message at all—but that she needed to convey to the Tsar and Tsaritsa that if they wanted to reply to this note, they needed to have that reply finished by three so I could take it when I went out for meat.

So the note was delivered to the Tsar and his anxious Empress. At the time I was not privy to its contents, nor to the discussions within the family thereof. I don't know what Nikolai and Aleksandra talked of. Oh sure, I glimpsed the words of the note when I took it out of the bottle stopper, but this one was in French too. I could not make out a word. Translated, however, the June 25, 1918, note sent to the Romanovs reads thus:

> With the help of God and your sangfroid, we hope to succeed without taking any risk. One of your windows must be unglued so that you can open it at the right time. Indicate which window, please.
>
> The fact that the little Tsarevich cannot walk complicates matters, but we have taken that into account, and I don't think it will be too great an inconvenience. Write if you need two people to carry him in their arms or if one of you can take care of that. If you know the exact time in advance, is it possible to make sure the little one will be asleep for one or two hours before the escape?
>
> The doctor must give his opinion, but in case of need we can provide something for that.
>
> Do not worry: no attempt will be made without being absolutely sure of the result.
>
> Before God, before history, and before our conscience, we give you this solemn promise.
>
> An Officer

Although at that time I didn't know what was said specifically in the second letter, it soon became apparent that our rescuers were progressing with their plan and circling ever closer toward our salvation. Sure, I perceived this because the entire Imperial Family took on an air of near gaiety, a lighter tone such that was otherwise seen only when the Heir was in good health and spirits. And just as I was not witness to the Tsar reading the note, nor was I witness to him replying to it. I assumed then, as I still do to this day, that they commenced a reply almost at once, because for the rest of the morning, while I busied myself helping Kharitonov, all the Romanovs were busy with their books and their diaries and their letters. *Da, da,* they wrote a good many letters from their captivity to Nikolai's mama, the dowager or as she was referred to, the older empress, who was under house arrest in the Crimea, as well as letters to Aleksandra's sister, Grand Duchess Ella, the nun, who was under arrest not far away in Alapayevsk, and to their friends like Anna Vyrubova and the such. That was how things appeared for the rest of the morning, business as usual. They went to great lengths to make it appear so. Several of the children even studied too, including Olga Nikolaevna, who at one point took her writing tablet, a French novel, and her French-Russian dictionary to her father for his assistance.

"Papa, I'm having trouble with this translation. Would you help me?"

"With pleasure, *dochka moya.*" My little daughter.

It seemed so natural that the Tsar would help his daughter with French. Nikolai, of course, spoke beautiful, proper Russian, and very nice English and French. But never German. No, I never heard him or his bride speak the language of her native land.

So Nikolai and his eldest daughter disappeared into his bedchamber ostensibly to study her French novel but surely to compose a speedy reply to the officer's note. Aleksandra was there too. Having returned to bed after the morning inspection because her head ached, she sat propped up, stitching away on her "medicines" as they composed their response, which was complete by one, when luncheon was served. This I know, because as the Tsar came into the dining room he sought me out, resting his hand on my shoulder, which he squeezed in a kindly, most fatherly manner.

"Leonka, would you be so kind as to assist me after the meal?" To distract attention, he quickly added, "I would like to move my writing table in order to take better advantage of the evening sunlight."

"*Da-s,*" I replied with a slight bow of my head.

We were all present for the meal, including Aleksandra Fyodorovna, whose head had cleared, not because of a decrease in barometric pressure but most likely because of the uplifting news. As always we shared the same table, master and servant, and we all did our best to ignore rank.

Well, our midday meal was indeed a thin cabbage soup, followed by a second course of vermicelli sprinkled with dillweed. And after we had eaten and Demidova and I had cleared the table, I immediately went to the Tsar's bedchamber, finding it occupied by both my master and mistress.

"How may I assist you, Nikolai Aleksandrovich?" I asked, standing in the doorway with my hands folded before me.

"Ah, Leonka. Excellent." He gazed at me with those remarkable eyes, then winked, which gave my heart a start. "I just realized this morning that the evening light would be much better for writing if I situated my table a bit to the left. After all, the electric lamps have not been so reliable as of late."

No, they most definitely hadn't. Not only was the power supply from the city dam most unreliable, so was the wiring of the house itself. Just last week several electricians had spent two whole days trying to correct the problem.

From the cushioned chair where she sat, needle in hand, Aleksandra Fyodorovna said in a distinctly loud voice, "Leonka, I have a small present for the father who gave us the *obednitsa* yesterday." She held up a small handkerchief on which she was stitching the twice transversed cross of Russian Orthodoxy. "I wonder if you would be so kind as to drop it by the church the next time you go for food?"

"With pleasure, Madame. I am to go this afternoon."

"How convenient. I shall be finished within the half hour."

The Tsar glanced toward the door, saw no guard, then reached for a book on his table. He flipped through the pages, coming to the very note the sister had brought earlier, and withdrew it.

"Hide this well on your body, young man. Our response is written on the same note," he said, his voice low. "Do it now, place it in your undergarments."

I did as ordered, opening my clothes and hiding the note on my body. As I buttoned up my pants, I looked up.

"You know what to do?" he asked.

Speaking words that the Yekaterinburg Soviet had strictly forbidden, I replied in a hushed voice, *"Da-s, Vashe Velichestvo."* Yes, Your Greatness.

The Tsar and I then played out the charade of moving the writing table, a fine piece of polished wooden furniture with a green leather top. And then I retreated. Toward two-thirty they all went out into the garden, including Yevgeny Sergeevich, who was greatly improved. They all went out except the Empress and one of her daughters, the second, Tatyana Nikolaevna. They remained indoors, where they conducted their spiritual readings, Daniel 16 to the end, as well as Hosea 1–5. This I know because the Empress herself told me, whispering that she would be praying for me.

And so it was that after I helped the Tsar's footman, Trupp, carry the wheeling chaise down into the garden, and after the Tsar himself carried down his fourteen-year old son, I returned to the kitchen. Shortly thereafter, I was escorted out of the locked rooms, past the guards, through the double palisades, and out the gates into the square of the Church of the Ascension. It never occurred to me to run, to flee, not then, nor any other time. I don't know why, but somewhere in my heart I felt my place was in there, with them, in that house that was so full of evil intent.

Well, that afternoon I again fulfilled my task. I encountered no problems. As instructed, I stopped by the church and delivered the handkerchief embroidered by the Empress herself. And I handed over the note dictated by the Emperor and handwritten by his daughter, Olga Nikolaevna. I gave it to Father Storozhev, and it reads:

> The second window from the corner facing the square
> has been opened for 2 days—day and night. The sev-
> enth and eighth windows facing the square next to
> the main entrance are always open. The room is oc-
> cupied by the komendant and his aides, who are also
> the inside guards—up to 13 at least—armed with ri-

fles, revolvers, and bombs. None of the doors have keys (except ours). The komendant or his aides come into our room whenever they want. The one who is on duty does the outside rounds twice every hour of the night, and we hear him chatting with the sentry beneath our windows. There is a machine gun on the balcony and another downstairs in case of alarm. If there are others, we do not know about them. Do not forget that we have the doctor, a maid, two men, and a little boy who is a cook with us. It would be ignoble of us (although they do not want to inconvenience us) to leave them alone after they have followed us voluntarily into exile. The doctor has been in bed for three days with kidney trouble, but he is getting better. We are constantly awaiting the return of our men, Ivan Sednyov and Klementy Nagorny, young and robust, who have been shut up in the city for a month— we do not know where or why. In their absence, the little one is carried by his father in order to move about the rooms or go into the garden. Our surgeon, Derevenko, who comes almost daily at 5:00 to see the little one, lives in the city; do not forget. We never see him alone. The guards are in a little house across from our five windows on the other side of the street, 50 men. The only things that we still have are in crates in the shed in the interior courtyard. We are especially worried about A.F no.9, a small black crate, and a large black crate no. 13 N.A. with his old letters and <u>diaries</u>. Naturally the bedrooms are filled with crates, beds and things, all at the mercy of the thieves who surround us. All the keys and, separately, no. 9 are with the komendant, who has behaved well enough toward us. In any case, warn us if you can, and answer if you can also bring our people. In front of the entrance, there is always an automobile. There are bells at each sentry post, in the komendant's room, and some wires also go to the guardhouse and elsewhere. If our other people remain, can we be sure that nothing will happen to them??? Doctor B. begs you not to think about him and the other men, so that the task will not be more difficult. Count on the seven of us and the woman. May God help you; you can count on our sangfroid.

And here I must pause in my story . . .

8

Misha pushed the *stop* button on his tape recorder, listened as the little machine clicked to a halt, and then sat back in his leather desk chair. The old man took a deep breath, held it, and finally exhaled. From this vantage—Lake Forest, Illinois—and this time—August 1998—it was all going fine, wasn't it? He was telling the story just as he should, right?

Oh, how he wished May were here. She would know. His wife who always had a word on her tongue would tell him whether or not he was saying too much, too little, or if he was getting it just right. *Bozhe moi,* my God, how he couldn't wait until this life was over.

He pushed back his chair, grabbed ahold of the edge of his desk, hesitated, and pushed himself to his feet. Then he just stood there. Everything used to be so automatic, now he had to think about every little step. He started to move his left leg, but then a bolt of pain stabbed his bad knee. Wincing, he leaned on the desk with one hand, hesitated, tried again. It was always like this, at first walking seemed impossible, but after the first few steps he seemed to be able to walk out of it. And so he proceeded.

He'd always been amazed that the slaughtered bodies of the Romanovs had remained hidden for so many, many years, and in fact he had often wondered if they'd ever be found, particularly within his own lifetime. And it wasn't until July 11, 1991, the day after Boris Yeltsin's inauguration, that a squadron of detectives, colonels, epidemiologists, and forensic experts headed out of Yekaterinburg toward the village Koptyaki. It was there, behind a fence, underneath a tent, and in the glare of all these lights, that the herd of Russian officials pulled more than a thousand smashed and crushed bones out of the mud. Even then they weren't sure what they found. Seeking the truth but lacking DNA technology, the Russian scientists developed a sophisticated technique of computerized superimposition, whereby their mathematicians matched photos of the Romanovs to the skulls they found. And that was how, Misha had read, they determined that skull number four—the very one that contained a desiccated brain shriveled to the size of a pear—was none other than Tsar Nikolai. Skull number seven, meanwhile, proved the easiest to identify because of its extensive and beautiful dental work. It was that of the Empress Aleksandra.

Ach, thought Misha, crossing the broad living room, as the saying goes, There exists no secret that will not be revealed. And those broken and bizarrely crushed bones found in that shallow grave quickly told the story that the deaths had not only been violent, but grossly brutal, which was absolutely correct because of course Misha had seen it all with his own eyes. The most shocking thing the Russian specialists discovered, however, was what they didn't find: the bodies of both the Heir Tsarevich Aleksei and Grand Duchess Maria. And so that was his job, Misha's. Now it was up to him to tell why the bodies of two Romanovs were still missing. His story, his truth, was what he would leave behind and it would be, he was certain, the definitive truth that would stand for decades if not centuries.

So sad, thought Misha as he hobbled along, so terribly sad. Not just the murder of the Imperial Family, but that the hatred of the Russian Revolution proved so barbaric and violent. *Slava Bogu,* thanks to God, that at least the Romanovs had finally been laid to rest in an Orthodox service just last month in Sankt-Peterburg. Misha had procured a videotape of the funeral, and May and he had watched it over and over, all of which filled them both with a sense of peace. And then a mere three weeks after the funeral in Peterburg, May herself had died, content with the knowledge that the revolution that had burned across their homeland was done and over.

With a heaviness that had hung from his heart since that night so long ago, Misha went about his business. He visited the downstairs powder room just off the central hall, and then briefly headed into the kitchen, where he poured himself a glass of water. Carrying the glass, he returned via the butler's pantry, a narrow room filled with stacks of fine china and rows of crystal glasses. As he pushed open the swinging door into the dining room and gazed upon the massive mahogany table, he was reminded of all the fancy dinner parties they'd hosted. Here had dined not only the crème de la crème of Midwestern aristocracy—the Wrigleys, Walgreens, Swifts, Cranes, Maytags, and so many more—but also such international luminaries as Walt Disney, Ella Fitzgerald, Katharine Hepburn, and even the Prince of Wales. But it had all been a lie. He'd convinced all of Chicago society that he'd not only bought an immense amount of stock for practically nothing at the very bottom of the Depression, but that he'd been one of the first investors in IBM, buying what would become a fortune in stock for just pennies. So that everyone would think him of good breeding, Misha himself had planted the rumor that his parents were minor aristorcrats who had been horrendously slaughtered by the *Bolsheviki.* And then Misha moved into a new life in America, going through the motions of great happiness, buying this huge house, playing golf at the exclusive Onwentsia Club, and throwing extravagant parties. Yet it had all meant nothing, nothing! No, everything that he saw was in the context of how ugly, how cruel, was this world and its human race. Try as he wanted, Misha could barely love even his own boy, that which his own seed created. He made an effort, sometimes with success, to care for his Peter, but every time he gazed into his face he saw but one thing: his own reflection. Absolutely, mused Misha, as he moved through the room. In his own child he saw living proof that he had survived, and it was almost more than he could bear, for Misha had never been able to escape from the belief that it should have been him who was shot in the basement chamber, it should have been him dead on that road to village Koptyaki.

His head hung low, his shuffle slow, Misha crossed into the living room, muttering as he so often had, "Lord forgive me. But first make me suffer. I am the devil's creation. Torture me and make me cry out for mercy, but make me suffer . . ."

Entering his office, he paused and admired the wall of books on his Nikolai and Aleksandra, some three hundred volumes altogether. His will stipulated that these should be donated to Yale for their—

Misha's eyes suddenly caught a magazine wedged between two books. Oh, my dear God, he thought, his heart jumping in pace, didn't I get rid of that? Apparently not. He placed the water glass on the edge of his desk, then pulled down a worn and well-read issue of *Esquire* magazine that had appeared five years ago. He flipped it open to a dog-eared page, and even though Misha had read and reread the piece, he couldn't stop himself from once again studying the article entitled, "What Really Happened That Dark Night?" Nothing before had ever come so close to the truth. Nothing had ever scared him so much, and his eyes flew threw the entire lengthy piece, scanning every paragraph, until he came to the last few.

> Although unlikely, one or possibly two of Nicholas and Alexandra's children could have survived that horrible night of July 16–17, 1918. Between the time of the execution and their nefarious burial miles away, anything could have happened. Many suspect a guard discovered that one of the girls was alive and pulled her from the truck as it passed down that dark, dirt road to the Four Brothers Mine. After all, while the

bodies of five Romanovs have recently been found and identified, the bodies of two of the children, Alexei and Maria, are still missing. Where are they? What happened to them? Yurovsky, the commandant in charge of the execution, later claimed to have burned them and scattered their remains, but this, say scientists, is doubtful, for it is impossible to completely cremate a body over an open fire.

The theories abound, of course. Some say that Maria was later spotted on a train headed for China. Others, including survivors from a nearby monastery, claim she wandered Siberia until her death in 1973.

While it is extremely unlikely that Alexei, a hemophiliac, could have survived the brutal events that took place in the basement of the Ipatiev House, one of the more interesting hypotheses is that he simply wasn't there at all. Rather, a handful of people believe that he switched places with the kitchen boy, Leonid Sednyov, who was about his age and height. Disguised, Alexei was then, they say, spirited out of the house just hours before his family was murdered. If the young Sednyov was killed in his place, if Alexei did in fact survive, if he did in fact go on to live to the age of 17, was he, as Rasputin had predicted, completely cured? And if so, how long did he live and where? Was he, as some suspect, the mysterious hermit monk sometimes spotted lurking in the forest outside Yekaterinburg? Perhaps.

Then again, we'll never know.

Misha slammed shut the magazine. He had to get rid of it. Sure, his granddaughter Kate might find a copy on her own, but he sure as the devil wasn't going to leave one right here in his office for her to discover. He'd been a fool to keep it here this long. And with that, Misha folded the magazine in half and threw it in his leather-embossed trash can. He'd been so thorough, tried to be so complete, and yet . . . yet . . .

He found himself leaning against his wall of cherished books.

These volumes, which included everything from the Tsar and Tsaritsa's last diaries to the letters of Queen Victoria, were like friends to him. Individually each one contained a snippet of the truth, while their knowledge combined did contain the greater part.

And it flashed through his mind: just a look. Sure, and rather like an addict his hands started shaking. Just one quick look.

Pulling a brass key from his pocket, he moved a few feet to the side and yanked out two books in particular, revealing a lock. He was just about to insert the key and unlock his vault when he caught himself. No, he thought. Not yet. If I go into that small chamber I'll be swept away by memories and I'll never finish the tape. And finish I must.

He slipped the key back into the pocket of his trousers, and parked the books back in front of the lock. He hadn't been in there since three days before May had died, when he'd brought his wife down for what turned out to be her final visit. Absolutely no one but May and he knew of the vault's existence, yet Kate, whom he loved so dearly, soon would. Within a short time the contents thereof would be all her responsibility. Misha only prayed that the audiotape he was now making and the sealed letter he'd left with his attorney would be enough to guide her.

In any case, it would soon be out of his control. He'd done everything he could not only during his lifetime, but to control things from the grave.

Sitting down at his desk, Misha took a brief sip of water. With a deep rumble, he cleared his throat. And then he pushed the button on the tape recorder and continued:

"Hi, my sweet Kate. It's me, your old Dyedushka Misha. I'm back. Is my story making sense? Are you able to follow everything? If there's anything that doesn't make sense, don't forget to check the documents in my dossier, okay, *malenkaya*?" Little one.

"You know, many people, many times have said to me how much Russians and Americans are alike. We both have such big hearts, we are both so welcoming into our homes, we are both so desperate to be liked. And sure, in these ways we resemble each other. I do not know—

perhaps it is because both countries are so vast and hold such a diversity of peoples, but . . . but the similarities stop there. The truth is that Americans cannot possibly begin to understand the depth of the Russian soul, the Orthodox soul. And this you must to understand. For my story to make sense you must comprehend that every Russian, in his heart of hearts, believes that sin brings suffering, great suffering. That in turn leads to repentance, and it is that very cleansing which eventually delivers one closer unto the feet of God Himself. Do not forget: sin, repentance, holy deliverance. Sin, torment and cleansing, purification. Sin, suffering, forgiveness.

"Clear?

"My passport says I am now an American, but in my heart I know I am and will always be *Russkie,* and like every other person of my country, I want to judge, I want to blame, I want to point away from myself, and say, There, that is the guilty fool, that person did that to me and my fatherland. He is at fault, not me! It's true, so very true, we Russians are peasants, mere peasants who will do anything to escape blame and responsibility, for we are still deathly afraid of our master's whip. But in fact . . . in fact the dynasty itself exploded for a myriad of stupidly brilliant reasons. Simply, it somehow stumbled upon a perfect, and yet altogether not random, chemical reaction: you take one part decent man but not enlightened ruler, one part heartbroken mother clutching for any way to save her son, two parts inbred dynasty and gossip-obsessed court, one part Great War, and three parts uneducated, worn, and hungry people, and—*boom!*—what do you get? Revolution, terrible, terrible revolution, of course! Any *eedee-ot* can see that.

"It amazes me still to this day how quickly the empire fell to pieces. One day the people are kissing the ground upon which the Tsar's shadow has fallen, the next they are hacking apart his body. Nikolai merely put down his scepter and walked away, and literally overnight a three-hundred-year old dynasty evaporated—*poof,* gone!—with no one lifting a finger to save it. Ironic that the Soviet Union collapsed just as easily, which proves it was no better, that the cure, *kommunizm,* was in fact far worse than the disease itself. Now, I can only hope, those days are over, and just maybe that's true. After all, it took nearly one hundred years for the insanity to fade from France after their revolution.

"So, anyway . . . where was I? Oh, sure," he said, leaning forward and checking the tape, which was whirring away. "I must continue my dark story. You must listen while I tell of the terrible things I saw the night the Romanovs were murdered. I have lived with this story every day, every moment of my life, yet never did I want these events to cross my lips. But now, because of recent developments, tell I must. You see, the night the Romanovs were killed, I chased after the truck that was overflowing with *troopy*—carcasses—as it slowly headed down that dirt road to village Koptyaki.

"But I will get to all of those gruesome details. Now, just listen as I return to the morning of June 26,1918."

9

It was a Wednesday. The previous day the second note had come so nicely hidden in the cork of that *chetvert* of milk, and then that afternoon I'd carried out the long reply. We were all quite hopeful, even quite expectant, that Wednesday morning. We'd had no news from the outside for weeks—no letters, no newspapers except an ersatz journal that consisted of three telegrams reprinted on some greasy brown paper—but suddenly there was that candle of hope. Perhaps the world had not forgotten His Majesty after all. Though the morning was hot—"Very hot again, 22½ degrees in the room," recorded Aleksandra in her diary—we were all quite eager upon rising, thankful to know that someone was apparently working on our behalf. Could it be that God had finally heard the long, sorrowful prayers of Aleksandra and her family? Had she finally got right her arrangements of icons?

I was in the kitchen stuffing the center of the samovar with twigs and pine cones. It was not quite seven-thirty. And the first of the Romanovs to go to the water closet that morning—accompanied by a guard, of course—was again the second daughter, Tatyana Nikolaevna.

Our eyes met and said the same things: yes, perhaps today was the day, perhaps by eve we would be free. Her fine lips pursed the smallest of smiles. Carrying a sponge, toothbrush, rubber traveling bowl, and a pressed white linen hand towel, she, with the guard right behind her, passed through the kitchen, past the twenty-three steps, and to the far corner of the house. In the back of my mind I heard the door of the water closet open, close, and knew that the guard was waiting right outside the door while the Grand Duchess was performing her morning ablutions.

Several moments later, however, I heard the door of the water closet thrown open, and then Tatyana Nikolaevna, like a fast moving summer storm, swept back through the kitchen, her eyes cast to the floor. There were bright blooms of red spread across her face—again, so much like her mother whose emotions manifested themselves physically—while behind her came the guard, laughing deeply as he stroked his stringy beard. What untoward actions had he taken? Had he cornered the young woman, tried to kiss her, as one of them had tried to embrace Maria just last week?

I glanced through the hall, into the dining room. I saw nothing, but heard a flurry of low voices, the swishing of dresses. A few moments passed before Nikolai Aleksandrovich himself came storming along the same route. Wearing his army tunic and tall leather boots, of course, he passed through the kitchen, his face grave. Behind him came the same guard, still laughing, still stroking his beard. Although I was all but invisible to both of them, I watched as the ex-Tsar moved with great determination into the water closet. He remained there longer than his daughter. A good deal longer.

I lit the samovar, vented the smoke out the window. I blew on the twigs, made sure the flame was fine and strong. And then I heard Nikolai Aleksandrovich emerge, heard him march my way, his pace steady, controlled, firm. Almost like a robot he passed me by, his face stony and void of expression. Many people have described the Tsar as such, that when bad news was delivered upon him they were surprised by his lack of reaction, lack of emotion. Some great ministers and foreign dignitaries mistook this as a lack of caring and feeling, a weak-willed passivity or deep-seated fatalism. But they were all wrong. Niko-lai Aleksandrovich was deeply emotional, extraordinarily caring. And also a firm believer that the Tsar of All the Russias must maintain absolute control—control of every little item on his desk, control of his own calendar and appointments, and above all, supreme among most manly things, control of his personal feelings. All this while deep inside so much was seething, all of which he expressed only to his wife. Yes, a passionate, loving man—which is made clear in the thousands of letters he left behind—but as he moved on by, not an inkling of emotion could I detect on that man's practiced face. I did notice something, however: his hands. They were blackened, and he was rubbing them together, trying desperately to wipe something away.

Unable to contain myself, I quickly peered into the center of the samovar and saw that the blaze was going well. I then glanced into the dining room, spying nothing. While all of the Romanovs needed a guard to escort them to the water closet or the bathing room, I did not. And so that is exactly where I went, to the very place where the Tsar had just gone on foot. Passing through the house, I reached the far corner, where I paused, heard the guards' deep voices—was that groggy one Komendant Avdeyev?—then reached for the door of the water closet. And thereupon entered a small chamber of surprise.

Russians can be witty. They can be cruel. And they find keen delight in the grotesque marriage of the two. Many things had I heard in jest about Nikolai—"We had a revolution not because we wanted a limited monarchy, but because we had a limited monarch"—but here on the walls of the water closet were things that my youthful mind had never conjured. On the wall across from the ceramic sink was painted a demonic man, his hair long and scraggly, his beard twisted and foul. He was naked, and rising from between his legs was a gigantic, erect penis which he was shoving into the crack of a woman who herself wore nothing but a large, bejeweled crown. Above him was written the name "Grisha," while on her crown was enscribed "Shura." Sure, in this tiny chamber the angry Red guards had portrayed the man they believed had soiled the dynasty and brought down the empire, Grigory Rasputin, fornicating with that traitor to the motherland, the German bitch, Empress Aleksandra Fyodorovna. Nearby, watching the scene with robust delight, was an effeminate, chubby, bearded man with droopy breasts—the Emperor Nikolai II—who sat in a tub overflowing with German marks and American dollars. It was done in big bold strokes of black paint. Permanent paint. That much was obvious because the Tsar had used a wet hand to try to wipe it away, though it had proved impossible to do little more than lightly smear the graphic mural.

But there was more.

Most of the guards had never before seen a toilet, let alone used one, and had taken to using this one by standing on the seat itself and squatting. In light of the numerous muddy footprints left behind on the seat, the Empress had had her maid place a cultured sign above the toilet that read: "Be so kind as to leave the toilet as clean as you found it." But that did little good, because most of the guards couldn't read, either. In any case, to the side and written directly on the wall was a little ditty:

TO ALL HIS PEOPLES NIKOLAI SAID
AS FOR A REPUBLIC, GO FUCK YOURSELVES INSTEAD
SO OUR RUSSIAN TSAR CALLED NICK
WE DRAGGED FROM HIS THRONE BY HIS DICK

To myself I mumbled aloud the last two lines—*"Tsaria russkogo Nikolu, Za khuy sdernuli s prestolu"*—and I began to shake. Such rudeness was unbelievable—to this day it's still forbidden in Russia to even publish the word *khuy*. And, I started to cry, not so much out of fear, but because for the first time I grasped how horrid a world lay ahead if, in fact, I survived.

Yes, the image and little ditty remained all the way to the end, and, in fact, were added to as the days fell away, with slogans like, "Crush the Crowns of the Tsar, Tear Apart the Old World," "Death to the

Blood Drinker," "To Hell with *Kapitalizm*," "Crush International Imperialism." All these did the Romanovs see in the water closet. Day after day, whenever they went to relieve themselves, they were surrounded with this hatred. I have no idea what they thought, what they felt, as they—father, mother, son, and daughters—went into that small chamber one after the other and sat there alone and half-naked as the hatred bore down upon them from all sides. And yet, the Romanovs suffered well. Not a protest did they make, not a word did they complain. They read their Bibles, they chanted their prayers, they bowed to their icons.

Yet that morning there was still a chance of rescue. And a chance meant hope. No, Nikolai did not want to be rescued from that special house and restored to the brilliancy of the Romanov throne, of this I am absolutely certain. If so many of his peoples felt locked in the chains of poverty, then he felt entrapped by the riches of the dynasty, which is to say that peasant and Tsar alike were liberated by the revolution. Yes, many have said, and I do believe it to be true, that Nikolai bloomed after his abdication.

The call of nature ruled all, of course, and one by one all of the Romanovs visited the water closet by eight of that morning, that is to say within the thirty minutes left before our inspection. Not a word of protest did they make, however—at least not outwardly, not that could be heard by any of their guards, or even us, their small retinue, consisting of Dr. Botkin, the maid, Demidova, the footman Trupp, the cook, Kharitonov, and me, the kitchen boy. I watched all the rest of them—the Empress, the Heir Tsarevich, and the other three daughters—as they passed through the kitchen to the facilities, escorted, as they all were, by a guard. To generalize, if they appeared full of trepidation as they headed for the toilet room, then they seemed shocked upon their return. In all that I've learned, the thing that surprised Nikolai and Aleksandra the most about his abdication, the one aspect that crushed their hearts, was definitely not the loss of power and wealth, but the realization of how widely hated they were. And by this I mean not by the court, but the *narod*—the masses—whose emotions were so deeply stirred by the centuries of inequity and darkly spiced by the poisonous propaganda of the *Bolsheviki*.

So the inspection that morning was a somber affair. The only visible sign of stress among the family were Aleksandra's eyes, which were swollen red, and her pale skin, which was all blotchy. But while she was deeply disturbed that morning, perhaps deathly afraid, she would not betray herself, she would not allow her captors that victory not simply over her persona, but most importantly over her faith in the greater glory of *Bog*. God. She knew as well that she had to be strong for her children, the children whom she had always tried to raise properly so that they would not folly in their wealth and exulted status. To them she wrote:

> Learn to make others happy, think of yourself last of all. Be gentle and kind, never rough nor rude . . . Show a loving heart. Above all, learn to love God with all the force of your soul and He will be near you . . . Your old Mama

Standing according to our rank, from Tsar to Tsaritsa, Heir to grand duchesses, then all the way from doctor, maid, and down to me, the lowest of all, that morning inspection was the most somber of any to take place in The House of Special Purpose. We stood in the dining room, in front of the large fireplace, all of us seething with rage and fear, but none of us saying a word, because we took our every cue from the Emperor and Empress. When they crossed themselves during a church service, so did we. When they dropped to their knees and bowed their foreheads to the floor, so did we. And that morning, during that inspection, both Nikolai and Aleksandra stood ramrod straight, their lips pinched tight like a champagne cork holding all within lest all explode. And so did we.

"*Noo . . . noo . . .*" Well . . . well . . . mumbled Avdeyev, looking us up and down.

Big and heavy was he, his hair a mess, his face unshaved. Actually his eyes were red as well, though certainly not from crying. *Nyet*, we knew there had been much drinking last night, for there'd been so much shouting, so much hooting and singing. And that was surely when the drawings had been made on the walls of the water closet.

"So . . ." began Avdeyev, his voice all coy, obviously fishing for some kind of reaction to the drawing and the ditty, "any questions, any problems?"

"*Nyet-s,* Aleksander Dimitrievich," respectfully replied the Tsar.

Avdeyev stared long and hard into Nikolai Aleksandrovich's face. One of the guards across the room openly laughed, and Avdeyev's bloated lips swelled into a puffy, purple smile.

"*Neechevo?*" Nothing? "Really? No questions of any sort?"

I glanced over, saw the Tsar's face bloom crimson, noted his chin begin to quiver. Was this it? Had the Tsar reached the end? Could he, would he, burst with this last teeny bit of needling? And if so, if he fell, what did that mean for the rest of us? What hope would there be?

"*Nyet-s, voprosov nikakix.*" No, there are no questions, tersely said the Tsar, holding his head as well as his voice steady, good soldier that he was.

Avdeyev shrugged and turned away, saying, "Very well, then go ahead and have your morning tea."

Groaning and rubbing his head, the *komendant* lumbered off, making his way back to the main guard room on this level, where, I imagine, he laid back down and went to sleep for a good long while.

Meanwhile, cook Kharitonov and I prepared the tea, which was served in the dining room. Black tea, black bread, and a bit of butter. They all sat down—the seven Romanovs, Dr. Botkin, and only reluctantly, only after all the others had taken their seats, Demidova and Trupp. Sure, cook and I brought everything out to the table and sat down as well. That morning we were short just three things, two teaspoons and one butter knife, so the cutlery went around the table. But it went around in silence, for hardly a word was spoken during the meager repast.

Immediately after breakfast Nikolai Aleksandrovich retired with his son to the drawing room, where they sat with Dr. Botkin, who, though much improved, was still weak from his attack of the kidneys. In his beautiful voice, so clear, so resonant, the Tsar read aloud, as was his frequent custom, and that morning he read to his son and his friend, Botkin, the twelfth volume of Saltykov, *Poshekhonskaya starina,* The Old Days of Poshekhonye. And soon the work of Russia's richest satirical writer—this one poking fun at the old landed gentry and bureaucrats alike—began to lift the morose cloud, filling the rooms of the Ipatiev House with small, but such significant peals of laughter.

And the womenfolk?

All morning they "arranged things." Aleksandra, her maid, and four daughters worked more furiously than ever, sewing secretively in near-constant shifts. I suppose given the notes we had already received and the very real possibility that we might at any moment have to flee, it seemed the only wise course. So Aleksandra disappeared into her bedroom, where in the heat of the summer she sewed away. A few minutes later Olga Nikolaevna went to assist her, an hour later Demidova, and so on.

Thus passed that painful morning, each of us in our own way trying to comprehend what lay ahead of us. Never, however, did I imagine so dark an event as would take place. Then again such a thing as a *chistka*—a cleansing, a liquidation—was a new concept, one that would be played like a black refrain throughout the history of the Soviet Union.

10

It was approaching the noon hour when a great *Slava Bogu* rose like a Gregorian chant. Yes, we all gave thanks to God when at midday Sister Antonina and Novice Marina came, bringing with them precious foodstuffs, including another priceless *chetvert* of milk. Cook Kharitonov and I were both in the kitchen when the visitors came, and again it was I, the kitchen boy, who received the goods from the sister.

"*Dobryi dyen*, my sons." Good day, said Sister Antonina, her stout little figure draped in black as always.

"*Dobryi dyen, sestra,*" I replied.

"With pleasure and by the grace of God Himself," she said, handing me a basket in which were nestled some eggs, "we humbly offer a simple token."

Kharitonov, who was boiling some water on the little oil stove, wiped his beaded brow, and said, "Ah, it is the good sisters of the world who keep our bellies full."

"Of course. Our chickens are our pride. And we have such good cows, such fresh grass as well. The novice Marina here," Sister Antonina said, indicating her shy, young apprentice, "is a very able milk-maid, isn't that right, *dorogaya?*"

Marina was dressed not as rigorously in black, for I could see waves of rich brown hair beneath her headpiece, not to mention her ankles at the base of her black frock. And she just stood there, her head bowed, saying nothing. Instead, she merely blushed the color of a summer sunrise as she carefully placed a glass bottle of milk on the wooden table.

"And today," continued Sister Antonina, "we have not only more milk and such nice fresh eggs for The Little One, but some cheese from our caverns as well."

"They are greatly appreciated," I replied.

"This I know."

I studied the sister's apple-wrinkled face, which was so darkly and tightly swathed by the black wimple of her order, and saw that her cheeks and nose were red and swollen with the heat of the day. Tiny droplets of moisture glistened on the surface of what little of her skin was showing, and my eyes traveled to her eyes, linking us in silent communication. Her long gaze, punctuated by one double blink, telegraphed all that could not be said.

Suddenly a guard appeared in the doorway, gun over his right shoulder, grenade on his belt. It was not the blond guard, but the beardless one with dark hair.

"It is not permitted to visit with the detainees!" he snapped, his voice surprisingly deep and gruff.

Sister Antonina turned on him with a practiced and extraordinarily effective weapon of her own, a grandmotherly smile. "Of course, my son."

"The *komendant* orders you to leave."

"*Da, da, da.* We're just going."

"Now!"

"I understand, my son." Sister Antonina then leaned forward and kissed me on each cheek, whispering in the faintest of angel voices, "Tell them to be ready as soon as tonight."

Yes, those were the very words she planted in my ear, which to this day have lived within my being like an ear worm, a refrain that sings over and over, and from which I cannot escape. The good sister followed after the lad, and I expected the novice to simply and silently patter after them both. Instead, however, Novice Marina, her head slightly bowed as always, stepped quickly toward me and, much to my surprise, reached to kiss me as well. Wondering what it meant, I stood there, quite surprised to feel her young, fresh lips upon first my one cheek, then the other. To further startle me, she reached for my hand and clasped her soft fingers around mine. Only in that moment did I understand the reasons for her affection, because in the slightest, most subtle of moves she transferred a folded envelope from her palm to mine.

"*Do svidanya,*" I muttered.

As she hurried off, I slipped my hand into my pants, depositing the folded envelope into the secret darkness of my pocket. Going about my business, I reached for the butter yellow ceramic bowl in which cook always made the blini the Heir so dearly loved. And into this bowl, its glaze all crackled, I placed the brown eggs of the monastery chickens. I stacked them slowly, neatly, one fragile oval shell atop the other. Glancing first over my right, then my left shoulder, I discerned no guards in the corridor, nor any lurking in the dining room. My eyes met cook's, and he gave me a slow, knowing nod as he went about his business of preparing macaroni for Aleksandra Fyodorovna.

I asked, "Will you prepare some of the eggs for Aleksei Nikolaevich's midday meal?"

"I think certainly."

I lifted the glass bottle of milk, finding it indeed as fresh and warm as a newborn. I checked the doorways once again, and pulled out the cork. As before, there was a tiny slit cut into the stopper, and I quickly pulled out the small note that was hidden there. I started to—

"Leonka," called a deep voice from the doorway.

I jumped, nearly spilled the entire bottle of milk, and did in fact drop the cork to the floor. As quickly as I could, I crammed the note into my pocket.

"*Sh-to?*" What?

I turned to see the Tsar's faithful footman, Trupp—Aleksei Yegorovich Trupp—standing in the doorway. He was an old man by then, somewhere over sixty, and had wiry gray hair and a healthy paunch. I think that he'd served not only during all of Tsar Nikolai's twenty-three year reign, but had also waited upon Nikolai's father, Tsar Aleksander III. A life without a tsar was simply impossible for Trupp, who had gladly shared the royal family's year-and-a-half imprisonment.

"Leonka," began the manservant once again, "if the nuns have brought more fresh milk, Yevgeny Sergeevich requests that you be so kind as to bring him a glass . . . to, ah, ah, soothe his stomach, of course."

"Certainly."

Trupp withdrew himself, which went quite against the worn-out protocol of the Imperial Household. Then again, these were extraordinary times and everything had changed. In previous times, however, a boy of my low status would never have been allowed to carry a mere glass or a simple plate to the dinner table or anywhere else within the royal apartments. Absolutely not. Back then, back in those days at Tsarskoye, everyone had a position and a purpose, and I would have remained entirely within the confines of the kitchen, which was in a separate building and attached to the Aleksander Palace only by tunnel. Any food that was brought to Their Highnesses or guests was done so by footmen like Trupp, who usually transported any nourishment with great haste, running through the long tunnel and down the long, straight halls of the palace. Upon entering the private rooms, however, one had to be quiet, for Aleksandra Fyodorovna hated the clatter of dishes, not to mention kitchenly smells, the likes of which now perfumed our daily existence.

But these were different days indeed. And I was no fool. It was my presence, not a glass of milk, that was requested.

I took one of the thin glasses, poured some thick, rich milk. And then I recorked the glass bottle and glanced once at cook, who nodded at me ever so slightly. I proceeded through the hallway where I slept, into the dining room where Anastasiya Nikolaevna still sat with her drawing tablet—this was the route, this was my course. The youngest of the daughters looked up at me only briefly, her face blank. She was learning quickly the language of mistrust, of course, for there was a guard standing in the far corner, a tall fellow with dark hair and a huge bushy mustache. And so I continued to the other end of the dining room, to the left, and into the long drawing room.

The three of them—Tsar, Tsarevich, and doctor—were in the alcove at the far end. This was where Botkin slept, next to the large wooden desk in the alcove. He was reclined there, while the Tsar sat alongside in a comfortable wooden chair and the Heir remained in the wheeling chaise. Nikolai Aleksandrovich continued the pretense of reading aloud as I circled the large potted palm, but then he stopped as I delivered the glass to Botkin.

"The *sestra* has just brought milk from the monastery, Yevgeny Sergeevich. It's still warm—she said it's fresh from the cow this morning."

"*Spacibo, molodoi chelovek.*" Thank you, young man, said the doctor, accepting the glass.

I turned to the Tsar, hesitated. Nikolai Aleksandrovich eyed the drawing room, then laid those magnificent eyes upon me. With a single nod, he bade me forward. I stabbed my hand into my pocket and snatched out the folded piece of paper and the envelope too.

"The paper was in the cork," I whispered. "And the other, the envelope, was given me by Novice Marina."

Nikolai Aleksandrovich looked at them both, and spying the handwriting on the envelope, muttered with a smile, "Ah, a letter from Anya."

He was referring, of course, to the Tsaritsa's only companion, her blindly faithful friend, Anna Vyrubova, the Cow, as the Empress referred to her whenever she was out of favor, which happened from time to time. But a loyal friend this Anya was. Persecuted too, for the entire country thought she not only worked hand in hand with Rasputin, but that the Empress, the mad monk, and Anya herself formed a poisonous camarilla bent on the destruction of Holy Mother Russia. For this Vyrubova was dragged from the Aleksander Palace and thrown into one prison after another, from the pits of the Fortress of Peter and Paul to Krondstadt itself. It was a miracle she survived at all—the starvation, the beatings, the filth, and the scourge. But she did survive; somehow she escaped an appointment with her own execution, went into hiding for several years, and then eventually fled across the ice floes to Finland, where she became a nun and lived all the way until 1964. And it is to Anna Vyrubova's credit that she was one of the few who worked secretly and continuously to save the Imperial Family, sending hundreds of thousands of rubles to secret agents in Siberia who, in the end, did little but pocket the fortune.

I leaned closer to the Tsar and quickly whispered, "Sister Antonina also said this, she said: 'tell them to be ready as soon as tonight.'"

How do I describe Nikolai Aleksandrovich's response? Was he stunned? Surprised? Excited? His eyes opened wider, remaining fixed on me as it sunk in, as he realized that their rescue could come as early as the day's end.

All he said was a deep, single word. *"Yasno."* All is clear.

I turned, retreating from the drawing room and my duties, and headed back into the kitchen, where I assisted cook Kharitonov in the preparation of our simple meals. Lunch was soon served, servants and royals sharing the same table.

And the third note, the one that I found like its predecessors, in the cork of the bottle? It reads:

> Do not worry about the fifty or so men who are in a little house across from your windows—they will not be dangerous when it comes time to act. Say something more precise about your komendant to make the beginning easier for us. It is impossible to tell you

now if we can take all your people; we hope so, but in any case they will not be with you after your departure from the house, except the doctor. Are taking steps for Doctor D. Hoping before Sunday to indicate the detailed plan of the operation. As of now it is like this: once the signal comes, you close and barricade with furniture the door that separates you from the guards, who will be blocked and terror-stricken inside the house. With a rope especially made for that purpose, you climb out through the window—we will be waiting for you at the bottom. The rest is not difficult; there are many means of transportation and the hiding place is as good as ever. The big question is getting The Little One down: is it possible? Answer after thinking carefully. In any case, the father, the mother, and the son come down first; the girls, and then the doctor, follow them. Answer if this is possible in your opinion, and whether you can make the appropriate rope, because to have the rope brought to you is very difficult at this time.

An Officer

This "Doctor D" to whom they refer—that was Dr. Vladimir Nikolaevich Derevenko who had been treating the Heir.

The Tsar often joked that their prison life was really more like one long trip across the ocean, each new day being identical to the previous. But not that one. A great stir in our routine had taken place and after the midday meal I heard many low voices and whispered discussions. Sure, they were trying to decide what to do, how to handle this, and what exactly it meant, this possibility of an imminent escape. At about two the entire household went down the twenty-three steps to take the fresh air; that is, we all went out with the exception of Dr. Botkin, Aleksandra Fyodorovna, and her eldest daughter, Olga, who remained with her mother to "arrange medicines." And there in the little garden, that scruffy yard, we were allowed to walk for two entire hours on account of the stifling heat. Paced in circles, that was what we did, particularly the Tsar, who never stopped moving. Sometimes he appeared animated and excited, while sometimes he looked worried and anxious. I think he was pondering, trying to foresee the events of the next few hours and days, though who could have guessed what the *Bolsheviki* had in store?

And the envelope that Novice Marina slipped from her palm to mine?

Truth be told, I never saw its contents, and unfortunately the letter no longer remains, or at least it has not surfaced from the bowels of the Soviet archives. I imagine Aleksandra ripped it up and flushed it, something along those lines, but it was most definitely from this Anna Vyrubova, the much assoiled friend. She was accused of many terrible things, but in the end of ends she was merely a simple, exuberant soul devoted to her friends, the sovereigns, and their well-being. True, she must have been a natural schemer, and an excellent one at that, otherwise how did she do it, how did she get all those letters to the imperial ones and all that money to the secret agents? Actually, it has never been clarified, for writing from the safety of Finland in 1923 all that Mademoiselle Vyrubova confessed was:

> Even now, and at this distance from Russia, I cannot divulge the names of those brave and devoted ones who smuggled the letters and parcels to and from the house . . . and got them to me and to the small group of faithful men and women in St. Petersburg. The two chiefly concerned, a man and a woman, of course lived in constant peril of discovery and death.

Though I was never to read the smuggled letter, I did see its effects, and exuberant effects they were. Gathered around the tea table that afternoon, the Romanovs ate their slices of bread and drank their black tea and surreptitiously passed the note from father to mother to daughter to sister . . . and so on . . . each of them not glancing at the words, but quickly holding the envelope to his or her nose and drinking in its scent. A marvel it was to them, something like a drug, something like a beacon that led back to the brightness of the dear past. I, who had driven the Heir in his chaise into the room, saw it all, saw their faces light up with shock and pleasure.

"Here, Leonka," Aleksei Nikolaevich whispered to me, handing me the envelope at the very end of the line, "smell this."

I held the paper to my nose, deeply inhaled, and . . . and my head bloomed like a flower, so rich, so sweet that . . . that I couldn't help but sneeze like a horse. They all burst into laughter, every member of the Imperial Family and those few of us who were left of their fifteen thousand servants.

"Boodtye z'dorovy, Leonka." Be healthy, blessed Nikolai Aleksandrovich.

One by one the others mumbled a similar blessing, while I wiped my nose and quickly handed back the note to Aleksei, who tucked it hidden by his side there in the wheeling chair.

Day passed into evening, and supper was served at eight. After the meal, the Tsar read aloud to Botkin, while Aleksandra wrote furiously on a pad, and Tatyana, Olga, and Nyuta pretended to darn some undergarments, but really "arranged." Eventually too Nikolai laid aside his book and took pen to paper writing not his diary, but a note, or more specifically a reply. *Da, da.* The following day when I carried out the reply to the third note I also carried out two replies to Mademoiselle Vyrubova's letter. Sure, both the Tsar and Tsaritsa wrote back, notes that still exist by the way, for rather than destroying them, the sentimental cow carried them all the way out of Russia, whereupon they eventually made their way to the preserves of Yale University in America.

To his friend Anya, the Tsar wrote:

> Thank you so much for your kind wishes, which we
> received only today. Our thoughts and prayers are al-

ways with you, poor suffering creature. Her Majesty read to us all your lines. Horrid to think all you had to go through. We are all right here. It is quite quiet. Pity we have not seen you in so very long. Kisses and blessings without end from your loving friend, N. Give my best love to your parents.

The Tsar's reply, of course, took him some time to compose. Yes, he was the careful one. Everything in its place, including words on a page. The Empress, however, was all heart, all emotion, and her reply, written in English, came out in one long gush:

My Darling, My Dear Little Owl, I kiss you tenderly. You are in all our hearts. We pray for you and often talk of you. In God's hands lie all things.

We received your letter, and I thank you from my heart. It was such a joy to hear from you. One has so much to say that one ends by saying nothing. I am unaccustomed to writing anything of consequence, just short letters or cards, nothing of consequence. Your perfume on the note quite overcame us. It went the round of our tea table, and we all saw you quite clearly before us. I have none of my "white rose" to scent this. Thanks for your own. The children and Father were so touched.

They say that life in the Crimea is dreadful now. Still Olga A. is happy with her little Tikhon whom she is nursing herself. They have no servants so she and N.A. look after everything. D., we hear, has died of cancer. The needlework you sent me so long ago was the only token we have received from any of our friends. Where is poor Catherine? We suffer so for all, and we pray for all of you. I read much and live in the past, which is so full of rich memories. I have full trust in a brighter future. He will never forsake those who love and trust in His infinite mercy, and when we least expect it He will send help, and will save our unhappy country. Patience, faith and truth. I won't speak of what you have gone through. Forget it, with the old name you have thrown away. Now live again.

I am writing this in my bedroom. Jimmy is sleeping on my feet, makes them hot.

I keep myself occupied ceaselessly. I read "good books" a great deal, love the Bible, and from time to time read novels. I also sew, embroider, paint, with spectacles on because my eyes have become too weak to do without them. I am so sad because they are allowed no walks except behind the house and behind a high fence. Father is simply marvelous. Such meekness while all the time suffering intensely for the country. A real marvel. The others are all good and brave and uncomplaining, and Aleksei is an angel. Many things are very hard . . . our hearts are ready to burst at times. The children are healthy. I am so contented with their souls. I hope God will bless my lessons with Baby. The ground is rich, but is the seed ripe enough? I do try my utmost, for all my life lies in this.

I am knitting stockings for The Little One, like those I gave the wounded, do you remember? I make everything now. Father's trousers are torn and darned, the girls' underlinen in rags. Dreadful, is it not? I have grown quite gray. Anastasiya, to her despair, is now very fat, as Marie was, round and fat to the waist, with short legs. I do hope she will grow. Olga and Tatyana are both thin, but their hair grows beautifully.

I feel utter trust and faith that all will be well, that this is the worst, and that soon the sun will be shining brightly. But oh, the victims, and the innocent blood yet to be shed! Oh, God save Russia! That is the cry of one's soul, morning, noon, and night. Only not that shameless peace. I feel so old, oh, so old, but I am still the mother of this country, and I suffer its pains as my own child's pains, and I love it in spite of all its sins and horrors. No one can tear a child from its mother's heart, and neither can you tear away one's country, although Russia's black ingratitude to the Emperor breaks my heart. Not that it is the whole country, though. God have mercy and save Russia.

I find myself writing in English, I don't know why. Be sure to burn all these letters. It is better. I have kept nothing of the dear past. Just burn these letters, my love, as at any time your house may be searched again.

We all kiss and bless you. May God sustain and keep you. My heart is full, but words are feeble things.

Yours, A.

P.S. I should like to send you a little food, some macaroni for instance.

Pathetic, is it not? A dethroned empress, herself a prisoner, wanting to send macaroni from Siberia. My eyes burst with pity even now. Odd this woman was, our Empress Aleksandra. So complex. As I've said, her greatest crimes were both her pride and her insecurity—which caused her to hold herself aloof from everyone but her husband and children—while her greatest gift was her compassion. I find it strange that such wildly different aspects could live within one soul, but then again a dog can be both black and white. I find it ironic as well that the Russian people of all classes merely wanted a tsaritsa of intense love and emotion, which was exactly their Tsaritsa Aleksandra Fyodorovna . . . and yet the more they disdained her, the more frightened and cold and distant she became.

Oi, such dark times were those, but over the months of captivity I shared with them, these were the Romanovs I came to know, and yes, the Romanovs I came to love. It was a captivity that grew more and more intense, from Tsarskoye Selo to Tobolsk and finally Yekaterinburg. And it was really only toward the end that I developed the clearest of pictures of the Imperial Family. I do remember in Tobolsk when one of the Tsar's aides-de-camp, a certain General Tatischev, commented on the very same thing, how he was surprised to find the family so intimate and sweet on each other. And to this the Tsar replied with that gentle, ironic smile of his:

> As my aide-de-camp over the years, you have had many such chances to observe us. Yet if you only now recognize us as we really are, how could we ever blame the newspapers for what they write of us?

11

A summer night in Siberia only comes with great hesitation. And that late June day was no different, for the evening passed ever so slowly. There was a brief but heavy evening shower that rode across town, a gust of cool wind, and a clear dusk that never wanted to give up the day.

That far north and that close to the summer solstice, it didn't fall dark until shortly after eleven, yet the Imperial Family retired well before that, which was odd. Shortly after nine the Heir Tsarevich was the first to bed, followed somewhat later by the girls. Often Nikolai would sit up reading in the drawing room, or Botkin and he would play draughts, the checkered black and red board opened upon the tea table, while Aleksandra would sit at the nearby large desk, laying patience. But not that night. By ten they were making their way to bed. I was thus quietly instructed as well.

All evening long there had been much discussion, to which I was not privy, but which I could imagine. Simply: was it possible that the rescue attempt would come as early as tonight? Yes, and on the sly we were all advised to be ready to flee, for the Romanovs were determined not to abandon us, the last of their faithful. It was, of course, most gentlemanly, most old worldly, of Nikolai to decide on this course, but it certainly wasn't practical. Seven posed a cumbersome enough problem, let alone twelve. Nevertheless, the decision came down the ranks, from Nikolai to Botkin to Trupp to Kharitonov to me.

"Sleep fully dressed," cook whispered to me. "Be ready at any moment."

"You mean, I should wear everything to bed?" I replied as I made my bed in the small hall between the kitchen and the dining room.

"Everything."

"Even my shoes?"

This threw him, and he thought for a long moment. Cook Kharitonov was a master at making a meal out of nothing—wild mushrooms folded into a blanket of blini, leftover rice and cabbage tucked into the warm, doughy heart of pierogi—but a strategist of deceit he was not. For a long somber moment he pondered my question before answering.

"*Nyet,* that would surely attract the guards' attention."

"Then I'll just have them nearby."

"Good. But if anything starts, we're supposed to run to their room and help barricade the door."

"Sure."

The electric light was extinguished, and I settled into one of the most uncomfortable, anxious nights of my life. Sure, it had cooled somewhat, but I was completely clothed down to my socks. Within moments I was broiling. I started tossing and turning, and grew all the hotter. I dared not cast aside my blanket, however, lest one of the guards make a sudden check. My mind began to spin, and so did Kharitonov's, I could tell, for on the other side of the tiny room the large man tossed and rolled as much as I.

So how would it happen? Would a band of loyal Cossacks ride into town, hooping and hollering, screaming and shooting into the sky? Would monarchist officers appear out of the woodwork and slit the throats of the Red Guards, one by one? I tried to imagine the scenario, if our secret rescuers would first take out the machine gun positioned on the roof, next storm the house, or if they would first attack the Popov House across the alley way, killing all the reinforcements. Then again, maybe an airplane would appear out of nowhere and the pilot would lean out, take careful aim, and let drop a bomb on the Popov House, blowing all the *Bolsheviki* to bits. A surprise from the air like that might be best, particularly since The House of Special Purpose had been rigged with an electric warning bell to summon all the guards.

Whichever way it happened, I was sure there would be much blood, and I pictured myself the hero, leading the grand duchesses out the window and down a rope of bed linens. On the other hand, the window might be too dangerous, for it overlooked the side yard and the Popov House. So . . . so I might have to lead the girls down those twenty-three steps and to some waiting horses or a motor vehicle of escape. I might even get a gun, I might even have to kill one of the Reds. And I imagined the Romanovs and me escaping with our lives—perhaps I'd be wounded, but not terribly so—and then the Tsar would make me a count or a prince or something. Sure. All night I stirred with the possibilities. All night I imagined killing someone. And all night I heard the handful of guards posted in the cellar directly below, heard their shouts, their laughter, their drunken bouts. Each time I thought it was the beginning of the end and my heart was fully roused, making it impossible to get any rest.

None of us slept. Or slept little. Once I heard a distant dog howl to the moon. Or was it a wolf who'd ventured as close as the city dam? Eventually Kharitonov began to snore and the guards below fell into complete silence, while outside the night slowly returned to the dead. I had no idea what time it was—only the landed gentry and the aristocracy carried watches—but it must have been close to two or three before my eyes fell shut.

While I later learned from a book that the Romanovs had all slept fully clothed and fully bejeweled that night, I have often wondered what they were thinking when darkness finally came. The girls, the boy, their parents—did they lie in their beds and pray for salvation? Did they smile at the thought of what might soon come their way? Did they weep with anxiety? I'm sure that Aleksandra, always plush with anxiety, spent the whole of the night worrying about her babies, her husband. If an escape attempt was made, would the guards pounce first and foremost on their hated Nikolashka, killing him dead? If the family fled in a mad rush, would The Little One bump a knee or an arm, thereby plunging himself into nightmarish pain and even death? Playing through every scenario from successful escape to hellish failure, the Empress recorded in her diary how sleep was not of interest.

> Colossal heat tho' rained a little . . . I went early to
> bed, but slept only 3 hours, as they made so much
> noise outside.

To this day I imagine the Romanovs lying there sleepless as they drank in every step, cough, word, bark, and stir of wind. I'm quite sure they tossed all night long, wondering, hoping, fearing. And a horrible night it was, followed by a long, horrible, hot day, which was in turn followed by another terrible night of heated worry, for on the twenty-seventh she recorded:

> 8:00 Supper. 23 degrees in the room. Scarcely slept.

Perhaps it was Aleksandra's bitter dealings with the aristocracy of Sankt-Peterburg that made her paranoid—high society thought her much too prim and constantly mocked her—but she was quite correct not to write all in her diary. In the old days, everything that could be used against her certainly had been. Consequently, she understood the dangers of writing a diary that was too specific. She had to be most careful, and for this reason it had become not so much a personal account, but a logbook of day-to-day events. Hence she recorded her work with her pounds and pounds of diamonds as "arranged medicines," and her mention of scarcely sleeping, of so much noise outside, refers to those nights when we all waited for the rescue that did not come.

At the same time, Nikolai Aleksandrovich proved himself not as savvy as his wife:

> 27 June. Thursday. Our dear Maria turned 19 years old. The same tropical weather held, 26 degrees in the shade and 24 degrees in the rooms; one can hardly stand it! We spent an anxious night and sat up dressed.
>
> All this was because we had received two letters in the last few days, one after the other, in wh. we were told that we should get ready to be abducted by some sort of people loyal to us! The days passed and nothing happened, but the waiting and uncertainty were quite torturous.

But why? Why in the name of God would he have recorded such things for the *Bolsheviki* to find and read? Was Nikolai Aleksandrovich so naive? That . . . that stupid? Or was he simply too much of a gentleman, too much an aristocrat of the Old World, too much of a tsar to even imagine that such a personal intrusion and affront was even possible?

So there we were, the morning of the twenty-seventh. The day was sunny and hot—twenty-two degrees by early morning—but there was no summer brightness from any of us. *Nyet,* we'd just woken from fitful dreams of hope and were still groggy with disappointment. For better or worse, our emancipation had not been attempted during the depth of the night and the waiting was, as Nikolai wrote, torturous. Whatever was to come, we all clearly understood it was the beginning of the end. Of course Nikolai and Aleksandra wanted their family to be rescued and carried to safety, but when they were faced with that very possibility they realized how utterly foolish and dangerous such a rescue would be. And when it didn't take place in those first few days,

Nikolai could see the darkness rumbling toward them, so much so that within a week or so he stopped writing his diary altogether, the very diary he'd faithfully written every day since boyhood.

We gathered under a gloomy cloud for our morning inspection and ate our bread and drank our morning tea with few words, but all of that was shoved aside for Maria's birthday celebration at eleven. The Tsar insisted, for both as a good father and a good soldier he was concerned about the morale of his little troop. Seeing how heavy our hearts were, he recognized that our spirits needed attention. Hence he issued a decree, beckoning Romanov and servant alike to wish the Sovereign's number-three daughter everything sweet and beautiful.

"A tea table in the late morning . . . how unusual," said Aleksandra Fyodorovna, surveying the spread before her in the drawing room.

"And why not?" pressed a beaming Maria, her eyes as big as saucers.

"That's right, why not?" seconded the Tsar. "After all, there's been a revolution."

"Oh, believe me, I know that." Aleksandra shook her head in bemusement. "Just imagine, everyone else used to have such interesting afternoon teas, but not us. We always had the same tea with the same breads, served on the same china, presented by the same footman. And it all happened precisely at the same time everyday. Why, I don't think anything had changed since Catherine the Great."

"No, I think you're quite right, my dear," replied the Tsar. "The palace ran on tradition alone."

Demidova, who stood next to me, volunteered, "I quite remember, Madame, when you tried to change a few things."

"I do too. Only too well, as a matter of fact. And wasn't that a disaster?"

"Wasn't it though!"

Later that day Demidova went on and on about all this, explaining that before the war the Tsar's tea, like everything else, had been an amazingly regimented thing: the doors opened at five, the Tsar came in, buttered a piece of bread, and drank two glasses of tea, not one more, not one less. On the other hand, Demidova had heard from other maids that the teas of the nobility had been infinitely more creative and extravagant, for it had been all the vogue to have a minimum of six different cakes at the tea table—chocolate, nut, berry, meringue, and so on.

Now looking down at the large knot-shaped sweet bread on the table, the Empress smiled in delight, and asked, "Tell me, cook, where on earth did you get such a beautiful *krendel*? Did the good sisters bring it?"

"*Nyet-s,* madame. I made it."

"Really?"

"Look!" exclaimed Anastasiya. "It even has raisins."

Aleksandra smiled. "You're a magician, Vanya. How on earth did you make it in such a small kitchen and how on earth did you come up with all the ingredients?"

Kharitonov humbly bowed his head, and said, "Leonka and I, well, we make do. We make do."

The truth of the matter was that while we had scrounged up a few raisins over the past few weeks, the *krendel* was missing cardamom as well as candied orange peel, items that had vanished from the markets months ago. Nevertheless, the entire household recognized the creation as quite a feat, particularly because it was made of the precious white flour we'd brought from Tobolsk and had carefully hidden in trunks and walls and even the back of the piano, all this lest it fall into the hands of the guards. However, the recent spat of fresh eggs and milk, not to mention a bit of *vanille* secretly brought by Sister Antonina last week, was more than Kharitonov could creatively resist. For days he'd been looking for an excuse, finally seizing upon Maria's birthday. Making do without an oven, the master of improvisation had cooked the sweet bread atop the oil stove just this morning, baking it between two iron pans that he had carefully cupped together.

Following the Tsar's lead, we rose to our feet, held hands, and bowed our heads as he intoned, "Gracious Lord, look down upon our dearest Maria with all of Your infinite kindness and wisdom. We beseech Thee to bestow upon Maria good health, long life, and great happiness."

"What about a husband, Papa?" interjected Anastasiya. "She wants to get married, you know, and have scores of children!"

"Anya, don't interrupt your father," chided her mother.

"But it's true, she wants to get—!"

"Anya!"

Nikolai Aleksandrovich crossed himself. "Hear our prayers, O Lord, and in these trying days protect our cherished daughter. *Ah-min.*"

All of us, even the one guard who stood in the doorway, likewise followed the Tsar's example, crossing ourselves and muttering a solemn chorus of, *"Ah-min."*

Nikolai embraced his daughter, wishing her birthday greetings, followed by Aleksandra, who made the sign of the cross over Maria and kissed her as well.

Usually birthdays were observed at a luncheon with many distinguished guests, a lavish table of much food, entertainments, and great gifting, for Russians are among the most generous sort, particularly when it comes to their children, whom they love to spoil and do so endlessly. In earlier times a young girl of the nobility would be showered with sable hats and coats and muffs, pearl necklaces and diamond earrings and so on and so forth. And even though such a celebration was impossible that summer day, hardly anyone seemed to notice.

The Empress poured the tea by her own hand, an event once seen as a great compliment to a guest but was now commonplace. Since the fine china was long gone, Aleksandra filled tall, thin glasses perched in metal standards with handles. There was no lemon, no cream. The cunning Empress, however, had secretly managed to preserve a few cubes of sugar, and that morning we were all issued one. I followed Aleksei's lead, pinching the cube between my front teeth as I sipped the tea, something that caught his mother's glare, to be sure, for it was a peasant's habit, something Aleksei had seen one of the guards do.

The *krendel* was cut and served. And then the gifting began.

Olga presented a novel in French, Tatyana a bookmark that she had painted with her own hand, Aleksei a rock he had polished like a sultan's jewel. A tablet of drawing papers came from Botkin, hand-knit stockings from Demidova, and a small bunch of flowers from Trupp. The baked delight, of course, was the gift from cook and me. And after all of us had made our presentations came the finale, several packages from Maria's parents.

"Here, my love," said Aleksandra. "Open this first."

The young woman did, finding enclosed a religious title, *Complete Yearly Cycle of Brief Homilies for Each Day of the Year.* Maria opened the volume, silently cherished the inscription, and then read it aloud.

"To Our Dear Darling Daughter from Your Very Own Loving Parents, Mama & Papa +, 27 June 1918." She folded the book shut, and leaned forward and kissed her mother. *"Spacibo, Mama. Ya ochen tebya lubloo."* Thank you, Mama. I love you very much.

"And what about me?" asked her father.

"Papa, of course!" she said, jumping up and planting a kiss upon his bearded cheek.

Nikolai embraced Maria, kissed her, and held forth a small box. "Here, my child. You must have something beautiful too, you know, otherwise good fortune will not follow you in the year to come."

"Oi!"

It was this gift that Maria had been waiting all morning to receive, for she was not simply a Romanov, not simply a Grand Duchess, but most importantly a young woman, who was well schooled enough to know how these things worked, that the prettiest gift always came last. And while what Maria found was no Romanov treasure, it was most certainly a thing of beauty, particularly during such dark days of imprisonment. The other daughters crowded around, and Maria lifted out a fine gold bracelet from which hung a simple charm of love carved from green stone.

"Oi, kakaya krasota!" Oh, what beauty, exclaimed Maria.

"Do you like it?" asked her father.

"I love it and I shall never, ever take it off!"

Maria jumped up and kissed first her father, then her mother, who fastened the bracelet on Maria's left wrist.

We all finished our sweet treat and single glass of tea. Conversation dissipated, and we servants, knowing our places, retreated. Only Dr. Botkin remained with the family in the withdrawing room, and soon we heard the sounds of the piano. It was a little program, first featuring the voice of Anastasiya as well as the Empress, whose contralto was so beautiful that she might have pursued a career in singing had she not been of such high estate. That was followed by the older pair, Olga and Tatyana, who played fourhand a beautiful piece, so sweet, so melodic, that it washed away any ill purpose from that house. Hearing the flow of the keys, the gush of the tune, I froze in the kitchen, gazed out the window, and thought for a few brief moments that maybe everything would be fine. *Da, da,* even the guards momentarily lost their anger, their burning zeal, for I noticed a few of them pause in their random patrol and gaze off in uncomplicated thought. All at once, and only that once, did things within The House of Special Purpose seem at peace.

But there were important duties to be done, namely there were "medicines" to be dealt with. And looming in everyone's mind was the essence of time, as promising as it was threatening. In short, the celebration of Her Greatness Grand Duchess Maria Nikolaevna's nineteenth birthday soon concluded and the feminine hands of the house resumed their deceitful needlework. By noon the rooms took on the air of a sweatshop, albeit a secret one.

Meanwhile, I wheeled about the Heir Aleksei, driving him from room to room. We played troika for hours, finding everything of interest when in fact there was nothing. Given our common age we were able to see things others could not, however, and as such the route around the dining room table became a troika track, the large potted palm in the drawing room became an oasis in the Sahara, and later the dogs, Jimmy and Joy, chasing and barking after us, were transformed into rabid wolves. Truth be told, we occupied ourselves for hours with a talent I have long since lost.

During all of this the Tsar negotiated a victory of sorts. Claiming that the hall where Kharitonov and I slept was insufferably hot, he successfully petitioned and received permission for the two of us to move to the other side of the house—to a room initially occupied by the Heir Tsarevich, who had since moved into his parents' room. While this small room was notably cooler than our little hallway, our comfort was not the Tsar's motive.

"It won't do to have me and all the women on this side of the house," whispered Nikolai Aleksandrovich with a wink as we carted our few possessions to our new chamber.

Sure, the Tsar needed all the muscle he could gather. And while I assumed that we were preparing for a fight or battle, we were instead retreating. After lunch the Tsar quietly pulled me aside.

"Hide these envelopes as you did before, *molodoi chelovek,*" young man, instructed the Tsar with a soft smile. "One is a reply, the other contains letters to be carried on to Sankt-Peterburg. Deliver them as you did before and you will have served us well."

So that was what I did. I hid the two envelopes in my undergarments, and when I went to the Soviet for more food from the cafeteria, I stopped briefly at the Church of the Ascension. Meanwhile, the Empress remained indoors with her oldest daughter, Olga, the two of them madly stitching their corsets, and the Tsar and others descended into the rear yard where they paced in the tropical heat of the Siberian summer. And I . . . I went out, delivering the envelopes to Father Storozhev. One contained letters to their dear Anna Vyrubova, while the other contained the reply to the loyal officers, in which I much later learned the Tsar tried to call off the liberation attempt:

> We do not want to, nor can we, **escape**, We can only be **carried off** by force, just as it was force that was used to carry us from Tobolsk. Thus, do not count on **any active help** from us. The komendant has many aides; they change often and have become **worried**. They guard our imprisonment and our lives conscien-

tiously and some are kind to us. We do not want them to suffer because of us, nor you for us; in the name of God, avoid bloodshed above all. Find out about them yourself. Coming down from the window without a ladder is completely impossible. Even once we are down, we are still in great danger because of the open window of the komendant's bedroom and the machine gun downstairs, where one enters from the inner courtyard. ~~Give up, then, on the idea of carrying us off.~~ If you watch us, you can always come save us **in case of** real and imminent danger. We are completely unaware of what is going on outside, for we receive no newspapers. Since we have been allowed to open the window, surveillance has increased, and we are forbidden even to stick our heads out at the risk of getting shot in the face.

And so it was that the Tsar, the Orthodox Tsar, put the squash on the rescue plans not simply because of worries for himself and his close family, not simply for we who served them, but for those thugs who guarded them and were soon to kill them. How could he have been so stupid? Couldn't Nikolai, didn't Nikolai, see the tidal wave of blood flooding toward them, toward all of Rossiya?

Oh, as the tragedies of Shakespeare have revealed, the fall of kings is but fodder for the richest of entertainments. The tumble of this Tsar and his consort was the grossest, however, and the conclusion of this story, I regret to foreshadow, was all the worse. In those days as the Imperial Family sat unknowingly waiting for their own executions, the Tsar's younger brother, that sweet, dashing Grand Duke Mikhail, was taken out into a field and shot like a dog. And the Tsaritsa's sister, Grand Duchess Yelizaveta? She and a handful of other Romanovs were thrown alive down a mineshaft, with hand grenades and burning brush tossed in atop them. Unfortunately, they lived through it all, singing praise to the Lord, until hunger itself took them days later. This we know to be true, for dirt was found in their stomachs once their bodies were exhumed.

Such were the times, so black, so crazy. *Kakoi koshmar* . . . what a nightmare.

12

Lord, forgive me. But first make me suffer. I am the devil's creation. Torture me and make me cry out for mercy, but make me suffer . . . for history shows that it was my grave error that precipitated the murder of the Tsar and his family. Yes, my dear granddaughter, Katya, I confess that it was my stupidity, an ignorant decision by a lowly kitchen boy, that gave the *Bolsheviki* the excuse they had been seeking . . .

By July 5 the revolution was collapsing in all directions. The *Bolsheviki* were terrified, for their defeat seemed but days away. The Germans controlled the Ukraine, the English had landed in the north, the Japanese had invaded the Far East, and the American marines were on their way, albeit slowly. Why, even in Moscow itself there was a revolt of the Social Revolutionary Party against Lenin and his depraved cronies. In other words, Lenin and the *Bolsheviki* were not only cornered, but desperate, which naturally made them more dangerous than ever.

It was a Friday, not hot, not like the days before, but a pleasant thirteen degrees. The rains resumed, which would pose a problem for the night of July 16–17, yet on the fifth things seemed ready to burst with hope and promise. Not only had the vulgar Avdeyev and his crew been replaced by a new *komendant* and new guards, but Sister Antonina and Novice Marina arrived, their arms laden with a bounty of wondrous supplies. They had not come for days, and suddenly they appeared, smiles beaming upon their faces as they carried in foodstuffs, the likes of which we hadn't seen for months, not since we'd been carried off from Tobolsk. Instead of just milk and a meager basket of eggs, now there were two *chetverts* of milk, one large basket containing a *chertova dyuzhina*—a devil's dozen—of fresh, warm eggs, not to mention a glass bottle of thick cream, a generous amount of *tvorog*—farmer's cheese—and even enough meat for six day's soup.

"*Oi!*" I gasped, as I helped the good nun and her novice into our little makeshift kitchen. "*Tak mnogo v'syevo!*" So much of everything.

Sister Antonina, tiny and round as she was, squinched up her nose like an old hedgehog, and said, "During Avdeyev we brought this much and more every time. But there was a toll, per se."

"What?"

"*Da, da, da.* At the outer gate, at the inner gate, as we walked past the guards' room—they all took as they pleased."

Novice Marina, her voice small, asserted, "It's true—they wouldn't let us pass otherwise."

"Now that we know the way is clear," beamed the good *sestra*, "next time we will bring even more!"

When we walked into the tiny kitchen, cook Kharitonov saw the goods and was beside himself, putting aside his boiled potatoes and immediately bragging about what he would make.

"Maybe even some meat pierogi!"

I placed the larger of the baskets upon the kitchen table and fetched a bowl for the eggs. As I unloaded them, the young Novice Marina stepped forward, clutching dearly one of the *chetverts* of milk, which she lifted unto my hands. I gazed into her eyes, perceived the most subtle of nods, which sent a rush of excitement up my spine.

And, yes, the tiny pocket cut into the cork did in fact contain a note, the fourth and final one the Tsar was ever to receive. No sooner had Sister Antonina and Novice Marina departed, than big Dr. Botkin appeared in the kitchen doorway. Everyone was hoping for more news from the outside, and he pushed up his gold spectacles and studied me quite eagerly.

"Would you be so kind, Leonka, as to fetch a glass of water for Aleksandra Fyodorovna?" he requested, his dentures oddly clicking as he spoke. "Her eyes are aching, and I have prescribed valerian drops to calm her nerves."

"Certainly," I replied.

I did as requested. As before, I removed the cloth covering the crock of water, ladled a glass of fresh, cool water, and set upon my way to the bedchamber. As I traversed the dining room, I fell under the stern eyes of one of the new guards. Did he know? Could he guess? *Nyet,* that would be impossible. I just had to maintain a certain composure, and I continued through the doorless passage into the girls' room, finding the three older grand duchesses on their beds reading and Anastasiya on the floor playing with Jimmy, her little King Charlie. Next I proceeded into the corner chamber, that of Nikolai and his consort. The Empress herself was reclined atop her bed, one hand over her closed eyes, while Aleksei sat in his nearby bed, making a chain out of a piece of copper wire. The Tsar was there too seated in a comfortable chair by the window, reading another volume by Saltykov.

"Ah, Leonka, *spacibo bolshoye."* Thank you very much, said Nikolai, rising to his feet, at the same time brushing back his mustache with the back of his hand. "Here, let me take that."

I approached him, handing him the glass of water.

In the most quiet of voices, he asked, "Did Sister Antonina bring something today?"

"Da-s."

I immediately reached into my shirt, where I had hidden the small folded note. Just at that particular time came frightful coughing from the room of the grand duchesses. We all knew what that meant.

The Tsar whispered, *"Bistro."* Quickly.

I heard them now, the heavy steps of a guard marching our way, and I nearly panicked. Finally my fingers found the small, folded paper, and I ripped it from my clothing and stuffed it into the Tsar's hand.

"Ah, good morning, *komendant*," said Nikolai, palming the note to his side and into his pocket. "The heat has finally broken, has it not?"

I turned around, saw the new *komendant*, Yakov Yurovksy, who just the day before had replaced Avdeyev, the Red pig. This new keeper was a trim man, not too tall. He had thick black hair, a black goatee, nice eyes, small ears, and a distinct, rather unpleasant voice that sounded as if he spoke through his nose.

"Good morning," said the dark one, so very matter-of-factly, as he held forward a wooden box. "I have here in this wooden casket the items of value that you gave me yesterday."

Aleksandra, never one to hold her tongue, gazed at him from her bed, and all but hissed, "We gave you nothing. What you have is what you took from us."

That was yesterday's incident. Yurovsky had arrived midday, and that very afternoon he and another had gathered the Imperial Family and demanded their personal jewelry "lest it tempt the guards."

"You took all the jewels we were wearing," continued the Empress, "except two bracelets from my Uncle Leo and my husband's engagement ring—things that cannot be removed without tools."

"I have done so for your own protection."

"Protection? From what, your people? I'm afraid you're too late. Our trunks in the shed out back have already been looted."

"An unfortunate incident," replied Yurovsky, his eyes spitting hate. "But it will not happen again. Comrade Avdeyev and some of the other house guards have been removed and sent to the front for actions unbecoming the revolution."

Ever the gentleman, Nikolai said, "I pity Avdeyev, but he is to blame for not restraining his people."

"Perhaps, but that is not your concern."

"In any case, we appreciate your attempts to restore order."

Yes, even the Tsar loved to feel the whip of authority and control. He disdained slovenliness and disorder, and in those first few days he appreciated the soldierly conduct of this new commandant, Yakov Yurovsky. Little did the Tsar or any of us know that Yurovsky was totally committed to one thing and one thing only: the "difficult" duties of the revolution, that is, murder.

Along with Yurovsky came an entirely new interior guard made up of "Letts." These guards, these emissaries of the underworld, however, were not made up only of Latvians, who played so strong a role in the Cheka, the forerunner of the KGB. No, this new group of burly men comprised a strange mixture of Magyars, Germans, Austrians, and Russians, a vile mixture of men divorced from God and country and certainly Tsar. In spirit they were all true revolutionaries, men who had thoroughly justified killing as a means to an end. The only consolation I have found is in my books, where it is written that all these men died the most hideous deaths, including Yurovsky himself, who died from a wonderfully painful cancer that curled up his throat in 1938. Not only that but he lived and suffered just long enough to see his beloved daughter, Rima, tossed into one of Stalin's gulags, where she languished for another twenty years.

Placing the wooden casket upon a table, Yurovsky opened it, and instructed, "You are to verify my list and verify the items in the box. When you have done this, I will seal the box."

"And then what will you do with our things?" said Aleksandra, her irritation clear as she rose from the bed. "Take them away again? Allow your soldiers to steal from us as before?"

"*Nyet*. I will leave this box here in your room and here on this table. It must remain sealed, however, and this I will check each and every day. I assure you, there will be no incidents, not as long as you do not provoke them."

"The only incidents have been due to the incompetence of your people. We, on the other hand, have been more than cooperative."

I could see that Yurovsky would have loved to have slapped her, but instead he held himself in check. Perhaps he was laughing on the inside, chuckling because he knew that a bullet was coming her way. And yet he forestalled any provocation. He merely nodded as he reached into his pocket and pulled out his trump card. You see, he was conniving to win their trust, angling to make their murders as easy as possible, for he was well aware that lambs were easier to lead to the slaughter than wolves.

"I believe these are yours," he said as he placed a handful of silver spoons upon the table.

Aleksandra looked at the silverware, her eyes wide with surprise. "Why . . . why, yes. Wherever did you find them?"

"They were stolen from the shed and buried in the garden."

"Our gratitude," said Nikolai, stepping forward. "So let us have a look at your list and the contents of this box. You have our word of honor that the seal will not be broken."

Right then and there I watched as Nikolai and Aleksandra reached into the small casket and withdrew a packet. They poured out its contents—their most personal jewelry—exposing nothing fancy, not by any means. Nice pieces they were—rings, simple diamond earrings of maybe 15 carats each, lockets, gold bracelets, gold chains with crosses. The former Tsar and Tsaritsa sorted through it all, made sure each piece was listed. Several minutes later, they slid their belongings back into the packet, which Yurovsky took and placed inside the wooden casket.

"I will place the spoons in here as well." The *komendant* did just that, then sealed the box with a piece of wire and some red wax. "As I said, this box is to remain on this table and is to remain sealed. I will check it everyday, and if I see that it has been tampered with I will remove it."

Aleksandra Fyodorovna smoldered. You could see it in her face, which blossomed a blotchy, angry red. Nikolai Aleksandrovich, on the other hand, never wavered, never betrayed his inner thoughts, and was as usual amazingly self-controlled and circumspect.

"We understand," he calmly replied, though I'm sure inside he too blazed with anger.

Yurovsky turned to leave, but rather than disappearing like a quick black cloud, he eyed the boy and descended upon him. I watched as the Emperor and Empress stiffened but said nothing.

"And how are you feeling today, Alyosha?" asked the *komendant* as he seated himself on the edge of the Heir's bed.

Aleksei glanced at his parents before replying, "I am well, thank you."

"Are you walking yet?"

"I have been able to stand, but not walk, not as of yet."

Yurovsky, once a watchmaker, later a photographer, and still later a medic, loved to dole out advice, and said, "Well, you must get plenty of rest and eat lots of eggs and meat so as to get your strength up, agreed?"

Aleksei nodded with the grace of his father, though he said nothing further, for he was infused as well with his mother's pride.

The Heir's dog, Joy, came trotting in just then, and the *komendant* rose from the edge of Aleksei's bed and gave the pup a pat on the head.

As he headed out of the room, Yurovsky said, "Well, I'm quite sure your four-legged friend here will watch over you."

How did he do it? With blood on his mind, how did Yurovsky go about interacting with this husband and wife and these children? *Da, da, da,* once I made my grave error, it was this Komendant Yurovsky himself who went about so calmly orchestrating the execution. It was he as well who fired the first shot. And it was he who led the haphazard burial team off into the pine wood.

In any case, the minor incident with Yurovsky was soon overshadowed by hope, hope provoked by the final note that Sister Antonina and Novice Marina had just smuggled in. As with all the others, it too was in French, and it too survived those awful days:

> The change in guards and in the komendant pre-
> vented us from writing to you. Do you know what
> the cause of this was? We answer your questions. We
> are a group of officers in the Russian army who have

not lost consciousness of our duty before Tsar and Country.

We are not informing you in detail about ourselves for reasons you can understand, but your friends D. and T., who are already safe, know us.

The hour of deliberation is approaching, and the days of the usurpers are numbered. In any case, the Slavic armies are advancing toward Yekaterinburg. They are a few versts from the city. The moment is becoming critical, and now bloodshed must not be feared. Do not forget that the Bolsheviki will, in the end, be ready to commit any crime. The moment has come. We must act. Rest assured that the machine gun downstairs will not be dangerous. As for the komendant, we will know how to take him away. Wait for a whistle toward midnight. That will be the signal.

An Officer

And here I must ask, Is the wisdom of my years clear now? Have I not seen things that no human should?

13

"Wait for a whistle toward midnight . . ."

Such enticing words. To the ends of the earth Romeo could have thus enticed his Juliet, Heathcliff his Cathy, even Zhivago his Lara. Such promise lies in those words, such hope, such beauty. Aleksandra, herself, whispered how she hoped for three hundred loyal officers to come charging into town, whooping and hollering and whisking us all to safety. So excited, so agitated was she, that in those final days the Empress scarcely rested or slept, fidgeting and turning with every sound. The Tsar, meanwhile, never stopped pacing. In the dining room, in the drawing room, in the garden he paced his soldierly step, back and forth, back and forth, waiting, praying, hoping. And eventually despairing, for he understood that his fate, which had long been waiting on the horizon like a black storm, was finally and at last set to arrive.

True, just then and for a few days that followed, our candle of hope burned so bright, so strong. We found hope in everything, from the heavy evening rains that cooled the air, to our dinner table, which was spread with more plentiful food than we had seen for months.

The nights of July 5 and 6 we were again secretly advised to sleep fully clothed, which in fact we did. And again none of us slept well, listening as we did for that blasted whistle, which was never to come, not ever. I don't know quite what happened, why this attempt to rescue the Romanovs never materialized. Perhaps the tsarist plot was discovered. Perhaps the officers lost their nerve. Perhaps their leaders were killed. Or perhaps they simply ran away with the pile of money sent by Anna Vyrubova. But something went terribly awry.

That night I lay on my bed, my ears stretching for midnight hope, yet only hearing the stomp of the guards outside and fighting cats and a woman screaming at her drunk husband.

"Borya, get inside at once!"

Once I was awakened by the report of a gunshot, a sharp blast that split the night. I sat up in my makeshift bed, a pile of blankets on the floor, and saw cook Kharitonov stir as well. Was this it, the beginning of the loyal officers' siege upon our prisonly house? Were we about to be carried away by faithful Cossacks? But then there was nothing. Kharitonov just rolled over, tumbled back into sleep. And I just sat there, staring at the room's lone window that was veiled in lime. The minutes crawled past, and I lay back down on the floor, overcome with a sense of hopelessness and eventually exhaustion.

Toward morning came the sound of war. And it increased every day from then on. Of course we could see none of this, not simply because of the double palisade surrounding The House of Special Purpose, but because of the limed windows. But like blind people we became particularly attuned to noises from beyond. Each time there came the sound of something momentous—the sound of hooves, the rumble of a motor lorry or two—a great pause passed through the house. The Emperor would cease his pacing, the Empress her secret stitching, Demidova her cleaning, and Kharitonov his chopping. What was that, a military or civilian wagon? Red soldier or White savior? Was it the time of our rescue or the time of . . .

We heard nothing more, not ever again, from these so-called Officers. The Empress became so nervous and the Emperor so frustrated, that he finally wrote a note begging for information. It was this note, entrusted to me by the Tsar and discovered by Yurovsky that provided the excuse the *Bolsheviki* had been searching so hungrily for.

But why was there no rescue? *Why?* Earlier, that past winter in Tobolsk town, the Romanovs could have easily escaped. The troops assigned to guard them had been nearly all won over by the Imperial Family's charm, and Nikolai could have effected escape by simply and quickly leaving town, fleeing to the great north and into the depths of Siberia. But the Tsar nobly felt an obligation not to stir up trouble, not to leave Russia, and so . . . so by the time they'd been transferred to that Red hotbed, the city of Yekaterinburg, it was too late.

But . . . but why did no rescuers appear by the light of the summer moon? By that July there were only several hundred Red troops in all of Yekaterinburg. The Whites, only twenty miles away, had seized towns all around and were poised to attack from any number of directions. We all knew the city was destined to fall any day. So why was nothing attempted? In those few days that followed there came through our single open window only tidbits of normal life and no whistle. Locked in The House of Special Purpose we waited. And as the time went by our hope fell away. It was on Thursday, July 11, that we finally realized just how desperate, even hopeless, our situation truly was.

To break the tremendous boredom, the Heir and I were once again playing, not troika or English tank, our two most favorite games, but elevator. One of the doors off the dining room was a pocket door that, much to our amusement, slid sideways in and out of the wall rather like an elevator's. And Aleksei, seated in the wheeling chaise, and I, by his side, pretended we were riding all the way to the top of one of those new American buildings that rose so high above the ground—twelve floors!—and, they claimed, scraped the sky. We weren't even to the fifth floor when we suddenly saw the grand duchesses and Dr. Botkin hurrying through the dining room.

Aleksei said, "Hey, something's going on."

The Heir pointed with his right hand and I, the consummate companion and lackey, immediately obeyed. I pushed him off our make-believe lift, steered him quickly through the dining room, through his sisters' room, and into his parents'. There we found the Emperor and Empress, all the girls, and the doctor staring at the one open window, a look of great grief upon all of their faces.

"What is it, Papa?" demanded Aleksei. "They're not sealing the window again, are they?"

The Tsar silently came over, rested his hand on Aleksei's shoulder, and softly, almost painfully, replied, "No, they're putting some kind of covering over it."

In a kind of shock we watched as two ladders were thrown up against the side of the house and three workers lifted a heavy metal grating. With no small effort, they attached the bars to the outside of the window frame. The limed-over windows were terrible enough, but this was worse, for within a matter of ten minutes we were securely behind bars. Wasn't it through this window we were supposed to flee? Wasn't our path to freedom now completely blocked? Was rescue now impossible?

"Oh, Nicky," gasped Aleksandra as she clung to her husband's arm.

Bit by bit, day by day, our world was shrinking. No longer did it seem as if we were merely under house arrest. Now, looking through those black iron bars, we all realized we were imprisoned, locked in a kind of grand cell from which there might well be no escape.

Nikolai, stroking his mustache, said, "And with no warning . . ."

"You don't think our . . . our friends on the outside have been discovered, do you?"

"There's no way of telling, though the guards certainly seem afraid of something. In any case I'm starting to like this Yurovsky less and less!"

Behind us came steps, and the *komendant,* entering the room, said in that nasally voice of his, "Do you have a comment, Citizen Romanov?"

The Tsar turned around, and asked, "Do you really have such fear of our climbing out or getting in touch with the sentry?"

"My orders are to guard the former Tsar."

"As I've said, I would never leave my family."

"I have my orders." Yurovsky then held up a small leather box. "I found this in the service room, stolen I believe from your trunk."

Nikolai took the box and opened it, revealing his gold watch. "Thank you for returning it."

"I will allow you to keep it in your possession, but for security purposes I suggest you wear it at all times."

Yurovsky turned and departed, and the Tsar took his watch and fastened it around his left wrist. A beautiful gold watch it was, naturally of the finest quality, and he wore it unto his death, when it was taken as a brilliant souvenir from his dead body.

"Oh, Nicky . . ." said Aleksandra.

The Tsaritsa felt the pains of the world in her head, her back, and in her legs. And Nikolai helped his beloved back to her bed, where she reclined and stayed for the rest of that day and, actually, almost for the short remainder of her life.

It was about then that our dear Dr. Botkin began his prophetic letter, the famous one found after the night of treachery. He began it at about this time and was still working on the wording all the way to the end. In fact, he was still writing it that night when they were all called down to the cellar.

In retrospect it was clear that the end was rapidly approaching. Dr. Botkin foresaw that. I, on the other hand, never stopped believing that we would be spirited away. Then again, I was but a lad of fourteen, as naive to the depravity of mankind as I am wise today.

And so it is with great sadness that I proceed to Sunday, July 14.

14

A Sunday it was, just two days until the end.

For days we had not been visited by Dr. Derevenko, the Heir's physician. And for days now the Tsar had been requesting his presence.

"My son needs the attention of our Dr. Derevenko, who possesses a unique electric device. He uses this to massage my son's legs, you understand, and the results are quite good."

"And as I've told you before," countered Yurovsky, "this is not permitted."

Likewise the Tsar had been asking for a religious service, which had not been permitted for quite some time. Then all of a sudden that Sunday, the fourteenth, we were informed at morning inspection that we would be allowed a service to be performed by none other than Father Storozhev himself.

"He and the deacon will be here at ten this morning," said Yurovsky. "No conversation will be permitted."

"Understood," curtly replied the Tsar.

Morning tea and bread were served immediately after the inspection, and the announcement of the religious service caused a great stir at the table, albeit a quiet one, for a guard stood at either end of the dining room. That left us not much to talk about except the weather, and a beautiful summer's morning it was, the sky having cleared after another night of heavy rain and the temperature now a cool, pleasant twelve degrees. As soon as breakfast was concluded, however, everyone scattered. Kharitonov, Demidova, and I went about cleaning the table and doing the dishes, while Aleksandra and the two younger girls, Maria and Anastasiya, set up a small altar in the drawing room. They cleared the large desk and decorated it quite nicely, spreading one of the Empress's shawls over it, then arranging their favorite icons, including Saint Feodor's Mother of God, perhaps the Empress's most treasured possession. Adding a nice homey touch, Anastasiya placed a few birch branches here and there, for whether of high or low estate Russians are a mystical sort, bound like pagans to the wild nature of their motherland.

At this time the Tsar retired to his bedchamber, presumably to sit with the Heir, perhaps even to read to him. This, however, was not the case. A few minutes later Olga slipped into the room, and it was then that they wrote the final letter to the "Officer." It had been ten entire days since we'd last heard anything from the outside, ten entire days of waiting for that bloody midnight whistle, and the Tsar wished to inform those on the outside that the conditions within The House of Special Purpose were deteriorating, rapidly so. Of course the Tsar, always cautious, controlled, and particular, was not a quick writer by any means, and it took him a good long while to draft the six or seven lines. Then, of course, Olga had to translate it into the French, so this entire process took all the way up until the service itself.

Shortly after ten the servant Trupp brought the brass censer with burning coals, handing it to me in the kitchen and requesting, "Please deliver this to father, who is in the guard's room."

I did as told, carrying the brass censer, suspended as it was by three chains. A rich plume of heavenly smoke billowed out as I walked through the house and to the guard room, where I found Yurovsky and a guard, plus the two from the church, Father Archpresbyter Storozhev and Father Deacon Buimirov. The two religious men were already vested, their gold and red brocade robes flowing to the ground, and Father Storozhev was in conversation with the *komendant* himself.

"So what is the matter with your hands?" asked Yurovsky with a small smile. "Why is it that you keep rubbing them?"

"I'm trying to ward off a chill, for I fear the return of pleurisy, from which I have only recently recovered," replied Father Storozhev.

"Ah, now of these things I know, for not only am I a trained medic, but I myself have had an operation on my lungs."

Yurovsky proceeded to dole out his free advice, and when he was finished we were told to proceed into the living room. First went Father Archpresbyter, then Father Deacon, Yurovsky, and finally me. Just as we entered, Nikolai Aleksandrovich, dressed in his khaki field shirt, khaki pants, and his high leather boots, came through the doors from the dining room, the two younger daughters behind him.

"Well, are all of your people present?" asked Yurovsky.

The Tsar nodded toward those at the front of the room. "Yes, all."

The Tsaritsa, wearing the same dark blue cotton dress she'd worn for weeks, was seated next to the Heir, who was in the wheeling chaise and wearing a jacket with a sailor's collar. The older daughters stood nearby; all four girls had changed and now were dressed nearly identically in dark skirts and simple white jackets, the same simple jackets that usually hung at the foot of their cots.

The Tsar took his place at the head of the family. On the edge of the living room stood Dr. Botkin, Demidova, the tall Trupp, the short and stocky Kharitonov, and me, the youngest and the last. Once we had assumed our positions, the *obednitsa*—a liturgy without communion—began, but here I should take care to add that there was one more person present: Yurovsky. In a complete affront to rank and etiquette, the *komendant* took great care to stand right up there at the front.

Severely tested as they were, the Romanovs were not simply more pious than ever, they were more grave and serious. The last time they had been allowed a religious service, the Empress and Tatyana had sung along with the priest. Even Nikolai Aleksandrovich had sung, his bass voice lively and vibrant as he had intoned "Our Father." This time, however, none of them sang along, not even the Empress with her beautiful contralto, and when Father Deacon chanted instead of read "Who Resteth with Saints," the entire family dropped to their knees. Standing behind them, the rest of us, from Botkin on down to me, immediately followed their example.

Afterward we lined up according to rank to kiss the holy cross that Father Deacon held in hand. Nikolai Aleksandrovich went first, but he hesitated, which even I, way at the end, took note of. Peering around, I tried to see why the Tsar seemed to be taking such a long time with Father Storozhev, to whom he was offering his thanks. And then I understood, the Emperor wanted to pull his note from his pocket and ask Father Storozhev to deliver it to those loyal to him. But this he could not do, for Komendant Yurovsky had so positioned himself to oversee and overhear *everything*.

And so this, unfortunately, was how the last note fell into my young hands.

15

The fifteenth, a Monday, was a cool, damp morning that slowly bloomed into a beautiful day. By noon all of Yekaterinburg was bathed in lovely summer sunshine. Other than that, there was nothing remarkable about the start of the day, nothing to make us suspicious. It was only after lunch, when four charwomen from the labor union were admitted to clean the floors, that events took a serious turn. These women began washing the floors in the Tsar's bedchamber, and Yurovsky stood near them to make sure there was absolutely no conversation between them and the young grand duchesses, who were helping move the furniture and talking gaily amongst themselves. Laughing, the girls were. While this was taking place, the Tsar and Tsaritsa relocated to the living room, where Aleksandra rested on the couch and Nikolai sat in a chair in the far corner, a novel propped in his lap.

By word of Trupp, I was beckoned from the kitchen to the Tsar, who in a quiet voice, asked, "Leonka, was there no sign of Sister Antonina this morning?"

"She did come, Nikolai Aleksandrovich. She and her novice came shortly after breakfast, only they were not allowed to proceed as far as the kitchen. Komendant Yurovsky wouldn't let them past the guard room, which is where I went to get the foodstuffs. I met them there."

"And why weren't they allowed any farther?"

"That wasn't clear, but Yurovksy asked them a great many questions and looked at everything they carried."

"I see. And what was it that they brought today?"

"A *chetvert* of milk, that was all. No eggs and no cream either. The *komendant* said there was to be no more cream. But . . . but . . ."

"But what?"

"He did ask them to bring a great many eggs tomorrow—no less than fifty."

"Odd. Very odd." Before continuing, the Tsar glanced across the room to make sure no guards had wandered in. "There was nothing else?"

"*Nyet-s.*" I whispered, "I checked the cork, but there was nothing."

"I see."

I quickly volunteered, "But I am to go to the Soviet cafeteria in an hour's time. Cook Kharitonov has received permission for me to get more bread."

"*Molodets.*" Excellent. "I have something I wish to send out." And then, exactly according to our short tradition, the Tsar entrusted me with a note folded into a small envelope. "I wanted to pass this to Father Storozhev yesterday, but that, of course, proved impossible."

I don't know what the note said, for I never saw the actual words, but I've always assumed it was in French, just like the others. More of the contents of this note I cannot say, for it alone has been lost to time, undoubtedly because of my stupidity.

So I took the note from the Tsar and kept it carefully tucked in my underclothing until it was time to leave. In the meantime, I was careful not to do anything to attract attention, and when the others went out into the yard for their afternoon walk, I headed off to fetch six loaves of *chyorny khleb*—black bread—from the Soviet. By that time the last two of the charwomen, Maria Staradumova and Vassa Dryagina, had completed their tasks and were also on the way out. As I came through the hall and reached the top of the short staircase, I saw them stopped at the front door.

"There is a new policy," explained Yurovsky, blocking their exit. "From now on, everyone coming into or departing from The House of Special Purpose will have to be thoroughly searched." The *komendant* looked up at me. "I'll get to you, young man, once I've finished with these women."

I started shaking. This couldn't be. I was to be searched? Panic shot through my body. *Gospodi,* what if they found the secret note I carried? Then what? Would I be thrown in prison? Shot? What would they do to me, to the Imperial Family? No, I couldn't let down the Emperor. I couldn't fail any of them. My task was far too important, too critical, too . . . I had to retreat, that was the only course. But where? I turned, started back to the kitchen. I could pull the note from my clothing, hide it somewhere in the house, then be on my way, and . . .

"Leonka!" shouted Yurovsky from the bottom of the stairs. "And just where do you think you're going? You must be on your way—some of that bread is for us too, you realize!"

There was only one logical explanation, and in a timid voice, I replied, "I was just going to go to the toilet, Comrade Komendant. Since you will be a few minutes with these women, I thought, well, I . . . I . . ."

"Fine. Just come right back."

Needing no other approval, I bolted. I ran from the front to the back hall, and finally into the small water closet with its toilet and wash sink. I all but slammed the door as I shut it and fastened the little eyehook, locking myself in. I turned, scanned the walls, which were covered with all those nasty pictures and words about the Tsar and Tsaritsa. There was, however, no little place to stash the note. No cabinet. No loose plank. What should I do, rip up the envelope and flush it down the drain? Tear it up and eat it?

Oh, if only I'd done one of those!

Instead my eyes fell upon a large pipe above the toilet itself. Convinced that I had no other choice, I pulled the note from my clothing, stood on the toilet seat, and tucked the note right back there, right behind the metal pipe. I jumped down and looked up, unable to see a thing. It would be safe there, at least until my return, and I unfastened the lock and pushed the door. Then stopped. Reaching back, I flushed the toilet, and was on my way again, confident I'd covered my tracks.

Before I left the house I was indeed searched, though not as thoroughly as I feared. In fact, had I still been carrying the note the *komendant* probably wouldn't have discovered it at all. I did overhear Yurovsky say to one of the charwomen, Maria Staradumova, that a good number of things had been pilfered from the family, which was so very unrevolutionary. Perhaps that was why he was searching everyone. But I doubt it. I think Yurovsky wasn't looking for little spoons or watches, skirts or leather boots, that kind of thing. No, I think he was looking for Romanov jewels. And I think that was why the Sister Antonina and Novice Marina chose not to come in that morning—they were afraid of being searched. Rather, they just left their goods. Who knows, maybe Sister Antonina was in fact transporting something more than a note, perhaps even a weapon. I have never found an answer to that question.

So I was searched and released without incident. I went directly to the Soviet, where of course I gathered the bread, three loaves for the guards and three for us. It was very tasty, nice and sour, though I knew the Empress wouldn't eat any, for she felt black bread was much too dense and gave her headaches. Then again, had she consulted Komendant Yurovsky he probably would have gone on at length with his advice. He probably would have stated that her headaches came from malnutrition, which they very well might have since the Empress ate so very little.

Having gotten out of the house undiscovered, I was feeling very smart as I returned. Very clever, indeed. There'd been a terrible crisis, and I, Leonka Sednyov, the kitchen boy, had solved it. The dreaded *komendant* had been about to discover the Tsar's secret dealings with his monarchist officers, and I'd saved the day entirely on my own. Yes, indeed. And a very fine officer I myself would make someday, of that I was sure. Once this revolution was over and once the Tsar was back in power again, I imagined that I was destined for great service, great reward, perhaps even great riches. Various members of the nobility, like Prince Orlov for example, had thus been so rewarded for their extraordinary services to their masters.

So I returned to The House of Special Purpose all but whistling. I delivered the three loaves to the guard room, whereupon Yurovsky quickly searched my body once again. Cleared, I proceeded up to the kitchen, where I put three loaves on the maple table. Next I headed directly for the WC, planning to fetch the note from its hiding place and secretly return it to the Tsar, telling him how I'd single-handedly averted disaster. So I went into the small WC, shut the door and dropped the hook into the little eye. I climbed atop the toilet, stuck my hand back there, but when I reached behind the pipe . . . I found nothing.

Nyet, nothing.

There was absolutely *neechevo* behind the pipe. I suppose it wasn't much more than an hour earlier that I had carefully hidden the note back there, but now to my dismay the little envelope had vanished. And so overcome with panic was I that I nearly vomited. I clawed at the walls, searched the floor, looked everywhere, hoping it had merely dropped out and was lying around. In desperation I pulled at the back of the toilet itself, even opened the tank, but there was no trace whatsoever of the Tsar's note to his loyal officers. My only hope, of course, was that the Tsar himself or someone else from the family had found it.

I hurried out of the water closet, through the kitchen, and into the dining room, where I found the Tsar and Tsaritsa playing a game of bezique.

"Do you realize Doctor Derevenko hasn't been allowed in once since the new *komendant?*" she bemoaned as she studied her cards.

"We will keep asking. And asking."

"Baby's going to take a bath tonight. Imagine, it's only his second since Tobolsk."

"In case you hadn't heard, the *komendant* says we bathe too much. We must stop this continual washing, it's not a good habit, or so he claims," said the Tsar with amusement. "After all he's—"

"—a trained medic."

They both started chuckling.

I cleared my throat.

Nikolai Aleksandrovich turned to me, and exclaimed, "Ah, Leonka, all is well?"

I felt their eyes upon me, both the Tsar's and the Tsaritsa's. So hopeful they looked, so yearning for good news. I wanted to cry, I wanted to shout out, for by the simplicity on their royal faces I immediately understood that, no, it wasn't them who had found and claimed the note! Dear Lord in Heaven!

Seeing my confusion, the Tsar asked, "Your trip to the Soviet for *khleb* was a success?"

Had there not been a guard by the window I'm sure I would have burst into tears and confessed my stupidity. Had we been alone I'm sure I would have dropped to the floor and admitted how terribly I had failed, blurting that the note most surely had fallen into the hands of the Reds who guarded us. As it was, there was nothing I could say, not only because of the nearby Lett with rifle and hand grenade, but . . . but . . . truth be told, because I was far too much of a coward.

My voice shaking, I muttered, *"Da-s."*

While the Empress was not a well-educated woman and by no means wise, she was extraordinarily perceptive, and if she called you a friend then she cared for you with her entire being. She knew something was wrong. And seeing me shake, she immediately rose to her feet and pressed her hand to my forehead in a smothering, motherly way.

"Nicky, the boy's burning up."

She immediately summoned Dr. Botkin, who pronounced the on-slaught of grippe, and as such I was immediately sentenced to the back bedroom, the far corner one. I was covered with blankets, offered tea and broth, both of which I declined. I just lay there, terrified of what I had done, what would happen, and wanting so much to confess and beg forgiveness. Instead I lay there all evening unable to speak. Much to my amazement, however, everything else seemed to proceed with complete normalcy. Aleksei did in fact have his bath, the family retired early, the wind came up, and somewhere in the depth of the night I heard both thunder and the report of artillery.

And I lay there, listening for that elusive whistle and praying, Please, please come tonight. Please come and carry us away this very eve . . .

By morning it seemed but a dream—or rather a nightmare that passed like the midnight storm—for nothing had changed. I woke cool and calm. First the Empress herself checked on me, feeling again my forehead, and then the doctor did likewise. I was pronounced healthy, surprisingly healthy. Meanwhile, it was noted that Aleksei had come down with a slight cold—caught from me, they speculated—and it was hoped he would recover just as quickly.

This was the sixteenth, of course. July 16. The day thereof. Yet as far as I could tell there were no suspicions, no thoughts or fears of what was to come. At least not by any of them, the family. This I knew because I studied them all day long, trying to figure out who had found this stupid note. I could learn nothing, however, and the time just progressed into another boring day. I suppose it was infinitely better that way, better they didn't suspect, better they couldn't conceive of anything as terrible as that which would transpire that very night.

That morning eggs, milk, and thread were again brought from the monastery. Sister Antonina and Novice Marina came early, but I did not see them. Rather, they left the foodstuffs with the guards at the front door. And while a good many eggs they did in fact bring, we received only ten. The evidence of the other eggs—all forty of them—I was to see only later.

Otherwise, for the rest of the day the Empress and Olga, her eldest, madly continued "arranging medicines." It was late that afternoon too that they completed the long and difficult task of individually wrapping every diamond in cotton wadding and then densely packing and stitching those little bundles between two corsets for the girls to wear. And just in time too. That night, when Yurovsky woke them, the grand duchesses would slip on their corsets, each of which was packed with no less than 10,000 carats. They would get dressed, sure that three hundred officers were charging to their rescue, and Aleksandra would think herself so smart, so clever.

And yet a horrific cloud of doubt must have hovered in the Tsaritsa's mind . . .

While Nikolai was a slave to fate, Aleksandra believed in the duality of the prophecies, that what was written in the Bible of ancient times applied as well to her, a fallen queen. In the afternoon while Nikolai was pacing outside in the garden for his thirty minutes, Aleksandra and her second daughter, Tatyana, remained inside reading of the prophets' gloom, including: "Though thou exalt thyself as the eagle, and though thou set thy nest among the stars, thence will I bring thee down, saith the Lord."

As for me, I became less worried as the day wore on. As far as I could see, no one in our suite had found the note, nor had Yurovsky or any of the guards apparently discovered it, for there was no recrimination, no horrible scene. Little did I know, however, that the note had in fact been found by the Reds and that the entire day telegrams were flying to and from Moscow demanding that Nikolai be "immediately destroyed."

16

Lenin denied it all.

During those tumultuous days, those violent days, when the outside world couldn't tell what happened to Nikolai and Aleksandra, Lenin claimed that the ex-Tsar was safe, that the rumors of their murders were only a provocation and "lie of capitalist press." But Lenin knew. Of course he did, for on that day, Tuesday July 16, 1918, he authorized not only the execution of Nikolai, but the entire family, including all the girls and the boy. That was what kind of man he was, a cold-blooded murderer. I spit on the bastard's body, which to this day lies like a pickle in a glass coffin on Moscow's Red Square. A shrine to a mass murderer, that's what it is.

I never learned who discovered the envelope I hid in the bathroom, but it soon fell into Komendant Yurovksy's hands, who in turn sounded the bloodthirsty alarm. And the discovery of that note from the Tsar to his would-be rescuers, his "Officers," caused a terrible fright among the *kommunisty*. Expecting imminent defeat and seeing monarchist spies in every shadow and around every corner, some of the Reds fled into the forest and hills. Others slipped out of town and secretly crossed over enemy lines, where the double-crossing bastards swore allegiance to the Whites. Yet others, a core group of Reds, gathered at the American Hotel, a fine brick building down by the train station. It was there, in room number three, that these bloodthirsty *Bolsheviki* celebrated, for at last here it was, their excuse, and to Moscow they issued an urgent request:

> . . . to destroy him and the family and relatives of the
> former Tsar . . . In case of refusal . . . we have decided
> to carry out this decree using our own forces.

Gospodi. Dear Lord. It was my fault that the note was found, that the plot to rescue them was exposed, and that the Tsar and his family were executed before they could be rescued. When I question myself, when I begin to doubt or even perhaps forgive myself, I take out my dossier. And I read these documents, and in each line I see the truth:

> The Presidium of the Ural Regional Soviet of the
> Workers' and Peasants' Government is at the tele-
> graph apparatus:
>   In view of the enemy's proximity to Yekaterinburg
> and the exposure by the Cheka of a serious White
> Guard plot with the goal of abducting the former Tsar
> and his family . . . For this reason: In light of the ap-
> proach of the counterrevolutionary bands toward the
> Red capital of the Urals and the possibility of the
> crowned executioner escaping trial by the people (a
> plot among White Guards to try to abduct him and
> his family was exposed and the compromising docu-
> ments have been found and will be published), the
> Presidium of the Ural Regional Soviet, fulfilling the

will of the revolution, resolved to shoot the former Tsar, Nikolai Romanov, who is guilty of countless bloody, violent acts against the Russian people . . .

We ask for your sanction . . . The documents concerning the plot are being expedited by courier to the Sovnarkom and the TsIK. We are waiting by the apparatus for advice. We urgently request an answer; we are waiting by the apparatus.

Facts cannot lie, and in them I see that the stupidity of a young boy hastened the murder of the Imperial Family of Mother Russia and their four loyal attendants. Eleven people in total. But my guilt is even greater, for the Romanovs were more than simply people. Nikolai, Aleksandra, and their five children were the ultimate symbols, both good and bad, of all that was Russia, and their brutal murders unleashed such chaos and darkness. Yes, regicide opened the door to fratricide, matricide, and patricide of unimaginable proportion. Some twenty, thirty, forty million souls perished under the Reds, helped along in part by me, Leonka Sednyov, the kitchen boy, for if the plot to save the Tsar had succeeded, what corner might history have turned? Might Nikolai have rallied his troops in the depths of Siberia and gone on to defeat the *Bolsheviki*? Would that gentle, misdirected Tsar have finally found the good direction he had searched for all along, and would he then have been able to lead his people and country back to sanity? I burn with the thoughts of what needn't have been and what might have been. And yet in a corner of my tired heart I still believe in the Russian people, that given the light, the life, and the opportunity a great future awaits them.

Meanwhile, of course, Yurovsky and the others were greatly dedicated to the destruction of the bourgeoisie and the creation of a workers' paradise, and yet . . . while they were most eager to murder the family to cement their cause, there was great hesitation on their part to take any definitive action. After all, Yurovsky, unlike many of those beneath him, was a professional revolutionary, and orders had to be issued and obeyed, the chain of command had to be followed. Consequently, many urgent communications were sent to the Red tsars in Moscow.

> To Moscow, Kremlin, to Sverdlov, copy to Lenin.
> The following has been transmitted over the direct line from Yekaterinburg: "Let Moscow know that for military reasons the trial agreed upon . . . cannot be put off; we cannot wait. If your opinions differ, then immediately notify without delay."

"Trial" was the code word for "murder," and the confirmation thereof did not come from Moscow until midnight, which was why the family was not led down those twenty-three steps until after one in the morning on July 17. In the meantime, Yurovksy went about preparing and arranging it all, getting everything ready. He chose a room in the cellar with no exit, a barred window, and soft plaster walls that might prevent ricochets. He ordered a truck ready to transport the bodies. Just in case any guards of the outside detachment might disagree with the executions, he had their commander, Pavel Medvedev, confiscate their Nagant revolvers, some twelve in total. So confident was Yurovksy of Moscow's approval that he even told Medvedev: "Tonight we will shoot them. Alert the detachment so they won't be alarmed if they hear shooting."

In my books I have since learned that earlier that afternoon Yurovsky and the murderers, all of whom were volunteers, not only agreed upon who was to shoot whom, but decided in an almost kind way that they should aim for the hearts so the victims wouldn't suffer. My fate was also decided then. Yurovsky and his Red comrades had no way of knowing that it was I who had been the secret courier all along, they had not an inkling that it was I who had hidden the note in the WC. Had they even suspected I would surely have been killed as well. Instead, they misperceived me as an "innocent" and decided there was no need to kill me, a mere boy, simply because of my association with the royals. Hence, my fate was cast, I was "saved," assigned instead to this long life of memory.

Some have written that it was the morning of the sixteenth that I was taken away, others the afternoon, but, no, it was that evening, just after dinner. Of course it was after dinner. I was washing the dishes in the kitchen when in came the guard, the young one with the blond beard, who was one of the few who'd survived the recent change in *komendanti*.

"The *komendant* requires you."

I all but panicked. "Wh-what?"

"Follow me."

Bozhe moi! My God! My first thought was the note, that I had been found out, and I all but dropped the dish in the metal tub. Too scared to say anything, I turned to cook Kharitonov, who stood stirring to-morrow's soup on the oil stove.

He stared at me, wiped his hands on his apron. "Well, go on, boy."

Demidova, the maid, came in just then, a stack of soiled plates in hand, and seeing the odd scene, asked, "Has something happened?"

"Leonka has been summoned by the *komendant*," explained Kharitonov with a shrug.

I pulled my hands from the dishwater and dried them on a towel. Was I to be interrogated? I was so afraid, so scared, but said nothing.

"Come," ordered the guard.

Trembling, I looked at Kharitonov and Demidova, yet knew I had no choice but to go, not realizing that my fate—life!—would be worse than anything I could yet imagine. And so I left the Imperial Family without the slightest farewell, which in turn has left my entire life incomplete. I followed the guard from the kitchen, through the back hall and out another door into the front of the house. He led me right into the *komendant's* room, where Yurovsky himself sat at the table, drinking his evening tea. I expected to be given quite a dressing down, but instead Yurovsky spoke quite calmly and evenly, not a trace of suspicion in that unpleasant voice of his.

"You are being removed from this house, young man. You are to follow this guard outside and through the gates. He will escort you to the Popov House, where you are to remain until further notified. Is that clear?"

This was the last thing I had expected, and I struggled to understand, struggled to make sense of this, and asked, "But . . . but why?"

"You are to wait for your uncle, who will come for you. He will then escort you back to your hometown."

Although I had no idea at the time, this was a lie, a very clean lie, and I said, "But . . . but, Comrade Komendant, what about . . . ?"

"Your services are no longer required."

"What about my things?" I asked, though I had but few possessions.

"One of the guards will bring them to you."

"May . . . may I say good-bye to the family and others?"

Yurovsky slurped at his tea. *"Nyet."* And then to the guard, he imperiously ordered, "Take the boy away."

I was thus herded out of The House of Special Purpose, too scared, too confused, to question or protest. What did this mean, that Yurovsky hadn't found the note after all? That I wasn't suspect? That I was really dismissed and was being sent home to Tula province? I knew the times, how difficult and hateful they were, and so I kept my mouth shut as I was escorted out of the house, down the outside steps, and through the double palisade. But, oh, how I wish I could have said good-bye, at least that, yet there was no way. Even then I understood. I was helpless, powerless, and as I followed the guard along the edge of Ascension Square and down the little lane to the Popov House, I realized that protest was as useless as . . . as trying to strip a naked man.

So I had no choice. I left. I was taken to the Popov House, where all the outside guards were billeted, shown a cot in a side room, and ordered not to leave. Years later, when all the books started coming out and the archives were opened, I learned how much my disappearance disturbed the family. Even Yurovsky commented on this, later writing:

. . . the boy was taken away, which very much upset the R—ovs and their people.

So they were fond of me, more than I could have ever imagined. Apparently they thought of me as one of their own, and Aleksandra herself was so concerned when I was taken away that she sent Dr. Botkin to speak with Yurovsky, who in turn recorded this conversation as well.

"But what about the boy," asked the good doctor. "Where is he? When is he coming back? His father is at the front, and Nikolai Aleksandrovich and his wife feel very responsible for him."

"You have nothing to worry about," replied Yurovsky, calming him down with another of his easy lies. "Leonka is visiting his Uncle Vanya."

By then, of course, Uncle Vanya was already long dead, killed Bolshevik style, that is, shot in the back of the head like a mad dog and dumped in a ditch.

Later, while her parents were playing cards, Grand Duchess Maria apparently went to the *komendant* as well, pleading, "Can you tell us, sir, if Leonka will be returning yet tonight?"

"He will not."

"Then tomorrow morning perhaps?"

"Perhaps . . ."

I sat terrified in my new quarters until one of the guards brought me my few things, whereupon I finally lay down. I curled up, using my jacket as a blanket, but of course I couldn't close my eyes, couldn't succumb to the lingering twilight of the Siberian night. And while the billeted guards were laughing and drinking in the other room of the Popov House, I crawled out of bed and went to the window. Across the alley and up the slight hill, The House of Special Purpose, massive and white, sat entirely dark, save for one window. It was the front room, that of the Emperor and Empress, and the limed panes glowed like a moon behind a slight veil of clouds. It was in that room and about at that time that Aleksandra Fyodorovna sat at the small writing desk, recording her simple last words in her diary:

> Yekaterinburg   16 JULY
> Irina's 23rd B.D.
> 11°C   Tuesday
>   Grey morning, later lovely sunshine. Baby has a slight cold. All went out 1/2 hour in the morning, Olga and I arranged our medicines.
> 3:00   Tatyana read Spir. Readings.3. They went out, T. stayed with me & we read: Book of the Pr. Amos & Pr. Obadiah. Tatted. Every morning the komend. comes to our rooms, at last after a week brought eggs again for Baby.
> 8:00   Supper.
>   Suddenly Leonka Sednyov was fetched to go & see his Uncle & flew off—wonder whether it's true & we shall see the boy back again!
>   Played bezique with Nicky.
> 10:30   to bed. 15 degrees.

Not quite two hours later the sound of a simple electric bell signaled the beginning of the end.

17

Even though I had been removed from The House of Special Purpose, I have read so many eyewitness accounts and studied so many documents, that in my mind's eye I can picture it all as if it were a movie. We know, for example, that by eleven o'clock Nikolai was asleep, having escaped into the depth of darkness, for sleep was his only refuge from depression. And I am certain that Aleksandra, who had been sleeping so poorly, was tossing and turning next to him, madly listening for that midnight whistle that was never to be heard. Otherwise, we know that the only other prisoner who was awake was Dr. Botkin, who sat at the large desk off the living room, writing a prophetic letter to some friend, a certain Sasha. Botkin never finished the letter, of course; it languishes in the Moscow archives, exactly where the doctor broke off . . .

> My dear, good friend Sasha,
>   I am making a last attempt at writing a real letter—
> at least from here—although that qualification, I be-

lieve is utterly superfluous. I do not think that I was
fated at any time to write anyone from anywhere. My
voluntary confinement here is restricted less by time
than by my earthly existence. In essence I am dead—
dead for my children, for my work . . . I am dead but
not yet buried, or buried alive—whichever, the con-
sequences are nearly identical . . . My children may
hold out hope that we will see each other again in
this life . . . but I personally do not indulge in that
hope . . . and I look the unadulterated reality right in
the eye. . . . The day before yesterday, as I was peacefully reading Saltykov-Shchedrin, whom I greatly en-
joy, I suddenly saw a vision of my son Yuri's face, Yuri
who died in battle in 1914. He was dead, lying in a
horizontal position, his eyes closed. Then yesterday,
again while reading, I suddenly heard a word that
sound like Papulya—dear Papa—and I nearly burst
into sobs. Again, this is not a hallucination because
the word was pronounced, the voice was identical,
and I did not doubt for an instant that my daughter,
Tatyana, who was supposed to be in Tobolsk, was
talking to me. I will probably never hear that voice so
dear or feel that touch so dear with which my little
children have so spoiled me. If faith without works is
dead, then deeds can live without faith. This vindi-
cates my last decision. When I unhesitatingly or-
phaned my own children to carry out my physician's
duty to the end, as Abraham did not hesitate at God's
demand to sacrifice his only son—

Hard and shrill, the electric bell rang with a chill just then, shattering the peace of that midsummer's night and interrupting Botkin
midsentence. He immediately put down his pen without the slightest
thought that he would never pick it up again. Instead, he focused on

the bell, understanding that something was quite wrong, for that was the alarm that roused them for morning inspection, yet here it was now approaching one at night. Concerned, Botkin slid back his chair and stood. He adjusted his gold wire-rimmed spectacles and pulled at his leather suspenders. He could hear noises from beyond—noises from the room of the guards—and he glanced into the living room, where the manservant, Trupp, had been roused from his sleep and was now propped up on his elbows.

"What's happening?" asked Trupp, his eyes puffy with sleep.

Botkin shrugged and ran one hand over his round balding head. *"Bog znayet."* Only God knows.

The door leading from the front halls rattled and opened, and Yurovsky emerged into the living room.

Botkin stepped forward, and asked, "What's the matter?"

The *komendant* calmly replied, "The town is uneasy tonight and it's too dangerous for all of you to remain upstairs. Would you kindly wake up Citizen Romanov and his family and ask them to dress as quickly as possible? For safety reasons all of you will be moved downstairs. This will only be for a short period, so instruct them not to bring anything at all along."

"Yasno." Understood.

As if he were inviting friends to the dinner table, Yurovsky's summons to mass murder was that easy, that simple. When the *komendant* disappeared, Botkin turned to Trupp, and the two men silently stared at each other, both of them wondering what this really meant.

Finally, Botkin took a deep breath, screwed up his eyes, and said, "I'll go wake them."

Wearing just an undershirt and his suspenders and pants, he crossed into the dining room, where he turned the switch for the electric chandelier. No sooner had the lights burst on than Nikolai appeared in the doorway on the opposite side of the room.

"What is it?" asked Nikolai, wearing his nightshirt. "We heard the bells."

"By orders of Komendant Yurovsky we are to dress and move

downstairs. He says it's for our own safety—apparently there's some sort of unrest in town."

"Unrest? What kind of unrest?"

"This I cannot say, Nikolai Aleksandrovich. He simply told me to wake you and the others, and that we are to dress as quickly as possible and move to the cellar. He also said this will only be for a short while and that we are not to bring anything."

Nikolai hesitated in thought before beckoning Botkin forward. "What do you think, could this be it? Could our friends be on the way?"

"Quite possibly, but it's difficult to say."

"Have you heard anything—shots, horses—anything at all?"

"*Nyet-s.*"

"Neither have we." Brushing his mustache with the back of his right hand, Nikolai stood in nervous thought. "Still, we must be prepared. After all, we can hear the fighting getting closer and closer. The town is sure to fall any day now."

"We can only hope."

"Wake the others and tell them to be calm but ready for anything," ordered the Tsar.

"Trupp is already up. I'll wake Demidova and Kharitonov."

Botkin moved toward the other rooms off the dining room, where the Tsaritsa's maid and cook slept. The Tsar, meanwhile, retreated to the room of his daughters, where all four of them sat up in their cots, the colored glass chandelier now ablaze overhead. Aleksandra, wearing a white linen nightgown, stood in the doorway of her bedroom, and even Aleksei stood there, balanced on one foot and leaning against the doorjamb.

"What is it, Nicky?" asked Aleksandra, her brow wrinkled with anxiety.

"Komendant Yurovsky has ordered us to get dressed and move downstairs. Apparently there's some sort of unrest in town."

Aleksandra audibly gasped and pressed a hand to her chest. "What do you think, could it—"

"I don't know the full story, but he says it's for our own safety. He claims it's to be only for a short while and that we're not to bring anything with us."

"Oh, Nicky, God has heard our prayers and they're coming! I just know it, they're coming for us!"

At this the girls began to move about and mumble with excitement, the vision of three hundred officers on horseback looming in their virginal minds. Nikolai, however, understood that the situation, whatever it was, was most precarious, and he turned and checked the dining room. No one was there.

"We can't let on to a thing," he commanded his small tribe. "We can't let them know our hopes. We just have to be alert and ready for any situation. And we all have to look out for one another. Understood?"

"*Da,* Papa," softly replied the children in near unison.

"The girls should wear everything, shouldn't they, Nicky?" pressed Aleksandra.

He thought for a moment, and answered, "Everything."

Of course they all knew what that meant. If the family was about to be rescued, they had to carry with them not funds for the Tsar to restore himself to power, but means for them to live. So the girls knew they should wear their diamond-packed corsets, which were not only awkward and uncomfortable, but difficult to put on and lace up. It would take quite some time.

Meanwhile, at the other end of the house Yurovsky paced about, complaining, "These Romanovs! They bathe so much, they read so much, they ask so many questions—and it takes them so long just to get dressed!"

Of course it did. The girls had never worn the corsets before and they were having trouble not only getting them on, but making them as inconspicuous as possible beneath their clothing.

"Do as well as you can, girls," instructed Aleksandra, her voice hushed, as she helped her daughters. "We can't let any of the guards suspect. And don't forget, we may have to move quickly."

Of similar heft was Aleksandra's corset. But that was not all she wore. *Nyet, nyet, nyet.* When it came to the Empress of Rossiya, she also wore a plate of fine gold weighing more than two pounds that was bent like a bracelet.

"Here, my love, let me help," said Nikolai as he slipped the plate up her thin arm, then pulled down the long sleeve of her dress.

"Does it show?" she whispered.

"Not at all."

Around the Empress's waist Demidova then fastened the large belt into which Aleksandra herself had stitched her ropes of beloved pearls, some the size of a robin's egg.

"Is that comfortable, Madame?" asked the maid.

"Just fine." Turning to her husband and son, Aleksandra said, "Don't forget your hats."

"Of course not," replied the Tsar.

Adjusting his own cap, Aleksei grinned, thrilled with the charade. "How do I look, Papa?"

"Perfect. Like a brave soldier."

Father and son wore their simple army clothes—coarse wool pants, field shirts, worn boots, and of course their forage caps, into which had been sewn those diamonds, rubies, emeralds, and sapphires that were too big for the girls' corsets. The remaining oversized gems— including a 70-carat diamond and 90-carat emerald—Aleksandra and her daughters had stitched into three traveling pillows, two of which she distributed to her daughters, one to Demidova.

"If they ask about the pillows," instructed the Empress, "tell them these are simply for our comfort while we wait."

When he saw his wife reach for her favorite icon, Nikolai said, "Sunny, my treasure, we're not to bring anything."

"But what about Saint Feodor's? I can't possibly go anywhere without it."

"Trust me, if fortune shines upon us and we leave this very night, I'll send someone back for it."

She hesitated, then replied, "Certainly, my love. You always know what's best."

"Papa, what about Jimmy?" begged Anastasiya of her tiny King Charlie. "Joy's outside and can take care of himself, but we can't leave Jimmy behind! If we do one of the guards will step on him, I just know it!"

"All right, but carry him snugly in your arms."

As if he were bestowing Easter blessings upon them all, the Tsar went from child to child, kissing them each. He ended with his wife, taking her into his arms, holding her tightly, and kissing her softly. Were their prayers about to be answered? Was their rescue at hand?

"We're all together, which is the most important thing. Everything's going to be all right," he assured her and the others. "Whatever happens, just remain calm. God will watch over us."

"As will Our Friend," said Aleksandra, referring to her Rasputin.

With the Tsar pushing his son in the wheeling chaise, the Imperial Family emerged from their bedchambers. It had taken them nearly an hour to get ready; it was nearly two in the morning. Full of excitement, full of hope, the Romanovs now proceeded into the drawing room, where Botkin, Trupp, Demidova, and Kharitonov were eagerly waiting.

This time the Tsar addressed everyone, saying, "Our fate is in God's hands, in whom we place all trust."

Nikolai gave Botkin the nod, and the doctor went to the outer door and called out that they were ready. The door immediately opened, and Yurovsky, appearing infinitely serene, beckoned them forward.

"Follow me. We'll proceed down the rear stairs and into one of the cellar rooms."

Somewhat earlier, perhaps about the time that the electric bells were sounded, I myself had climbed from my bed, for sleep could not possess me. I was much too afraid. Even though Yurovsky had said I was to join my Uncle Vanya, there'd been no sign of him, and I wanted to go back to them, the Romanovs, the only family I had in these parts.

So when I saw that the four other guards in my room of the Popov House had drunk themselves into deep sleep, I got up. I slipped on my jacket and carefully, quietly went outside. The rains of the previous days had stopped, and the night sky was clear and dark. I didn't know what or where I intended to do or go, but when I looked across the alley I could see the house blazing with electric light. Of course I knew which rooms were which, and I immediately saw the painted windows of the family's rooms glowing brighter than ever. I instantly understood that they had been roused for some reason, and my first thought was that the officers had indeed come to their rescue. *Gospodi,* Dear Lord, what joy! What happiness! I rushed up the alley, my happiness tempered only by the worry that I might be left behind.

Or was I all wrong?

Scurrying up the muddy alley toward the square, I suddenly saw a guard at the corner of the tall palisade. Recognizing him as part of the regular Red guard, I dipped behind a tree and into a cloak of darkness. A moment later the guard disappeared, and I scurried forward. It was in such secret fashion that I made it all the way up the alley and eventually onto the square. I hid behind a small Orthodox shrine, and while I could see the windows all glowing with light, I could discern nothing odd. There were no officers on horseback, no Cossacks whooping and hollering. Looking up at the roof, I could see a lone guard behind a machine gun. Everything appeared completely normal, which in turn led me to believe that if the rescue attempt hadn't already taken place, it was about to be launched.

Which is when I heard it. Not much at first, but it was a sound that grew by the moment. No, this was not the sound of three hundred officers on horseback galloping to the rescue of *Batyushka,* the Dear Father. It was the sound of a motor. At first I wondered if it was an airplane, but then I realized it was in fact an automobile or motor lorry, in itself a rarity in Yekaterinburg, particularly at that time of night. Finally I saw it, a single, bulky motor lorry emerging from one of the side streets and heading right across the square toward the house. In the dim northern night I recognized that the back of it was covered with a canvas roof. Could there be soldiers back there, a dozen or two sharp-shooters? As the vehicle approached, I hunkered down behind the shrine and saw that it was a Fiat. And as it passed I realized the rear of the truck was empty. Unable to suppress my curiosity I chased after the lorry as it drove directly up to the house.

When the vehicle stopped at the large, wooden gates, the driver leaned out and called, *"Troobochist."* Chimney sweep.

With this code word the gates were thrown open, and as the lorry rumbled forward I scurried along the far side of it, following it down the short hill and around the back of the house. When the clumsy vehicle pulled to a stop, I scurried off, taking shelter alongside one of the sheds.

Crouched in the darkness, I watched as several guards approached the Fiat truck. Words were spoken, so deep and cluttered that I could not understand a thing. And then all was silent. I saw several other guards move about, but little else. Twenty minutes passed, perhaps more, and I wondered what in the name of the devil I should do. I was stuck in my hiding place, too terrified to move for fear of being caught, for wouldn't they shoot me if they found me?

I finally heard movement from within the house, the sound of many feet on wooden steps, and I pushed myself as deep as I could into the shadows of that small shed. *Da, da, da,* that was a group of people descending those twenty-three steps, the twenty-three wooden steps that led from the main floor down the back of the house and to the scruffy garden. We had descended that staircase so many times, once in the morning and once again in the afternoon, and always gladly, for that was the route to fresh air and a walk outside. But not that night. Frightened, my eyes scanned the courtyard that was filled with a couple of wooden sheds and the big, silent truck. I heard them before I saw them—all the men with their boots and the women with their heels clattering.

Finally a side door was pushed open. First came Yurovsky. Then came the Tsar, wearing of course those worn, dark brown leather boots of his. They'd obviously left the wheeling chaise upstairs, and in his arms Nikolai Aleksandrovich effortlessly carried his beloved son and my friend, Aleksei. Both of them, father and son, were dressed alike in simple army hats and clothing. Next came Aleksandra Fyodorovna, wearing a long dark skirt and long-sleeved, light blouse, her long, thick hair put up on her head. She looked so old that night. So tired. Yet in the shadows of that night I thought I saw a glimmer of hope smooth her brow as she glanced around, perhaps looking for someone or something.

Next came the girls, Olga, Tatyana, Maria, and Anastasiya, all of them dressed in identical dark skirts and light blouses, all of them with nothing on their heads and of course no wraps on their shoulders. Rather than appearing exhausted, they seemed lively and eager. I saw that both Tatyana and Maria carried small pillows, and that Anastasiya cradled her treasured dog, Jimmy, who was so ominously quiet. Following them came Dr. Botkin, Demidova, who also clutched a pillow, valet Trupp, and cook Kharitonov. No one spoke. No one protested or sobbed. What did they think? What had they been told?

From my hiding place I watched as the line of Romanovs and the last of their faithful calmly and quietly followed Yurovsky along the back of the house. Aleksandra, who suffered off and on from sciatica, limped slightly, but she kept up, certainly spurred on by her ever-present faith. They were midway toward the other end of the house when I saw my favorite, Maria Nikolaevna, gazing up at the sky. I turned my attention upward as well, peered through the leaves at the dark heavens above, whereupon my eyes landed on a handful of stars. When my attention fell back to earth, I saw that Maria was no longer staring at the heavens, but gazing directly at me. She saw me there in the bushes, and for an instant that I can never forget our eyes embraced. Recognizing me but not daring to betray my presence, Maria Nikolaevna even cast me a small smile.

"This way," called Yurovsky, leading them into the far door.

Thus the group of eleven calmly disappeared into that mouth of death, proceeding back into the cellar and to a rear chamber from which there would be no escape. Losing sight of them, I scurried around, darting like a spy from shed to bush to tree to bush. And there, through a large open window covered with a heavy metal grating I not only saw all of them in that cellar room, but heard them as well. It was not that large of a space, not really, and held not a stick of furniture. The walls were covered in striped yellow wallpaper, the rear door to the storeroom appeared locked, and a single electric bulb hung from the low ceiling.

"There have been various rumors in the capitalist press as to your safety," began Yurovsky, spinning his lies with such great ease. "Because of this, we would like to take your photograph to reassure people in Moscow. Would you be so kind as to line up against the wall?"

That was all the *komendant* did, all he needed to say, to get this unsuspecting group to line up in a nice, easy firing line. Clearly pleased with himself, Yurovsky turned to beckon his executioners. At that moment, however, Aleksandra Fyodorovna, ever herself, clawed out at him.

"What, there isn't even a chair?" said the Tsaritsa with the last imperious comment of her life. "One isn't even allowed to sit down?"

Smiling to himself, Yurovsky hesitated but a moment, then left without replying, gently shutting the double doors behind him. I crept along, spied the *komendant* in the next room and through the open doorway heard him bark at a soldier.

"Apparently the Empress wishes to die sitting down," he said with a stout laugh. "Fetch me two chairs."

What did Yurovsky mean? What was he up to? Panic crawling up my throat, I moved back and peered through the grated window at the Romanovs. Should I shout out? Scream a warning?

One of the two doors was kicked open, and Yurovsky entered, smiling to himself as he delivered two chairs. Taking one of the pillows for supposed comfort, Aleksandra Fyodorovna sat in one chair near the window, while the other was positioned to her right for Aleksei. The Tsar carefully lowered his son onto this chair, and then the other members of the Imperial Family, photographed so many thousands of times, automatically assumed positions as though for an official portrait. Behind the Empress, yet more toward the middle of the room, stood the four daughters. Close by their side was Demidova, faithfully clutching her pillow as if it were a treasure, while behind Aleksei stood Botkin, Trupp, and Kharitonov. The Tsar himself stood between mother and son.

Once again, Yurovksy stepped out of the room, pulling shut the doors behind him. And then came the longest, oddest silence in which my heart began to beat ever so fast. Inside the chamber, not one of the Romanovs spoke. Aleksandra Fyodorovna did turn and gaze out one of the windows, searching, I'm sure, for those officers. About then Tatyana came over and placed her hand on her mother's shoulder, which Aleksandra took and reassuringly kissed.

Suddenly the lorry in the courtyard fired up its engine, its noisy motor roaring in the night. All at once, Yurovsky returned, throwing open the double doors into the small cellar room. He quickly moved in and ten henchmen, brandishing Nagant revolvers, awkwardly piled through the small opening behind him. Except for one, they were all the new guards, the so-called Letts. Crowded to the side as if an afterthought, I recognized one of the former guards, the young one with the blondish beard.

Calm and self-assured, the *komendant* unfolded a piece of paper, and boldly proclaimed, "In view of the news that your relatives both inside the country and from abroad have attempted to free you, the Ural Executive Committee has decided to execute you by—"

The Tsar cut in, his voice loud and desperate, *"Shto? Shto?"* What? What?

Rather surprised at being interrupted, Yurovsky cleared his throat and started over: "In view of the news that your relatives both inside the country and from abroad have attempted to free you, the Ural Executive Committee has decided to execute you by firing squad."

Horrified, Aleksandra Fyodorovna threw her right hand up, desperate to make her sign to her God. Olga, the eldest daughter, likewise attempted a plea to a greater mercy.

"Papa!" screamed Anastasiya, clutching her dog, Jimmy, against her chest.

His voice shaking, Nikolai turned slightly, muttering, "Forgive them Father, they know not what—"

Eleven people lined up in a small room as though for a photograph. Eleven assassins piled into a narrow doorway. The shooting began in nearly the same instant, and Nikolai *krovavyi*, the bloody, caught the first hail. All at once the blast of those eleven revolvers struck and lifted the Tsar off the ground, hurling him back through the air. His head exploded, showering his daughters with a coarse spray of his blood and brains. An instant later, Aleksandra, the *Bolsheviki's* hated German bitch, took a handful of bullets in the face and mouth, the force of which threw her back as well, her cross-making hand flailing upward, her chair hurling back, her feet flying overhead as she tumbled ass over head into infinity.

"Aim for the heart!" shouted Yurovsky.

A horrible wail of confusion rose in the room. In complete terror, the daughters ran about, screaming, begging, and shrieking. Botkin shouted and pleaded. Demidova wailed. Trupp and Kharitonov sobbed. Only poor Aleksei, stranded as he was, remained in place, clutching his eyes shut, grabbing at the sides of his chair as bullets whizzed all about him. The gunshots started coming faster, more desperate, but remarkably no one else fell. I heard the twinging of ricochets, saw sunlike sparks burst as bullets bounced off those corsets, so thick with jewels that they had inadvertently been made . . . bulletproof. Protected as they were by all those invincible carats, the girls were not granted a quick death. Rather it appeared as if God Himself were shielding them, and a great cry arose, not from the horrified victims, but their executioners, so sure were they of the divineness of these White princesses. Terrified, the guards started pumping the bullets faster, more desperately.

Finally big Dr. Botkin tumbled, a bear of a man who dropped to his knees and fell face first into death. I saw Olga running to the side, clasping her ears. Suddenly her neck was ripped wide in a streak of crimson, and she too dove into the beyond. Trupp, Kharitonov—they went next, paying in blood for their faithful service. As they fell, a devilish fog began to fill the room and cloud it with confusion, for all the modern smokeless bullets had been used up during the war. And then Aleksei tumbled from his meager wooden throne.

"Mama! Papa!" rose the shrieks of those girls.

I saw Anastasiya bending her head, shielding her Jimmy, shrieking hell and devil. I saw Maria run back and forth, then fall against the wall. And I saw Demidova holding that priceless pillow up like armor. And too I saw Tatyana's face and neck and arms blister with death.

Within moments, the entire room filled with smoke from the bullets. Yet still it went on, the shots slapping and hurling, biting and ripping. I heard the deep voices of the guards coughing and shouting, gagging and yelling, as they stirred up this black stew of pandemonium. And though the guards could no longer see their targets, it went on. And on.

Eleven men firing eleven guns for a minute is a lifetime. Upward of ten minutes is an eternity. But it took that long and longer to cut down those eleven victims. Eventually, the bullets began to slow and the smoke began to lift. Several of the men, vomiting and coughing on the acrid smoke, retreated into the hallway.

The clouds of death parted, revealing Yurovsky as he walked above the dead. Waving his hand back and forth in front of his face, the *komendant* peered down through the dimmest of light at the young Heir. It was then that I saw Aleksei, still moving, still treading life, still moaning and writhing as he clutched his father by the sleeve. Lowering his gun, Yurovsky placed the barrel on Aleksei's temple and blasted, once, twice. He and the guards, who had fetched rifles from the hallway, moved on through the room, discovering that even after all the shooting three of the sisters and Botkin were still alive, convulsing as they choked on their own blood. Approaching Tatyana, a dark-bearded guard raised his rifle and bayonet over her and plunged at her heart. Despite all his brutal virility, however, the dull blade bounced off her, and the young princess twisted and contorted in semiconscious pain. Confused and dismayed, the guard straddled her, clutched his rifle in both hands, and plunged again. And again met with no success. Unable to puncture her chest and clearly terrified by her immortality, the man whipped out a knife and quickly slit her throat, finally finding proof positive in her butchered neck that she was not the daughter of a demigod.

Suddenly a woman's voice screamed out, "Thank God!" It was Demidova. "God has saved me!"

I caught sight of the Tsaritsa's maid, who'd apparently only fainted and was now pushing herself from the floor, smeared with the blood of her masters. No sooner had she risen back to life, however, than a herd of men were upon her, and she fell once again and for all, screaming, screaming, screaming so horribly as she grabbed at the dull, rusty bayonets that punctured her full round body no less than thirty times.

For a brief moment there was silence and peace, which in turn was broken by a pathetic whimper and an animal-like cry. One of the guards went over to Anastasiya and plunged her throat with his bayonet. Miraculously, however, the cry grew but louder until suddenly the girl's tiny pet wiggled and squirmed from beneath the child's carved body. Seeing the little dog, now soaking crimson, try to scramble away, its back legs broken, the guard raised one of his heavy boots . . . and smashed little Jimmy's head.

All in all, it took twenty minutes before silence graced the basement chamber of The House of Special Purpose.

18

Hidden in the bushes, I stared off at the black sky, seeing nothing, neither star nor moon, but seeing again that which I had just witnessed: those twenty minutes. Hearing them too. *Da, da, da,* hearing their screams. Ever since, for eight decades now, I have daily seen this cinema of horror in my mind's eye, and I watch it from this angle, from that, and nearly go insane.

I find myself so angry. Angry at all the tsars of my Rossiya for driving my homeland down the dead-end path of autocracy. Angry at the *Bolsheviki* for not realizing that *kommunizm* is naught but a gorgeous dream that can never be. Angry at Aleksandra for being a supreme mother not to her country but her invalid son. Angry at Nikolai for not signing that one piece of paper that would have averted all. Sure, Russia in its own clumsy, inevitable way was stumbling toward a constitutional monarchy, and because Nikolai could not see this, because he could not sign a simple paper granting a ministry appointed not by him but by his parliament, he and his family as well as about forty million others were slaughtered.

The thick, acrid smoke had yet to clear before the henchmen were upon their victims, Red vultures picking at the Imperial Family as if they were carrion. While Yurovsky was going from body to body, verifying pulses and the sort, two of the guards were in the hall, still vomiting not because of the gore but because of the foul smoke from those old-fashioned bullets. The rest of the guards forgot every bit of their ideology and searched pockets and wrists and necks for trinkets and treasures. Greed was their strongest urge, and these henchmen fed furiously upon their victims. They wanted more for themselves, and so they feasted upon those they had killed for possessing too much. Only Yurovsky stood as the pillar of the ideal revolutionary, and he flushed with disdain upon seeing the joyful looting.

He shouted, "You are to take nothing! Nothing! Now I want half of you to go upstairs and gather all the sheets you can, and I want the other half to go out to the shed and gather the shafts from the troikas." When he saw hesitation among them, Yurovsky raised his gun. "Go!"

For a long moment, none of the guards left. Realizing he was losing control, Yurovsky took aim at one of the men.

"Leave!"

One by one, the assassins departed. Shaken by the disobedience, Yurovsky stood there, pistol raised as he guarded his royal kill. And because of this challenge, he never finished verifying the dead, specifically Anastasiya, Kharitonov, and Maria. Minutes later his men returned, and according to Yurovsky's directions the sheets were suspended between the harnessing shafts and the bodies loaded up. With the noisy engine of the motor lorry masking the commotion, the Romanovs and their small retinue were then carted out one by one and heaved into the back of the vehicle.

The entire time I sat there, hidden in the darkness, watching, seeing with my own two eyes, and yet not believing. Not a tear did I shed, not even then. Not a whimper did I cry. Somehow fear steeled me, protected me, for had I started crying I would have been pulled from my hiding place and killed as well.

Once the last of the bodies was heaped upon the pile in the back of the truck, the biggest of the guards pulled himself onto the truck. He scrambled over the dead, pawed at them like a mad dog, and laughing, reached into a pile of Romanovs. He threw aside an arm, tugged at a bloody dress, and seized upon a fleshy prize. A moment later he leapt up and held out his cupped hand as if it were full of gold.

"Now that I have touched the Empress's pussy I can die in peace!" he laughed and shrieked.

His joy was a call to chaos, and his comrades hooted with fiendish delight. All at once the lot of them climbed and clambered aboard, once again pulling at boots and necklaces, eyeglasses and especially watches, which Russians have always sought as a souvenir of death. Though they failed to discover the fortune of diamonds hidden in the royal corsets, the guards clambered over the carcasses of their history, desperately pawing for riches of any kind.

Suddenly Yurovsky charged out of the house, cocked his gun, and shouted, "The next man who takes anything gets a bullet in the head! Drop everything you've taken and get back inside—now!"

The frenzy came to an immediate but uncomfortable pause, followed by grumbling and some reluctant movement.

"I'll be checking each and every one of you, and should I find that you've taken anything—anything!—you'll be executed immediately!"

All of a sudden things began to fall. A bracelet. An amulet. Dr. Botkin's glasses. One of the traveling pillows. The guards dropped them back onto the bodies, and these things landed with soft plops upon the still-warm flesh. From where I hid, I sensed the bodies shifting as the guards clambered over them. The next moment I saw an arm slip out from beneath the canvas top, the gold watch on that arm sparkling in the night.

The guards did as they were told. All it took was terror to whip them into control, of course, and this team of executioners leaped to the ground and hurried inside. Thereupon big buckets of sawdust were carted into the cellar room. Brooms too. And mops. They had to obliterate all signs of the crime. The Whites would take the city any day, and the Reds couldn't leave any trace of the bodies or even the murders; all along the greatest danger to their cause had not been the possibility of Nikolai being restored to the throne—neither Red nor White wanted that—but the very real possibility of the Whites seizing the dead Tsar and his family and resurrecting them as martyrs to their cause. But of course there could be no martyrs if there were no bodies.

While all of this cleaning up was going on, I stared at the dead arm swinging back and forth, the gold watch on that arm ticking this way and that against the side of the Fiat lorry. As if mesmerized by Rasputin himself, I was drawn out of the darkness, and I inched forward. They say that a Russian cannot believe with his eyes what he cannot touch with his hand, and against my own will I was drawn forward. Without even thinking, I reached out. I reached out and clutched the arm of *Batyushka,* the Dear Father. I held onto his muscular arm for but a moment. And then I pulled at his watch. When my hands came away, not only did I clutch something as brilliant as the sun, but my fingers were sticky red with his death.

Minutes later, after great confusion, the motor lorry finally made its departure. Once again I trotted after it, hiding in the vehicle's night shadow as it passed through the gates. Of course I should have fled, but that never occurred to me. Not once. I should have taken off across the square, but somewhere I understood that the end of the tale had not yet come. And so like a pathetic dog I trotted after my dead master as the lorry moved through the dark, muddy streets of Yekaterinburg.

Da, da, da, like a faithful dog I chased after that motor truck that was overflowing with all those *troopy,* those bodies. With a driver, a single guard, and Yurovsky seated up front, the vehicle proceeded so very slowly that I had no trouble keeping up, and when it drove all the way around the far side of the race track, I took the shortcut and actually had to wait for it to pass. When it headed northward on the dirt lane to the village Koptyaki, I trotted after it. Usually it was only carts and wagons that moved along here, peasants bringing their fish or game to sell in town. But not tonight . . . not tonight . . .

I had no idea of its destination, but I ran after the motor lorry, and the vehicle barely creaked along, certainly not faster than a cart itself.

A few versts from town one of the wheels sank into a deep hole, then rose quickly out of it, hit a stone, and the whole back of the lorry bounced violently. That very instant a black heap of something was thrown from the rear of the truck, landing with a near silent thud on the dirt road. At first I couldn't imagine, but then it bolted through me, seized my heart. *Gospodi,* Dear Lord, one of the bodies had been hurled from the lorry onto the ground.

I froze in horror, then bolted forward, hurried to this sack of death lying so still in the rutted road to Koptyaki. *Da, da,* it was a body. That much was clear. And not Dr. Botkin. And not one of the ladies. No, it was the Heir Tsarevich Aleksei Nikolaevich. A rag doll of a body . . . that was all that was left. He was the mirror of me, this boy was. We were about the same height, the same age, and there he lay, twisted and crumpled, his military tunic torn, his face so . . . so . . .

Gospodi, Dear Lord, when I knelt to him I saw the side of his head all black and shattered. His right ear was gone, blasted away by the two bullets that Yurovsky had fired point blank into the side of his head. *Da, da,* the bullets had pierced the skull, not blowing it apart, really, but surely exploding through his brains and out the other side. But his face . . . it was . . .

My stomach turned, slithered like a snake up the back of my throat. I turned away, then immediately looked back. Yes, it was him, there was no doubt, even though it was almost impossible to tell, for they had slashed his face with bayonets, beaten it with rifle butts. Mother of God, this boy, who had so yearned to play *shahmaty,* well, there was nothing left to gaze at but slaughtered meat and bone hanging, dripping, into the earth of Siberia, so . . . so mutilated was he.

I couldn't move. I stared down at this grossly killed boy, the Heir to the throne of Russia, and the blackest of terrors filled my every pore. I wanted to die. I wanted someone to blow my own brains out, to blast this sight from my mind, but then . . . then the truck started picking up speed, started moving quicker. And all of a sudden another one fell out. I looked up the road and saw another body tumble from the back of the truck. It just . . . just fell like a sack of wheat onto the road.

I didn't know what to do. Once again I looked down to the Heir, saw his perforated body, knew that the future of Russia was dead beyond a doubt, and then I gazed up the road at the next dark pile that was yet another Romanov. I started moving, started running to the second body. The truck, oblivious, rumbled on into the madness of the night. Unbelievably, the second body moved and quivered and . . . and I wanted to scream out, to beg to God. It was the third child, Grand Duchess Maria who by some miracle was not only still alive, but trying to get up. She hadn't fallen from the truck but thrown herself, and when I reached her she was trying to push herself to her knees. Her long, dark skirt was torn, grossly soiled, her light blouse ripped and stained, but she wasn't crying. No, she had quite literally risen from the dead and she was as stunned as a newborn, shocked, even horrified, to find herself here on this earth.

Hearing my quick steps, Maria shook with fear. This most beautiful of girls, this protected princess, opened her mouth to scream. I saw that she was going to howl to the sky and moon and back, and I charged forward. As quickly as I could, I threw my hand over her mouth, gagged her fear, kept it bottled up inside the poor thing.

"*Eto ya!*" It's me, I hissed into her ear. "*Eto ya!*"

I gently lowered her back to the road, and Grand Duchess Maria fell weak and silent beneath my youthful power. She attempted to struggle but then, gazing up at me with those rich eyes, fell still.

"Leonka . . ." she gasped, clutching my arm.

Like the sternest of schoolmasters, I ordered, "Keep quiet or they'll come after us both!"

She understood, of course. At the same time I saw her eyes strain after the lorry that was carting away her family.

"Papa . . . Mama . . ." she moaned, her body now falling flaccid in my arms.

Only as I held her did I realize how badly she was bleeding. I didn't know if it was a bayonet wound or if a bullet had grazed her temple, but she was bleeding most profusely from the side of her head, from just above her ear. I touched her temple, sensed a long, deep wound, and then tore a swath of material from her skirt, which I wrapped around her head. Fearful that the truck would turn around and come back, I tried to help her get up.

"We've got to get off the road and into the woods," I said.

But when she moved, she clutched her side and cried out, "I can't!"

The bullets meant to kill her had instead struck her diamond-studded corset, the force of which had broken a number of her ribs. She started gasping for air, and as I held her, I saw she was bleeding terribly from her left leg as well. Raising her skirt, I saw two wounds in her left thigh, one on the front, the other the back. A bullet had apparently gone through her leg, perhaps shattering the bone. As she leaned upon me, I tore more of her skirt, then tied that strip around the top of her leg, tightening the tourniquet to stem the blood. I glanced way down the road, saw the vague, dark shape of the lorry slowing. Or had it stopped? Panic seized my throat. Had they discovered that not one but two of the Romanovs had fallen from the back of the vehicle? Were the Reds about to return and hunt us out? I had to get Maria Nikolaevna off the road and hide her in the woods. Somehow I found this strength. She was a big girl, and I turned around, pulled her up on my back. It was then, as I half-dragged her off the road, that she saw the other body.

"Aleksei . . ."

There was no way to soften the truth, not on that night, and I said, *"Ew-bili."* They killed him.

I kept moving, carrying the Grand Duchess into the woods, which were not really that thick. Behind a clump of bushes I found a pine, and there I placed Maria, lowering her to the sandy ground and then propping her up against the tree.

"My brother," she begged.

"Ew-bili," I repeated.

I wondered if we shouldn't just leave him for the guards to find. A decoy. And she understood this, the Grand Duchess did, for she saw the hesitation on my face.

"Bring him to me."

In all the time that I'd spent in The House of Special Purpose I'd never heard any of the Royal Family issue a command, particularly none of the children. Yet Grand Duchess Maria Nikolaevna so ordered me. Dead or alive, she would not abandon her brother. And so wasting no time, I darted through the wood and back onto the road. I glanced into the distance and sure enough, there was the truck, stopped or perhaps stuck. There was little time, and so I grabbed Aleksei by the shoulders and pulled the boy out of the road and into the pine wood, leaving a swerving tail of blood behind. Reaching the trees, I stopped and took off my light jacket, which I in turn draped over the boy's mutilated head. I then dragged him on, all the way to Maria, whereupon I laid him by her side. She immediately took his hand, then started to pull away my jacket.

It was my turn to order, and this I did, catching her hand, pushing it back, and commanding, *"Nyet-s!"*

She understood quite clearly, and she laid back, holding his hand, which she pinned to her chest. Her eyes blinked quite heavily as if she were about to fall into the most permanent sleep.

Suddenly her mouth moved, and she begged, "Please, you must go after them, after . . . after Tatyana . . ."

Tatyana? It couldn't be. My mind exploded—I'd seen her shot, I'd seen that guard attack her with a bayonet, or was I all wrong?! Could she have been protected by her corset as well?

I demanded, "She lives as well?"

She gazed weakly at me. "You must go. You must bring her."

She slipped away then, Maria did. At first I thought she'd simply expired on the spot, but then I saw her chest rise and fall, albeit quite slowly. Whether she was passing into some kind of shock or she was about to die I couldn't tell, but this much I knew—I had to find out if indeed the Tsar's second daughter, Tatyana, was still alive.

And so I said, "I'll be back."

Her head slowly rose and fell.

"Trust me, I'll be back to take care of you. Just don't try to move. Just wait. I'll go see if your sister is . . . is . . ."

"Go," she pleaded with the last of her strength. "Go now."

"I'll be back," I chanted yet again, making a pledge as much to my-self as to the Princess.

Those were my last words to her before I scrambled out of the woods. I had no idea how much blood she'd already lost, just as I had no idea how much longer Maria would live. I was so young and knew so little of such things.

So . . . I left her. I did exactly as the Grand Duchess begged, no more, no less. I abandoned her, which of course turned out to be the stupidest thing. I followed her command, hurried to the road, where-upon I saw all that blood pooled like motor oil on the dirt. I knew I couldn't leave such an obvious sign, so I returned to the edge of the wood and took a large branch. And this branch I dragged over the blood of Aleksei and Maria so as to obscure it. Which I did. I swirled the dirt around, buried the redness as best I could, and then . . . well, then I threw the bloodied pine bough into the bushes and started run-ning after the motor lorry, the engine of which coughed and sputtered in the distance. Already the depth of darkness had passed, and in the faintest of early light I could see it, that clumsy truck laden with all the bodies.

I ran and ran, my mind on fire. The vehicle passed over a railway embankment, and I was just catching up when suddenly I heard all this commotion. I heard shouting voices, the stomp of many horses, and I ducked behind a clump of birches. From nowhere a convoy of men, as many as twenty, charged out of the night. Most of them were on horseback, a few in small horse-pulled carts, and they were shout-ing with the drunken revelry of revolution. And murder.

"Give us Nikolashka!"

"Off with his capitalist head!"

"Death to the blood drinker!"

I quickly understood that this haphazard detachment of Reds had been told they would get the honor of killing the royal ones, not sim-ply burying them. When they found out, however, that their hated

Nikolashka and his traitress whore, the German bitch, were already dead, there was a fiery roar of disappointment and anger.

One of the men shouted, "We were told you would bring them to us alive!"

"We wanted to kill them!"

"You tricked us!"

They were so angry and so drunk that a second blood bath—Komendant Yurovsky's very own—began to quickly boil. Someone fired a shot into the air. Another lowered his pistol and fired into the back of the truck itself.

Fearing the worst, Yurovsky shouted, "Long live the revolution!"

With that he ordered the driver, Comrade Lyukhanov, to move on. The convoy of men had no choice but to follow the motorized transport. And neither did I. Once they were all well under way, I emerged from behind the birches and ran after them. It was easier, of course, than ever to follow them, for the road was in terrible condition, which forced them to drive slowly. Plus the men made such racket. In such a way did I follow them for another twenty, thirty minutes when suddenly the lorry came to a sudden halt. The road had narrowed and the truck itself had become horribly stuck in the mud between two trees. They couldn't budge it, not an inch, for the vehicle had sunk so deep. Sure, there'd been so much rain and now there was much mud. A whirlwind of shouting ensued—everyone had an opinion, of course—and Yurovsky and the other fellow in the cab of the truck climbed out. A great effort was made. Everyone pushed, but to no avail.

By this time I was able to get quite close. Too close, really, but I was desperate to find out if Tatyana lived as well. I positioned my young body behind a pine, and in the gray morning light I watched as first one, then two men jumped onto the back of the truck. I think they just wanted to see the bodies with their own eyes. But then one of the peasant men, groping for the touch of a royal bosom, reached into the bodice of a grand duchess and came up not with a breast, but a handful of bloody jewels.

"Brillianty!" he screamed with shocked glee.

With the diamonds finally discovered, a handful of men swarmed over the bodies like hungry maggots. Panicking, Yurovsky started jumping around, shaking his pistol overhead and screaming. He fired once into the air, and the comrades slithered off the truck like scared rats.

As for the lorry, it was quite obvious the vehicle was going nowhere. Yurovsky was desperate. Things couldn't be going much worse, and he waved his gun around and ordered the men to transfer the bodies from the lorry to the carts. Because the horse-drawn carts were so small, however, they had to split up the bodies—two on that cart, three on that, one over there—and in that way Yurovsky didn't realize that Aleksei and Maria were missing. *Nyet, nyet, nyet,* the *komendant* was so busy waving around his pistol and trying to control these men that he didn't even count all the *troopy,* not just then, not just yet. And as soon as he was told the bodies had all been reloaded, off they went in single file through the woods.

The morning light was filtering softly through the trees by this time, and soon the mistakes began flowing like a mountain brook. Not five minutes passed before this line of murderers and murdered took a wrong path and became lost in the wood. To complicate matters even more, they came upon a group of peasants from the nearby village Koptyaki.

Threatening these simple people with his pistol, Yurovsky shouted, "There are Whites everywhere out here, so you'd better get home before we shoot you all!"

Finally, just as the northern morning sun was climbing into the sky, this convoy of carts and horses and men reached the ruins of the Four Brothers Mine, named after a cluster of old pines, where gold had once been sought.

"I want you three men," Yurovsky shouted, his pistol ever in hand, "to patrol the area and shoot anyone on sight."

Hearing this, I slunk into some deep bushes, crouched down, and watched the Red bastards handle the Imperial Family like slaughtered animals.

It was a fiasco, a farce right from the beginning. This area, this place, was only a few versts from village Koptyaki, a hamlet of a few dozen wood huts, and before the Romanovs were even stripped of their clothing the entire village knew that their Tsar had been murdered and where he was to be buried. Furthermore, the Four Brothers was an open mine, not a tunnel, but a big hole. It was a pitshaft, actually, and not very deep, not really, maybe some twenty feet at most, and the bottom of it was filled with water, very cold water. In short, it was the stupidest place to think of burying anyone, be he peasant or king.

Komendant Yurovsky ordered the bodies unloaded, and the men eagerly swarmed upon Nikolai, Aleksandra, the girls, the others. They dragged the Imperial Family and their attendants off the carts and threw them in a pile like game from an imperial hunt. It was then that I realized they were dead, all dead, including of course Tatyana. I saw her heaved atop and knew without doubt that she was gone.

"I don't want anyone to be able to identify these bodies," shouted the *komendant*. "So I want you to strip them all. What you can't pull off, we're going to have to cut away."

And this these animalmen did, pulling and slicing boots and jackets, blouses and shirts from the hated Romanovs. Soon there were diamonds spilling from the corsets into the mud, which sent an electric charge through the men all over again. Working with great frenzy, they found the gold on Aleksandra's wrist and the ropes of pearls around her waist. When one of the men couldn't get a ring off Aleksandra's finger—the one given her by her Uncle Leo—he took out his knife and cut the finger clean away. Sure. I watched as he yanked the ring free, secretly stuffed it in his pocket, then tossed aside the manicured finger; months upon months later, Investigator Sokolov, whom the Whites brought in to try find the imperial remains, found this very finger, which to this day remains preserved in a jar of alcohol in Paris.

Altogether it didn't take the Red barbarians long to strip their victims, and soon the Imperial Family and their servants were lying about this way and that, naked in the mud. Yurovsky then ordered a big bonfire built, and this his men did as well. They built this fire and threw the clothing into the flames.

It was then of course that they discovered that two of the Romanovs were missing. Yurovsky . . . he went crazy. He started running around screaming. He counted the bodies over and over. Then he . . . he called for two guards. He gave them two horses and told them to ride off and . . .

Oi, I have lied so much and for so long that I have almost forgotten the real truth, which is so difficult to let pass my lips. But . . . but I . . . I started running then. I looked back only once. Big Dr. Botkin—two men started to drag his naked body toward the opening of the mine. They each had him by a foot, and they were pulling him face down. Later, much later, this Sokolov man also found Botkin's dentures all caked with mud. Eggshells too. Sokolov found lots of eggshells, which turned out to be the very ones the good Sister Antonina and Novice Marina had brought. Hard cooked, the eggs meant for food for the Romanovs had instead nourished their killers.

As for the bodies . . .

Well, they were never found there. Later, once Yurovsky and his men had burned all the clothing and had tossed the *troopy* —the carcasses—into the mine, the guards hurled in hand grenades. But they couldn't seal it up. It was impossible, for the ground was too tough. And this terrible thing that was supposed to be so secret? Well, the Four Brothers Mine proved to be only the first grave of Tsar Nikolai, his family, and faithful. And it turned out to be their grave for less than thirty hours.

Da, da, da, and as those awful men dragged along faithful Dr. Botkin, I ran. I ran through the wood and straight to her, straight to Grand Duchess Maria Nikolaevna, whom I had left bleeding there in a wood and against a pine.

19

So I charged through the woods as fast as I could, knowing that anything could happen. I could be caught by the Reds and shot. A villager could see me and turn me in. Maria could be dead by the time I reached her. But I was determined to keep my promise. And I did. I returned to that spot in the pine wood where I had abandoned Grand Duchess Maria.

At first I wasn't sure if she was still alive. She sat just as I had left her, propped up against the tree, her eyes closed, her hands wrapped around her brother's. Rushing up to her, I dropped to my knees, reached out and gently touched her on the shoulder. Her eyes fluttered, then opened.

"Ah . . . my Leonka."

Almost immediately she drifted away again, tumbled back into shock. Sure, I knew she needed immediate medical help, but I also knew that I had to hide her better. So I picked her up. I picked her up in my arms and carried her as far as I could into the wood. When I could go no more, I found a tree that had been half-blown over. Its roots had been lifted up and there was a den of sorts beneath that. It was into this dark corner that I placed the Grand Duchess. As carefully as I could, I laid her down on the soft dirt floor. She moaned, but nothing more.

"I'll be right back," I whispered.

Wasting no time, I returned to the Heir, whom I also gathered in my arms. I carried him too. With my jacket over his head, I carried his lifeless body all the way to the hidden den, and there I likewise placed him.

Turning to the Grand Duchess, I touched her on the shoulder, and said, "I'm back. I brought your brother."

But there was no response of any kind. She'd lost so much blood that she was no longer conscious. And I understood she was dying. I didn't want to leave her again, but I had no choice. She needed medical attention. She was dying and needed care that I didn't know how to give. And so I hid Maria and Aleksei. I covered the opening of the den with branches, and departed once again.

I raced along, thinking I would go directly to Father Storozhev. But as I approached the city, I looked down and saw that my shirt and pants were smeared with blood. There was no way I could go into the center of Yekaterinburg looking like that; I'd be picked up by the Reds in an instant. So I had no choice. I went to my only other friends, the only others I could trust. I went all the way around the edge of town to the monastery, where I found the good Sister Antonina and Novice Marina, who had already tried that morning to bring foodstuffs to The House of Special Purpose. Instead of being able to deliver their goods, however, they were turned away and told never to return. Not ever. A few hours later the entire town was abuzz, everyone saying that something horrible had happened to the Tsar and all the rest of us.

Upon seeing me and my blood-stained clothes, Sister Antonina gasped and crossed herself, whereas Novice Marina, who'd assumed me dead, all but screamed.

"Leonka, my child!" cried the sister, crossing herself. "What's happened?"

I started to cry. Immediately the sister took me into a windowless chamber, and it was there that I explained the events of the night. I sobbed. Sure, with tears in my eyes I told them of the murders, of how I'd found Aleksei and Maria, of what I'd seen at the mine, and I begged for their help, begged for them to come at once.

"I don't know how much longer Maria can last!"

They wasted no time. Sister Antonina and Novice Marina flew into action. They gathered up bandages and other medical things, and I led them around the edge of town and into the wood. All the way there Sister Antonina kept chanting prayers, begging for God's mercy and crossing herself. It seemed to take forever, and I worried the whole way that we would be discovered, but finally we made it to the hidden den, whereupon we found the first light in the nightmare.

20

When I lifted aside the boughs I'd placed over the hidden den, the light of God cut through the day and struck her face. Immediately the girl's eyes opened and the slightest of smiles graced her face.

Upon seeing us Maria said, "What, brought others to see me, have you, Leonka?"

"Everything's going to be all right," calmly replied Sister Antonina.

At once the sister, so short and round, descended into the den, and with her merciful hands she started treating the wounded young woman. First she carefully examined the gash on the side of Maria's head, next she checked the bullet wound in her leg.

"You did very well, Leonka, very well, indeed," muttered Sister Antonina with approval, for somehow I had managed to stem the flow of blood.

She then turned to Aleksei, his head covered by my jacket. And it was just as I had told her, the poor boy was hopelessly dead. This she verified. The sister lifted up a corner of the jacket, gasped, made the sign of the cross, and covered him once again. There was no time to waste in grief, this the old sister clearly knew, and she beckoned her assistant into the den.

"Come, Marina."

The young novice descended, and thereupon the two of them set upon Grand Duchess Maria, cleaning her wounds, bandaging her arm and thigh, and comforting her with their few supplies. The two women of the cloth made an easy team, and their hands worked quickly and confidently. Much to my surprise, it was soon apparent that Sister Antonina knew about the corset of diamonds.

"Let's get this thing off you, *dorogaya moya*," my dear, said the nun, untying Maria's undergarment. "Lying on all those stones can't be comfortable."

Immediately Maria twisted to the side, and she protested, "But . . ."

"Don't worry, they'll be perfectly safe, just like the rest."

At first it didn't make sense. Sure, I knew that Maria, like her sisters, was covered in *brillianty*. But I didn't understand how Sister Antonina knew about them as well, not at least until the following day. Only then did I learn about everything else, all the jewelry that had been hidden away. The suitcases of Romanov jewels. While one had remained in Tobolsk, the second, weighing over a *pood*—some thirty-eight pounds—had already been brought to Yekaterinburg.

Without turning to me, Sister Antonina ordered, "Leonka, my young one, we're going to have to cut away the young woman's corset. Please turn away."

I wasn't in the little den. The space just wasn't that big. I was simply looking in through the roots. But rather than turn away, I covered up the little entrance. I laid branches back on the opening and left the sister and novice to attend to the Grand Duchess, which they did very well. They spent a long time cleaning and dressing her wounds and administering what medicaments they had brought. They fed her water too. And broth. And bread.

During this entire time I hid in the wood, but I did not sleep. *Nyet, nyet, nyet.* I watched. I hid in brush and watched for the Reds, who were sure to sweep the area, searching for the two missing young ones. But the Reds never did come. No. They furiously searched the road and the town, but they never ventured that far into the wood. And in an attempt to cover up his gross error—imagine, he'd lost two bodies!—Yurovsky conceived of the famed Yurovsky Note in which he claimed to have burned the two missing bodies. This, however, was yet another clean lie, for virtually no sign of any bodies was ever found, not even a single bone. It was a stupid lie too, for it is impossible to completely burn bodies over an open flame.

I finally settled against a birch, slumping against its peeling bark. Nearly an entire hour passed before Sister Antonina and Novice Marina emerged from the hidden den.

"How is she?" I asked, rushing up to them. "Will she live?"

"She rests comfortably now," replied Sister. "And with the grace of God, all will be well."

"Slava Bogu." Thank God.

"Now it is time to bury The Little One. Would you be so kind as to fetch him, Leonka?"

And that I did. I fetched the body of my friend and master, the Heir Tsarevich Aleksei Nikolaevich. His sister Maria had fallen into the deepest of sleeps, and so it was just the sister, novice, and I who blessed him and gave him back to the earth. I carried him out of the den and laid him on the ground. As the two women cleaned and comforted his horribly damaged body—Sister Antonina ripped away part of her own garments and wrapped him in it—I carved his grave in front of a clump of three white birches. But it was not a deep grave, merely adequate, a shallow wound, since all I had to dig with were several branches and my bare hands. Then as the sister chanted prayers and blessings, Novice Marina and I buried the boy, though we did not make a cross.

"Better that we not mark the spot," recommended Sister Antonina.

And she was right at that. We put the boy to rest there in the soil of his Holy Mother Russia, the very soil which he himself had been born to protect, then covered him and hid the grave beneath branches and leaves so that the Reds could never find him, never bother him again. And he lies there hidden in that wood, undisturbed today, of that I am quite sure.

Then Sister Antonina scurried off to check on Maria. Like a mole dressed in black, the sister crawled into the hiding spot beneath the tree roots. When she emerged a few minutes later, however, the concern was rippling across her face.

"She rests well, but her wounds weep oddly and I worry of infection," reported the old nun. "I must return to town for more medicaments. Marina, you are to stay by the girl's side. And, Leonka . . ."

"I will guard them both."

"Excellent." She turned to go, and over her shoulder called, "I will be back before the fall of night."

That was her promise, but sadly those were her last words to us. Neither Novice Marina nor I were ever to see her again, for someone informed on Sister Antonina. Some Red spy saw her creeping back into the town, saw her torn, dirtied habit, and knew something was up. And so Yurovksy sent his henchmen, those thugs from the Cheka, the political police of the Reds, to question her. They found fear in her eyes and blood on her garments, and they brought her in. Not a thing would she tell them, however, not even when they tortured her. They asked and pushed and cut on her, but she didn't say anything about the Heir or Grand Duchess, of course, or even the fortune of gems. Two days later, rather than waste a bullet on her, the Reds tied a heavy metal stove grating to her and dropped her to the bottom of the River Ityesk.

Yes, such terrible things that went on . . .

Ever hopeful, however, Novice Marina and I waited, watching and attending to the Grand Duchess's every need. Night came and passed. So arrived the next day. Still there was no Sister Antonina. We knew something was wrong, terribly wrong, and yet by sun fall we had even a worse problem: Grand Duchess Maria had developed a very sudden, very high fever. Within an hour's time she started to burn up.

"Get me some fresh, cool water, Leonka!" demanded Novice Marina. "Quickly!"

I rushed to a nearby stream and fetched nice, cold water, which we fed the Grand Duchess and used to cool her brow. But it was not enough. Her temperature kept rising. The very following day we were so worried that I snuck into town myself. I left Marina and the Tsar's daughter, and went off in search of the medicaments. Of course I was very careful, and in my own secret way I found the path to the Church of the Ascension. I wanted to speak to Father Storozhev, but he was off at the jail, trying in vain to win the freedom of Sister Antonina, who was then still alive. Not trusting anyone else, I left, having found nothing with which to heal the Grand Duchess. My thought was that I would return to the church the next day, and so I headed back to the wood, bringing with me only some cheese and bread. Our only hope, it seemed, was to keep Maria strong enough that she might live yet another twenty-four hours. Instead, her temperature kept rising and she ceased taking even water.

By the following morning her breathing had grown more difficult and she was lingering on the very edge of life itself. Both Marina and I understood the end was at hand. Kneeling beside the Grand Duchess, I clutched her hand. Novice Marina knelt next to me, chanting prayers and crossing herself repeatedly.

"Leonichka," Maria said, opening her eyes and using the softest diminutive of my name, "thank you for watching over me . . ."

"This is all my fault!" I confessed, my eyes flooding like the mightiest of Siberian rivers. "Your father entrusted me with a note, which I failed to deliver. I'm sure it fell into the hands of the Reds and—"

"Sh, my friend, there's no need for that . . ."

My tears came stronger than ever, and I bowed my head before the last of the Imperial Family. Did she not know, did she not see what role I had played in the end of her entire family? Had the shock of that night wiped clean her memory?

"You don't understand, Maria Nikolaevna!"

"I understand everything . . ."

"No, no you don't! I was supposed to deliver that note, I was supposed to rally the three hundred officers!"

"Yes, and this you tried to do with all your heart. The Lord God sent you to try to save us, and this you attempted. Father was most grateful for your help."

"No, Maria Nikolaevna! No, you don't understand!" I pleaded, bowing my head over and over to her. "I failed! You do not understand!"

"I understand that you blame yourself for events beyond your control."

"Please forgive me!"

"There is nothing to forgive."

"But . . . !"

I clutched Maria's hand as tightly as I could. As she faded away, I tried to tether her to this world. But she did not want to be kept here.

Maria's eyes then closed and slowly opened, and she said, "Three hundred years ago my family made this country strong and stable . . . but we should have left long ago. Better I should die. Better we should fade away."

"No!" pleaded Novice Marina, breaking her chanting. "Do not leave us, Your Highness!"

Yet perhaps she was correct. Perhaps Maria was wise in her words, for she clearly understood that the time of the Romanovs was finished. Besides, who knew what would have happened had the last daughter of the last Tsar survived? I don't think she could have rallied the troops, for she was too young. Rather, I think she would have rallied only confusion and despair. Meanwhile, every Bolshevik on earth would have hunted her and any future offspring down.

The Grand Duchess faded into delirium, and just when I thought we'd lost her, she rallied her strength. Beckoning the novice and me closer, Maria Nikolaevna commanded us with what would be the greatest tasks of our lives.

"Marina," began the Grand Duchess, her voice so very faint, "you perhaps know where our riches are hidden here in town?"

"*Da-s, Vashe Velichestvo.*" Yes, Your Highness, replied the young woman. "I am aware of what we have guarded at our monastery."

"Then this you must do—you and Leonka must gather it all.

Every bit that is here in Yekaterinburg and, if you can, that which is still in Tobolsk. You must then bury it all away again. You must keep it someplace safe. And once this terror has left our land and once my family has had a proper Orthodox burial, then I beg you to return all of these treasures to the people of my country. It is to be a gift from my family to our people. Understood?"

"*Da-s,*" both the novice and I replied.

And so it was that Grand Duchess Maria Nikolaevna, third daughter of Nikolai and Aleksandra, married the Novice Marina and me in both duty and fate. Which is to say that we both escaped that time and place with one entire suitcase of Romanov jewels, which we have ever since guarded so carefully. You see, as we fled through the Siberian woods to Shanghai and eventually America, I, Leonka, became Misha, whereas Marina became May, and jointly, in time, we became husband and wife.

But that fateful morning, Maria Nikolaevna lasted only moments longer. She who was born in a golden palace expired shortly thereafter on a pile of leaves, there in that filthy den of tree roots. I myself was clutching her hand when she opened her eyes for the last time. Our eyes met and held and I understood she was leaving.

"*Nyet!*" I cried, falling upon her.

This was how I caught her last breath. She exhaled . . . I breathed in . . . and she was gone. That peacefully. That easily. And so ended the family of the last Tsar, the humble Tsar Nikolai II, and his devoted consort, Tsaritsa Aleksandra.

Ah-min.

21

"But, Katya, *moya dorogaya vnoochka*..." Kate, my dear granddaughter, continued Misha, seated at his office desk and clutching the microphone in both hands, "that's not quite the end, for the Romanovs have now been buried a total of three times. In other words, Rossiya still does not know what to do with her last Tsar and where to place him in her ugly history. Yes, such devilish things have been done to the bodies of the Tsar and his family."

Misha sighed, caught his breath, and gazed at his wall of books on the Romanovs. He was almost done, almost to the end, determined to make his granddaughter understand the complexities of the revolution and the fall of the Tsar. And he was doing just that, wasn't he?

"Well, the very day after they were dumped down that mine, the Tsar and his family were brought back to the surface of the world again. Yes, it's true, we learned all this not only from the Yurovsky Note of 1920, but also from those guards, who were later thoroughly interrogated by the Whites. And that next day the Romanovs were indeed resurrected. Because so many townspeople knew what had happened and where the bodies of Nikolai, Aleksandra, and the others were buried, the Komendant Yurovsky recognized the necessity of transferring the corpses to another location. On top of that, Yurovsky's idiots, those Reds, had made such a mess of the area at the Four Brothers Mine that even a blind man could have found the bodies! So Yurovsky and his men returned to the mine and fished out the Romanovs. One of the *Bolsheviki* was lowered to the bottom of the pitshaft, where he stood in freezing water up to his waist. He started with Tatyana, tying a rope around her young, naked body. Giving a signal, the young princess was then hoisted up. And so it went, one by one. And because the bodies had been in this chilled, fresh water, they were all pink and fresh looking, like naked babies, their cheeks nice and rosy. They were all pulled out, of course, except the tiny dog, Jimmy, who was found only months later, nearly perfectly preserved.

"*Oi,* it was such a farce! What idiots those Reds were! They tossed the murdered ones in the back of a truck and headed off, intending to bury them in a deeper mine near the Siberian Highway. Along the way, however, the motor lorry kept sinking in the mud because, of course, it had rained so much. Finally it went in up to its axles, becoming hopelessly mired. The Reds jumped out of the truck, scratched their stupid heads for a few minutes, and then pushed and pushed to no avail. Eventually Yurovsky decided they needed to lighten the load, and so they pulled off the bodies, tossing the Tsar and his family on the side of the road like a pile of logs. Again they pushed and pushed, this time freeing the vehicle. By then it was dawn of yet another day, and Yurovsky and his idiots were so exhausted, do you know what they did? They threw the Romanovs and their retinue in the shallow muddy hole left by the truck! True, it's true, Katya! Yurovsky thought himself so smart, pleased that they were killing two hares with one shot. And so they tossed them in the shallow hole, Romanov and servant piled this way and that, and then they doused them with sulfuric acid to make them unrecognizable. Finally, they covered them with mud and clay, threw some railroad ties over this grave, and ran the motor lorry back and forth to pack everything down. Can you imagine? And it worked. It worked for almost seventy-five years! Investigator Sokolov searched the entire area and even had his picture taken standing atop those very railroad ties—but never thought to look beneath them!"

Caught up in his anger, Misha fell silent. He could go on for hours. So many stories. So many horrors. But enough. He was so tired . . . so very, very tired.

"But here, *dorogaya,* I must draw to a close." He took a deep breath, gathered all his energy just to hold himself together. "And so this is my story, the one I've never been able to tell. I apologize. I apologize for my lies, but we were so afraid, your grandmother and I. You must understand that she was but a simple novice, so sweet, so pretty, and I was but a plain kitchen boy. And these things we could not tell you because we were ever afraid of the *Bolsheviki,* ever afraid that they would not only come after us, but later, after both you and your father. This was a real danger too because the Reds were doing this, they were going after Russians everywhere, even killing one of their own, that *kommunist* Trotsky, in Mexico. This is exactly why the Tsar's sisters fled so far as well—Ksenia to England and Olga eventually to Canada, where of course she died above that tiny barber shop.

"But I apologize both for me and your Baba Maya. Because of our fears we presented ourselves to you as a lie. Yes, my beloved wife was none other than the young, innocent Novice Marina.

"Well, my dear, I shall end now. I've instructed my lawyer not to give you this tape, nor the key and combination to my vault, until I have died. Which means that by the time these words reach your ears I will have left this earth to join your grandmother. Be confident, my sweet one, in our love for you. Be strong in our faith in your abilities. There is nothing more precious in the world than you, our lovely granddaughter—not even the Romanov gems that you will soon see. Since the early death of your father, my son, seventeen years ago, you have burned like a bright star in our lives, your grandmother's and mine. Our sincerest thanks for restoring in part our belief in the goodness of the world.

"Oh, but I hesitate to say good-bye . . ." Suddenly he felt hot tears flood his eyes, and he crudely blotted at them. "There are so many more stories. So much more to tell." His voice began to quiver. "But enough . . . enough . . . *ya tebya ochen lubloo*. I love you very much."

Realizing that he could no longer control himself, the old man quickly flicked off the tape recorder. He mopped his eyes, then slumped forward, resting his forehead in the heels of his worn hands. It had been harder than he thought, but he'd done it, gotten through it all. Yes, he'd given his granddaughter a thousand truths.

He wanted to sit there, basking in his memories, both horrific and wonderful. But now was no time to linger. He was so close, so very close, and he had so little left to do.

Pushing himself on, Misha popped the cassette out of the small black machine. He picked up his gold pen, gathered his thoughts and energy, and on the tape itself, wrote, "For Our Katya." He then slipped the tape into the envelope he'd already addressed to his granddaughter, sealed it, and placed the packet in the center of his desk. Sure, he thought. Everything was in order. He'd gone through all his papers, all his files. He wanted to leave behind as clean a trail as possible. There was no sense in making this difficult for Kate, no sense making it more complicated than it already was or would be.

Misha rolled back his chair, braced himself, and then pushed himself to his feet. He sensed himself teetering and leaned over, placing both hands on his desk. So old, he thought. So much time had passed, so many things had happened. Sometimes he felt like he could live another century, other times, like now, he felt as if he had but minutes left.

As he carefully moved to his built-in bookcase, a jolt of pain bit his left knee, his bad one, and he stood still. Then proceeded. Reaching into his pocket, he pulled out a key, one that he always carried on his person. He next reached up to the wall of books, where he pushed aside two volumes and revealed a brass lock. When Misha inserted his key and turned it, a well-oiled and well-balanced three-foot section of the entire bookcase, stretching from floor to ceiling, began to swing out. He pulled it fully open, revealing yet another door, a metal one, with a brass handle and a dial lock. He'd had this hidden vault installed sixty years ago when May and he had bought this house. Now he spun the dial to four numbers—1-8-9-4, the year of the Tsar's ascension to the throne—and immediately there was a gentle, pneumatic sound and the door moved slightly. Misha pulled on the handle, swinging forward the thick, heavy door. The first thing he did was hit a light-switch, revealing a walk-in safe some six feet deep and five feet wide. The only other person in the family to know of its existence was, of course, May, and together they had come in here three or four times a year, not simply to check on things, but to marvel at the treasures and bathe in bittersweet memories.

Misha had never worried about being robbed. If the house had been broken into, the thieves would have gotten only the inconsequential stuff—the silver flatware, the tea set, some of May's day to day jewels—but not this, the secret heart of his life's work. At first glance the contents of the vault seemed pathetic, for on the left hung a rack of old clothes, a raincoat, suit, and pants for him, a dress, hat, and a coat for Maya. On the right stood a rack of shelves filled from floor to ceiling with boxes, some small, some large. Beneath them, resting on the floor were three bankers' boxes that contained sundry documents.

In the beginning, May and he had sold hardly any of it, no more than a small bag or two of insignificant diamonds. They'd used that money not only to escape Russia, but to launch their lives in America. Later on, of course, Misha had sold more of the loose gems, none of them of historical value, using the cash to buy sundry Fabergé items that the cash-poor Soviets—not to mention the defrocked Russian princes—were selling all across Europe.

Oh, yes, thought Misha, reaching for a box on the fourth shelf. He quite liked this one, and he pulled the cardboard box halfway out, opened the lid, and revealed a gray jewelers' bag inside. Flipping that open, he gazed upon a Fabergé box some twelve inches long and four inches deep that was covered with lapis and diamonds. Before it was hidden away here it had sat for several decades on Tsar Nikolai's desk. Fabergé had been a master of combining styles from different periods, turning objets d'art into functional things of beauty, what he termed *objets de fantaisie*.

Oh, and this one, thought Misha as he closed up that box and reached for another. This one was May's favorite. Lifting another jewelers' bag into his hands, he felt something heavy and egg-shaped, which he slid into his palm. It was a large gold egg encrusted with a multitude of double-headed eagles—the emblem of Imperial Russia—that were fashioned out of platinum and hundreds of diamonds. And like all of the fifty-six eggs Fabergé had created for the Imperial Family, this one too contained a surprise: Misha tipped back the top of the egg and a diamond encrusted Orthodox cross popped up. It made him laugh, just like it always did. Created as an Easter present to mark Aleksandra's conversion to Russian Orthodoxy, the egg had the year 1896 drawn in rubies on the back.

Upward of twelve Fabergé eggs had vanished during the flames of the revolution, and yet Misha and May had secretly managed to obtain seven of those. And all seven of them were in here. Reaching for the box to his right, Misha opened it, revealing another egg, this one in green enamel atop a solid gold pedestal. Flowers fashioned from gold and platinum, rubies, sapphires and, of course, diamonds, covered the egg. When Misha tipped back its lid he found a gold perfume bottle inside, its cupola top encrusted with a frosting of tiny diamonds. He gently laid it down, then quickly opened the lids of the next two boxes. Opening the inner boxes of each, Misha reached in and felt the shapes of two more eggs swathed in jewelers' bags. Without even opening them, he turned his attention to the smaller box on the next shelf down. Opening the cotton bag inside, Misha slipped a diamond some two inches in diameter into his palm. He slid the diamond back in its bag and surveyed the wall of shelves. Five shelves, to be exact, all lined with similar boxes, some sixty or seventy. It was all here, the contents of the entire suitcase he and May had carried out of Russia, all of the gems carefully catalogued and packed. Many, he knew, dated back to the time of Peter the Great. One piece of jewelry, an emerald the size of a silver dollar that was in turn surrounded by a halo of 20-carat diamonds, had been a gift to Ivan the Terrible.

Incomparable treasures, all of them. Collecting and guarding them had occupied nearly his entire life, and now that he had succeeded in his duties he felt, surprisingly, a sense of pride. He had pledged to bury these things away not only until the fall of communism, but until his Nikolai and Aleksandra received a proper Orthodox burial. And now that these both had happened—what miracles!—he could rest with a degree of peace. His beloved Kate would have to oversee the final step, returning all of this to Russia, and he had every confidence that she would execute the transfer in a timely manner.

This room held the climax of his story and his life, thought Misha. Everything he recorded on that tape was to prepare his granddaughter for this room and its priceless contents. How much was all this worth, three, four, five hundred million dollars? A billion? Certainly somewhere in that range. And that was his reason for telling Kate his version of the final days of the Tsar—simply so that she could and would understand the meaning, the purpose, and the true value of all these jewels in this room. Misha was laying at Kate's feet not unfathomable wealth, but overwhelming, mind-boggling responsibility, and he had to make sure she understood every ramification.

As much as he wanted to go through every box and admire every gem, there just wasn't time. It had taken years for May and him to catalog it all, examining and weighing every stone, describing every *objet,* and then recording it all in a jewel book. May even insisted on drawing a facsimile of every piece, which she carefully did, and that log was there, right over there on the shelf. *Oi,* so many memories, mused Misha as he closed the boxes one after the other.

He even started laughing.

Turning, he looked at the rack of old clothes and chuckled aloud. May and he had been so very afraid, not just in the twenties and thirties, but especially right after World War II and into the fifties. Accordingly, they had taken every precaution, and Misha reached for his raincoat, finding it oddly heavy. Squishing the material between his fingertips, he sensed a band of small, hard objects running all the way around the neck. Stones. And not mere stones, but diamonds. Similarly, May's dress over there held an entire panel of secret *brillianty* and the hem a great circle of them. Scattered through these clothes were some ten pounds of gems, hidden away like this in case May and he had suddenly needed to flee. In a separate codicil to his will he'd left note of this too, so Kate wouldn't simply throw these clothes in a bag and drop them at the Goodwill.

But enough of this. He had to be going, his end was imminent. There were but two things Misha wanted from this room, and he reached for a bankers' box on the floor and pushed aside its cardboard lid. Inside, carefully wrapped in cotton towels, he found a small red tin box, a bit rusty at the edges, its cover embossed with the imperial double-headed eagle and lettering that read TOVARISCHESTVO A. I. ABRIKOSOVA V MOSKVYE—The Goods of the A. I. Abrikosova Company, Moscow. Opening the old candy box, Misha gazed down upon its contents—some bits of wire, a tiny chain, two small rocks, a flattened coin, and some rusty nails—and his eyes blistered with tears. It had been terribly stupid of him back then, but he hadn't been able to flee Yekaterinburg without these things, so priceless were they to him. Odd, mused Misha, how all of that seemed just like yesterday. He so clearly remembered sneaking late one night into The House of Special Purpose—then deserted by the Reds—and snatching this bric-a-brac, the treasures of a little boy, from its hiding place behind the mopboard.

He closed up the old candy box, bent slowly over, and reached for something else. This time his gnarled fingers wrapped around a dark brown glass vial, small and corked tightly, and he carefully held it and the tin box as he closed up the vault. What a job, what a task, he mused as he glanced about the room one last time. Now there was just one more thing he had to do: commit a fantastically great sin, the greatest of all.

Moving with determination, Misha flicked off the single light and swung shut the vault door and secured it tight. He then stepped into his office and pushed the bookcase back in place. Once it was locked, once he'd positioned the books so that they covered the lock, he slipped the brass key back in his trousers.

If only he could whisk through time and return to that night. If only he could reverse the flow of time and make the right choices, the right decisions, then perhaps he could change the outcome of it all. Like a mad river, however, time rushed in only one direction, and there was no turning back to the dark events of July 16–17, 1918, just as there was no turning back his decision now. No, thought Misha. He knew what he had to do, what must be done. He'd felt so guilty, so awful ever since that heinous night, but eighty years of suffering were not enough. He was not ready yet for forgiveness, for holy deliverance. He must sin again so that he would suffer not just in this life, but in the life hereafter and forevermore.

Misha, feeling every creak in his weary body, sat back down at his desk. He placed the old red candy box before him, opened it once again and admired the bits of bent and rusty things. Picking out a flattened coin, he was instantly transported—*"Just look at what Papa's locomotive did to this kopek!"*—and instantly saw that bed, that room. But it was like torture, this memory of his. He could remember it all, see it all like a movie, but he couldn't return and participate in the actual events.

He had so long ago decided just what must be done and how, and for so many years had been so determined, that his actions now were nearly automatic. The time had finally come. May had died. And he'd fulfilled a pledge he'd made long ago in a Siberian wood. *Da, da, da,* he'd accomplished everything that he possibly could, including, of course, telling a thousand truths just so he could get away with one singular, gross lie. Sure, that was exactly what the audiotape was: one enormous lie. From now and hopefully forevermore his Kate would believe that he, Misha, had been none other than the young Leonid Sednyov, when in fact nothing could have been further from the truth. Of course he'd been there, but not as the little kitchen boy. It was May herself who'd come up with the idea of supplanting one lie with another, of crafting a story so close to the truth that no one would ever doubt that it was in fact the truth. And Misha had told the tale perfectly, doled it out so convincingly that neither his granddaughter nor the world would ever know what really happened on that awful, awful night. Now there was nothing left for him here in this life except, perhaps, forgiveness, which is the last thing he desired or felt he deserved.

With that, Misha uncorked the small vial of cyanide. He swirled it a bit, then poured its contents into his glass of water, and saw the life and death therein whirl into eternity, his own.

"Please, Father," he muttered in near silent prayer, "do not forgive my sins."

Not wasting another second, Misha lifted the glass to his lips and drank it down in two bitter gulps. Almost instantly he was blinded by an atomic-like flash of blazing red light and his weary body slumped forward onto his desk.

EPILOGUE

Saint Petersburg, Russia
Summer 2001

As she sat in the Winter Garden of the Astoria Hotel, Kate Semyonov barely noticed the extravagant lunch of caviar and blini, smoked sturgeon and champagne laid before her. Likewise, she barely paid attention to the conversation of the three other people at the table even though they spoke exclusively in English.

Suddenly she realized they were all looking at her, waiting for a reply of some sort. Kate blotted her mouth with her napkin, tried to think of something to say, and then simply confessed.

"I'm sorry, I think I'm a little jet-lagged," she said with her trademark broad smile, which happened to be her best defense. "What did you say?"

Dr. Kostrovsky, the director general of the Hermitage Museum, replied, "We just wanted to go over your schedule for the next few days."

"Oh. Sure, of course."

Her mind was anywhere but here in this spacious, elegant dining room with its glass ceiling, marble floor, and arcing palms. Rather, all she was thinking was how she could possibly escape. She looked from Dr. Kostrovsky, a heavy man with gray hair and a goatee, to his deputy director, an elegant blond woman by the name of Dr. Vera Tarlova, to Mark Betts, the head curator from the Art Institute of Chicago. No, thought Kate, I can't do this right now. There's something much more important that can wait no longer. I've come all this way, and I've got to take care of it now.

Mark, a tall, trim, balding man who'd accompanied Kate from Chicago, said, "Doctor Kostrovsky was just saying that tomorrow morning we'll have a private tour of the exhibition, followed by a luncheon with the city mayor, and then—"

"You know what, Mark? I have a splitting headache right now," lied Kate. "I don't know if it's because of the long trip over or because all this is just a little bit overwhelming—you know, being here in Russia—but I think I need to go lie down for a while."

"If that's what you want, of course."

Kate turned to the two Russians. "I'm sorry Doctor Kostrovsky and Doctor Tarlova, but would you excuse me?"

"Absolutely. But are you in need of a physician?"

"Just a little rest, that's all. I'll leave all the planning to Mark. Anything that's okay with him is perfect for me."

"Then we'll see you tonight for the performance at the Mariinsky?"

Oh, shit, thought Kate, how she wished she could get out of that one. There was no way, however, she could opt out, for not only had they reserved the tsar's box for her, not only had they called in their best performers to dance *Swan Lake,* but the entire performance was in her honor. Yes, she was being feted as a hero for precisely following her grandparents' last will and testament. Changed in the 1980s upon the death of their only son, Kate's father, Mikhail and May Semyonov did not simply name Kate as their sole heir, but also instructed her to return the fortune of Romanov gems to the Russian people, designating Saint Petersburg over Moscow for the site of their permanent exhibition.

In light of the recent death of our cherished son, we hereby bequeath to our beloved granddaughter, Katherine Semyonov, our home in Lake Forest and all its contents except those items manufactured in Russia by the jeweler Carl Fabergé. All of the Fabergé pieces and sundry gems in our home vault, we bequeath to the Russian people; these items are to be held for safekeeping at the Hermitage Museum, the Winter Palace, St. Petersburg, Russia. This transfer shall take place only when and if both of the following two criteria are met: 1) the Communist government of Russia is no more, 2) the family of Tsar Nikolai and Tsaritsa Aleksandra have been given a proper Orthodox burial. These items are to be considered as an inviolate gift from the last royal family to its people and are for display and collection purposes only; they are not to be sold at any time. Until these requirements are fully met these items will be on temporary loan to the Art Institute of Chicago.

As for our financial resources, including all stocks, savings accounts, bonds of any sort, etc . . ."

"I can't wait," said Kate, her smile as broad as ever.

A few more pleasantries passed amongst them, and then Kate escaped, passing from the elegant dining room into the gilded marble lobby of the hotel itself. The past three years had been nothing but a whirlwind, beginning with the death of her grandparents and the revelation of the Romanov fortune stashed in Misha's office. There'd been so much publicity—*Dateline, Larry King Live,* and others—followed by the exhibit The Secret Jewels of Nicholas & Alexandra at the Art Institute of Chicago. And now this, the opening of the permanent exhibit of the gems in a hall specially renovated in the Winter Palace.

As she neared the front entrance, she was tempted to bolt right then and there. It was, however, the sight outside of the limousine and bodyguard assigned to her that stopped her dead cold. If she went out there, they'd not only insist on driving and accompanying her, but they'd also make a full report to her host, Dr. Kostrovsky. And she couldn't risk that. She'd have to sneak out a side door. But first she had to change, get out of her navy linen dress and fine leather heels.

Entering the small elevator near the front desk, she rode the lift to the fifth floor, the top. Her room was the best in the hotel, arranged by Dr. Kostrovsky himself, and consisted of a suite with an entry hall, living room, spacious bedroom, and an enormous bathroom, all of it filled with antiques, all of it overlooking Cathedral Square. Before the revolution this chamber had been used by various princes and counts; later Hitler himself had planned to stay in this very corner suite after his victory over Russia, which had never materialized.

Kate was a beautiful woman of thirty-five, five foot eight inches tall, and noticeably thin. She wasted no time changing from her fine clothes into her typical garb of well-worn jeans, brown leather clogs, and a beige cotton twinset. She had rich, thick brown hair, brown eyes, and a nose that she could and did scrunch up at a moment's notice. Her upper lip was straight, even flat, just like her grandfather's, and she grabbed a tissue and blotted off most of her lipstick. Wearing only a simple pair of sterling hoop earrings, her gold wedding band, and the gold bracelet always worn by her grandmother, she headed out, convinced that she looked less like an heiress and philanthropist—she'd inherited well over $100 million—and more like a student. Well, she granted as she slung her black purse over her shoulder, maybe a graduate student.

Rather than return to the main lobby and risk running into Mark and the others, not to mention the bodyguard, Kate wove through a series of corridors. She passed into the adjoining Hotel d'Angleterre, and a few minutes later emerged onto a side street that jutted off from the enormous St. Isaac's Cathedral. Flagging down one of the small, pale-green taxis took but moments.

"*Vam kooda?*" Where to? said the burly, baby-faced driver.

"Vot zdes addres." Here's the address, replied Kate, handing him a slip of paper.

He glanced in the rearview mirror. *"Vyi otkooda?"* Where are you from?

"Ya Amerikanka." I'm American.

For the next ten minutes Kate carried on a reasonable conversation in Russian, which she'd learned not only from her grandparents but in a series of college courses. And while she spoke little more than excellent kitchen Russian, her accent was nearly perfect, or so said the driver two or three times.

Bouncing around in the small taxi, Kate was driven down Nevsky Prospekt, the city's main avenue. The sky was clear and blue, the sun bright through its rays soft in the northern sky, and Kate kept her eyes on the apple green Winter Palace and ensuing Hermitage as they drove around the front of the extensive, regal complex. Passing neighboring palace after palace—once the glittering homes of the richest of the grand dukes but now housing such centers as The House of Scientists—the driver turned left across the Troitsky Bridge. As they reached the other side of the Neva River, Kate's eyes focused on the Peter and Paul Fortress, where Nicholas and Alexandra had been reburied nearly three years earlier. Dear God, she thought. I have to go there. I have to visit and pray and light a candle. Or was there already an official ceremony planned? Yes, if she remembered correctly the patriarch of the Orthodox Church was coming from Moscow to lead a service to commemorate the wondrous deeds of Kate's grandparents.

The driver swerved over some tram tracks, around a park, past the city's only mosque and its pair of towering minarets, then crossed Kamennoostrovsky Boulevard and turned into the dumpy courtyard of a building. Puddles and broken bricks littered the space, two children played on a pile of dirt.

"Priyekhali?" We've arrived? asked Kate.

"Da," replied the driver, pointing to the door.

Kate paid in dollars, which the driver was only too glad to accept, and climbed out. This was the real reason she'd come to Russia, not the opening of the exhibit, not all the grand celebrations, but this, perhaps her very last chance to peel away the final layer of the many truths and mistruths fed to her.

The half-rotted door to the crumbling apartment building flapped open, though it was obviously meant to be bolted. Kate pushed it back, proceeding into a dingy lobby of sorts that was lit by a single, naked bulb. A row of heavy wooden mailboxes hung on one side, and she checked. Yes, the name was there. Dear God, thought Kate, she'd been so scared, so frightened that she might be too late.

Kate swatted a mosquito from her neck—she'd read somewhere that they bred year-round in the water-logged basements of these two-hundred-year-old buildings—and headed up the worn stone steps, which were low and easy. The cast-iron railing was half-broken away, the window at the top punched with a hole, and she mounted the second flight and came to the first door. Once again Kate looked at the address, and then pressed a buzzer, which rang so loudly she could hear it inside. As if in reply Kate heard a television inside being turned down. When there was no further sound, Kate pressed the buzzer again, and a moment later heard shuffling feet. A few moments passed before the inner door was opened with obvious difficulty. The outer door, however, remain solidly locked.

Finally a frail woman's voice inside, said, *"Kto tam?"* Who's there?

Kate was about to reply in Russian, but stopped herself. If it were really her, she would understand English.

"A friend from America."

For the longest time there was nothing, no reply, virtually no sound of movement from within. Kate, finally sure that this was all a folly, was about to call out in Russian, when finally she heard a heavy bolt unlatched. The thick, padded door swung open, revealing a hunched-over woman, her gray hair skewing this way and that. Her eyes, foggy with age, studied Kate for a long, suspicious moment. Finally the old woman's eyes bloomed with tears and she reached out and grasped Kate's hand with every bit of her pitiful strength.

Oh, dear God, thought Kate, her eyes likewise filling with tears, it's her, it's really her. "Perhaps you don't realize who I am, but—"

In hesitant but excellent English, the old woman said, "I know who you are, dear Katya. Of course I do, and not just from what they write of you in these newspaper stories, either. *Da, nyet.*" Of course not. "No, you should not have come . . . but I prayed with all my heart that we would somehow meet, which of course, was so very selfish of me." She shook her head in disbelief. "Yes, it's really you, and yet . . . yet how did you even think to come looking for me."

With a trembling hand, Kate reached into her purse and pulled out a cassette tape. "My grandfather left this for me."

"I see . . . Now come in, my child. Come in quickly. We have much to discuss and you can't be seen standing out here."

The old woman, frightened by the ghosts of Stalin and the like, all but yanked Kate inside. As the woman bolted shut the door, Kate stepped into a tiny, windowless living room, no more than six feet by eight. One door led to a minute kitchen with a table and stools on one side, a bathtub on the other, while another door led to a slender bedroom with a single bed and the apartment's only window.

Suddenly the old woman was before Kate, taking Kate's hand, then touching Kate on the shoulder, the cheek, the forehead, all the time muttering in Russian.

"Gospodi, eto 'vo ne mozhet byit . . ." Dear Lord, it can't be . . .

And then she was crossing herself, bowing her head, and kissing not only Kate's hand, but the cuff and next the sleeve of her sweater. When the diminutive woman started to drop to her knees, Kate took her by her thin shoulders and pulled her back to her feet.

"No," begged Kate. "Please don't."

"It's a miracle!"

Kate glanced to the side, saw an old black-and-white TV, the volume turned down but the picture still flashing. On the old couch Kate saw two magazines, which not only featured pictures of the soon-to-open exhibit of Romanov gems, but Kate's own photograph as well.

"So it's really you?" asked Kate.

"Yes." And touching Kate's wrist and finding the gold bracelet with the jade pendant, the old woman gasped. "Your grandmother gave this to you?"

"I received it upon her death three years ago."

"Peace at last." She crossed herself. "How did you find me?"

Kate shrugged. "After my grandfather died, I cleaned his office. I went through everything, and I was just about to empty his trash can when I found an article speculating what really happened the night the Romanovs were killed. There were several different theories, but one thing in particular struck me—it talked about some survivors from a nearby monastery."

"Ah, I see . . ."

"I saved the article, and then when my grandfather's story started to fall apart, I looked it up again. I called *Esquire,* the magazine that had originally published the article, and tried to track down the woman who had written it. But I couldn't find her—she'd left the magazine years earlier—and so I started doing some research on the Internet."

"The what?"

"I used my computer."

"Wh . . . what . . . ?" She gazed at Kate with confusion. "You have to forgive me, I so seldomly speak English."

"I started doing some research using my computer, but I couldn't find mention of any monks who might have survived until even as recently as the sixties. In fact, the only thing I could find about a monastery in Yekaterinburg was this."

From her purse Kate pulled a short article, the headline of which read, "Ancient Yekaterinburg Resident Attends Romanov Funeral."

The old woman took it and shook her head. "My eyes are no good anymore. What's it say?"

"When the Tsar and his family were reburied here in Saint Petersburg, a British man wrote about it for a London paper. He also did a short side piece about a milkmaid who claimed to have worked at a

Yekaterinburg monastery when the Romanovs were under house arrest. He wrote how she attended the Orthodox burial of the Imperial Family here in town."

"I should never have gone. I . . . I . . . was just going to watch the procession from afar. It was right across the park, just here at the fortress. And when I saw it all, I fell to my knees and started to crying. They were ordering me away, but in my weakness I begged. One of the fathers took pity on me and allowed me to attend."

"So it's true, then?"

The old woman nodded. "This man, this British writer—he was there, writing about the funeral, and then he followed me back here to my apartment."

"I know. I looked him up. He's the one who gave me your address."

"I knew I shouldn't have talked to him!"

"You didn't tell him that your father was British, did you?" pressed Kate.

"No, of course not. I only told him part of the truth." She hesitated before confessing, "I . . . I told him I worked as a simple milkmaid at the *monastir*."

Finally understanding how it all fit together, Kate said, "At first I didn't quite get it. The story on the Internet said your name was Marina, and I knew right away that it was just too much of a coincidence. I kept reading and rereading the article, and then I realized I didn't understand because he didn't understand, this man who wrote the article. He thought you worked for some monks at a monastery, but you didn't, did you?"

"No, of course not. I worked for the sisters at the other monastery."

"Or as we would call it in English, the convent. And you didn't simply work there, but you studied there, correct?"

"*Da, da, da.* I was a lay sister."

"So you're not the milkmaid Marina from the men's monastery, but the Novice Marina from the Novotikhvinsky convent, or as you would say in Russian, the Novotikhvinsky woman's monastery."

"Yes, my child." The old woman took Kate by the hand, leading her into the tiny kitchen. "Here, come sit."

By the simplicity of Marina's words, Kate knew she was telling the truth. And as she sat down on a small stool, Kate sensed there were but only one or two more truths in this nesting doll of deception. She was, at last, that close. Yes, thought Kate, this old woman now putting on a kettle of water for tea, now shuffling for two chipped teacups, was most certainly the daughter of an Englishman and Russian woman.

In her bones, in her soul, Kate knew the truth, but her mind, so weary of deception, threw out a test. "Who did your father work for?"

"Papa? He was a diplomat. He was posted out there in Yekaterinburg at the consulate."

"Under whose tutelage were you at the monastery?"

"Sister Antonina."

"What did you do first thing in the morning? What were your primary responsibilities?"

"My responsibilities?" She pulled a small sugar bowl from the shelf. "Oh, I see. You test me, do you not?"

Kate said nothing, just sat there.

"Well, sometimes they had me assist in gathering the eggs, but yes, this is truth—I always, always milked the cows because, of course, my hands were then young and nimble."

So it was all just as Kate thought. And now that she had the truth, or the most of it, she started to cry not out of grief, but fear. Meanwhile Marina went about making tea, as any good Russian did upon the arrival of a guest. She even put out a plate of three meager biscuits.

Finally sitting down opposite Kate, Marina asked, "Who else knows? Have you told anyone?"

"No, not even my husband."

"Excellent. And you mustn't, my child. For your own safety you mustn't ever. Have you any children?"

Kate nodded. "Twins, a boy and a girl. They just turned two."

"How wonderful," beamed Marina. "But you must protect them, do you understand? Your grandparents put snakes between you and the truth to protect you, and now you must do exactly the same for your young ones. Am I clear?"

"Absolutely."

"I read in the magazines about you. I read that your father died in a car accident, and I wondered if you knew. How much did your grandfather tell you?"

"Not everything, of course. As I said, he told me some stories—or rather he recorded on tape what he said was the truth. And at the time I believed it all. Then something happened, which in turn caused me to doubt him, and not much later I began to look for you." Kate looked up, looked right into Marina's foggy eyes, and said, "You see, my son is a bleeder."

"Gospodi." Dear Lord, gasped Marina, yet again crossing herself.

Overwhelmed with the responsibility of taking care of her aged grandparents, explained Kate, she'd put off starting a family of her own.

"I've only been married five years."

It was odd, she continued, how she shied away from kids until the deaths of her grandparents. After that, she wanted a family right away, and a mere year later she'd given birth to her Andrew and Melissa. The twins at first appeared beautiful and healthy, but then Andrew bumped his head, which resulted in a horrendous bruise.

"When he was diagnosed, I grew suspicious of everything that my grandfather had told me."

"But what about him, the boy child?"

"He's okay. It's still a serious condition, of course, but there are treatments now for hemophilia. There's even talk of a cure using genetic engineerng. So there's no immediate critical problem, not really."

But the discovery of her boy's affliction led Kate to do her own research. It was just too much of a coincidence. And her initial studies led her away from her mother.

"I was told that Dad died on his way back from the club when his car swerved off the road and hit a tree. I always assumed he was drunk. At least there were those hints. And he probably was. But when I found his death certificate it stated that he died of a brain hemorrhage due to a lack of clotting, so it's obvious now that he was a mild bleeder, that he swerved off the road, struck a tree, hit his head on the steering wheel, and died before help arrived."

Marina, her eyes wide, sat crossing herself.

"That's when I really knew," continued Kate. "Hemophilia is caused by a defect on a single X chromosome, which is why women are almost always only carriers and not sufferers, since we have two X chromosomes and therefore a double copy of the clotting factors. The healthy one can make up for the other. So my son inherited a defect on his X chromosome from me, because as the daughter of a hemophiliac I'm an obligate carrier. And my father inherited it from his . . ." Kate stopped. "I can't even say it out loud. It's too frightening."

"And you mustn't ever, my child. This is a brilliant truth that must be buried away like a terrible evil."

"When I first started researching all this, you know, I thought it meant that my grandfather was him, their son. But that's impossible, because genetically hemophilia couldn't follow that path, right?"

She stared in surprise at Kate. "Your grandfather was most definitely no Romanov, I can assure you that."

"But if you're the real Novice Marina, not my grandmother, and my grandfather was Leonka, then—"

"Ach . . . the newspapers claim your grandfather said such things. Did he really?"

"Of course he did. On the tape he told me all about how Sister Antonina and you carried the rescue notes, hidden in the cork of a milk bottle, into the house, and that he, the kitchen boy, delivered them to—" Terrified by the look on Marina's face, Kate suddenly stopped. "Wait a minute, don't tell me that's a lie too? You and the nun did sneak the notes into The House of Special Purpose, didn't you?"

"Why . . . why, no."

"But . . . but then who did? There really were rescue notes, and they still exist, I've seen copies of them. So if you didn't smuggle them in, who did?"

Marina hesitated before saying in the quietest of voices, "Why, your grandfather of course."

"What? But that's not what Misha said. He told me someone else snuck the notes into the house and that he found them in the corks of the . . . the milk bottles. He said that was his job. As the kitchen boy, it was his duty to . . . to . . ." A horrible thought struck Kate. "Oh, my God, my grandfather was their kitchen boy, wasn't he?"

"Heavens no, not at all," mumbled Marina, shaking her head. "There was a young kitchen boy, this Leonka, but I have no idea what happened to him. He was removed from the house just hours before the execution, but after that he vanished into the oblivion of the revolution."

Suddenly Kate felt ill. She had thought she finally held the truth, the complete truth, of her family. But, no, her grandfather's deception was as deep as it was insidious. And yet if Misha wasn't Leonka, the Tsar's kitchen boy, then who the hell was he?

"Wait a minute . . ." began Kate, desperate to piece it all together. "My Grandfather Misha was there, I know he was. I mean, he had to have been. How else would he have known all those things, all those details?"

"Oh, yes, my child, he was most definitely there . . ." said Marina with a sad sigh.

"Tell me."

"Ach, there are some stones better left unturned, certain wolves better left unprovoked."

"You don't understand—I have to know." Kate, seeing a chink of weakness in the old woman's eyes, pressed on. "For me to keep my silence, I have to know the all of it. I have to know the truth of both my grandmother and my grandfather, otherwise I'll keep searching. If you don't tell me, then I'll keep asking around. I'll ask all sorts of people and reveal things I shouldn't, but I'll keep hunting until I have it, the absolute truth."

"Oh, my child . . ." she muttered, now gazing at the floor, staring at nothing. "Please, I beg you, please . . . if your grandfather didn't tell you, then don't ask me."

"I mean it, I won't give up."

"I worry that the truth will be poison to your soul."

"Tell me!"

"So be it . . ." quietly said Marina, reaching out with a gnarled, bony hand and touching Kate on the arm. "However, please do not harshly judge your grandfather, for he repented. Agreed?"

Kate blurted an expedient, "Agreed."

"Well, then . . ." The old woman hesitated one last time, finally spitting it out like bitter medicine. "Your grandfather was one of them, one of the guards. He was barely a man back then, and his name was Volodya." She nodded. "I can still picture him, still see him quite clearly—young, cute Volodya with the blond hair."

Dear God, thought Kate, her stomach clenching horribly. Her grandfather was that devilishly clever to have so twisted the story? To make her see him as he was not? And yet . . . yet in an instant she understood it could be no other way. Yes, Kate was surprisingly sure of it. Her dear grandfather had been one of them, one of the Reds. The next moment everything came flooding in, finally making such perfect sense, and Kate saw it all in her mind's eye, not just the truth, but an image of her grandfather back then, back there . . .

Afraid of what she was asking but unable to stop herself, she said, "A beard . . . did he have a beard?"

"Why, yes."

"A blond beard?"

"Exactly," reluctantly confirmed Marina. "He had blond hair and a thin blond beard and was the youngest of them all, a lad of barely twenty, if that. Maybe only eighteen or nineteen, I don't know. Everyone lied about everything back then—particularly boys whose fathers had died in war—but this Volodya was one of the original interior guards. And the Tsar and Tsaritsa so trusted his innocent face—why, from time to time your grandfather even entertained the Heir, even played chess with him—which was why the *Bolsheviki* used him."

"What do you mean, used him?"

"The rescue letters—they were all fakes. In an attempt to trick the Romanovs into an escape attempt, the *Bolsheviki* wrote the notes themselves. They then used your grandfather to smuggle the notes in and out of The House of Special Purpose."

"Oh, God." Remembering what her grandfather had revealed in his tape recording, Kate said, "And that night . . . the night the Romanovs were murdered . . . he . . ."

"Exactly," continued Marina. "One of the executioners, a Hungarian, backed out, saying he couldn't shoot women and children. This was just an hour or two before the Romanovs were led to the cellar, and Volodya, drunk on ideology and desperate to prove himself not only a true man but a real revolutionary, volunteered. At first they said no, he was too young, but soon Yurovsky relented, for there was no one else at so late an hour. They just needed someone to pull a trigger." The old woman shook her head. "Before this, Volodya had never killed . . . and I know in my heart of hearts that he repented every day since."

No, he suffered, thought Kate. Every day of every week since then, he suffered. And as if some horrible bandage had been yanked away, there it was, now exposed, the festering wound in her grandfather's soul, the very one he had never permitted to heal. With all her being, Kate didn't want to believe this—her grandfather capable of murder?—yet at the same time she couldn't help but know in her heart of hearts that it was in fact the truth. It just made too much unbelievable sense. Kate's mind whooshed through it all, but unlike Tsaritsa Aleksandra, who had always found hope in the face of such undeniably dark logic, Kate saw it plainly before her. Here at last was the source, at last she had found it: the Artesian well of her grandfather's self-hatred.

"Who was he assigned to kill?" asked Kate, her voice trembling.

"Why, Grand Duchess Maria, of course. His orders were to aim for the heart so as to make the kill quick and clean. When it all began, however, he panicked. He panicked but he did as ordered: he aimed and fired through the foul smoke at the young princess. But there was so much chaos. Truth be told, only God knows whose bullet struck whom in that mayhem. In any case, when your young grandfather wiped the smoke from his eyes, he saw Maria lying on the floor, completely still, completely dead."

"Dear God . . ."

So he was there. So he'd killed. And so, thought Kate, recalling her grandfather's thick gold watch, he'd looted.

"What happened?" pressed Kate, still unable to make sense of it all. "How did . . ."

"Just listen . . ." continued Marina. "About an hour later the truck loaded with the bodies set off with three men seated up front—a driver, a guard, and Yurovsky himself. Since there was no more room in the cab, Volodya—that is, your Dyedushka Misha—was ordered to the back, where he stood guard over the dead ones as the vehicle slowly made its way out of town on the road to the village of Koptyaki and the Four Brothers Mine. Later he told me that if he'd had a bullet he would have killed himself right then and there. Regardless, it was only when the truck passed the racetrack on the edge of town that they encountered the first of many problems. All month there had been heavy rain, and when one of the wheels sank into a muddy hole, the truck became stuck for the first time that night, and Volodya jumped off the back, he jumped onto the ground."

And looking at the wheel he immediately saw the problem, and shouted to his tovarishi *in the cab up front, "It's not so bad, comrades. Let me give a push!"*

The driver, Lyukhanov, put the lorry in reverse, rolled it back a bit, then jabbed it into first gear. Volodya leaned into the rear bumper and pushed with all his strength. In one great heave the vehicle rolled up and out and raced ahead. A few short moments later, however, the left rear tire struck a rock and the entire lorry bounced up. The force of the jolt in turn caused something to be thrown off the back and onto the dirt road. He couldn't believe his eyes—one of the bodies! Terrified, he froze. Finally Volodya rushed to it, discovering the Heir Tsarevich Aleksei Nikolaevich.

He was dead, half his head blown away. Volodya looked up and was about to call out to his comrades when suddenly another body fell to the ground. Hurrying to that one, he discovered that it was the body of Grand Duchess Maria Nikolaevna, the very one he'd been assigned to kill! Then as if she were a ghost come back to haunt him, she suddenly moved, rolling her head to the side and looking up at him.

"Help . . ." she gasped. "Please help me!"

From the truck Lyukhanov leaned his head half out the window, and called, "You okay back there, Volodya? You still with us?"

He stared at the young woman bleeding so horribly on the ground. He'd held the fate of her life in his aim once before . . . and here he held it once again.

"The Lord Almighty had seen to a miracle," gushed Marina. "He was giving Volodya a second chance. A mere hour or so earlier he'd been this young woman's murderer . . . and suddenly he had the chance to redeem himself—he could be her savior!"

Kate looked up. "You mean—"

"In the split of a second, actually . . ."

. . . actually without even thinking, he looked after the lorry, which was slowly motoring away, and called, "I'm still with you . . . just keep going!"

He made his decision just like that, just that quickly.

"I've got to hide you away!" he whispered to Maria.

She nodded but couldn't get up, for she was so badly wounded and had lost far too much blood. And so he dragged her off into the wood, leaning her against a pine. He brought her brother too, lying him nearby.

"If I don't go with them," Volodya said, "they'll come back for us both. Just wait here and stay calm—I'll be back as soon as I can."

And knowing that he had no other choice, he left her.

"Yes," said Marina, "that's exactly how it happened. So as to keep the truck from turning around and discovering what had happened, your grandfather ran through the night and rejoined his comrades—

his *tovarischi*. He jumped on the back of the truck and stayed with them all the way to the Four Brothers Mine too. When Yurovsky finally discovered that two of the bodies were missing, it was this Volodya who quickly volunteered to take a horse and ride back to town to see what had happened. Instead the guard Volodya Subottin disappeared for all of time."

"He rode directly to the Grand Duchess Maria and her brother?" Kate half-begged.

"Absolutely. He went straight to them. And once he had moved them to a better place of safety—in a hole beneath the roots of a fallen tree—he secretly made his way back into town, where he fetched Sister Antonina and me."

The story that Misha had told her, realized Kate, had been so very close to the truth. In many ways it had been the truth, just deviously shaded and twisted here and there so as to deceive in the most subtle but ultimately profound ways.

"So the two of you went back and treated Maria, right?" asked Kate. "You cleaned and bandaged her wounds. But did Sister Antonina later return to town?"

"Yes," confirmed May. "She went back for more medicine, for more bandages so that we could keep the girl's wounds clean."

"And there she ran into horrible trouble?"

"Horrible, horrible trouble. Unfortunately the Reds caught her, questioned and tortured her, and—"

"Drowned her?"

"Exactly." Marina took a deep breath. "Furthermore, the Grand Duchess soon came down with a horrid fever. Her wounds had become infected and there was nothing we could do. Volodya and I were with her the entire time. Actually, Volodya rarely left her side except to fetch fresh water or scurry off in search of food. There was not much we could do for her, not really, just make sure that she was comfortable. We needed to get her to a hospital, we needed to feed her medicaments, but all we could do was pray for a miracle, and the two of us knelt by her side."

"You can't leave us," begged Volodya with tears in his eyes. "You can't!"

Hour by hour Maria's breathing had been getting more and more difficult. Hour by hour her temperature had been rising. For nearly thirty hours she'd taken nothing but water and a little bit of broth Volodya had managed to get from the closest peasant hut. By the fourth day she was lingering on the very edge of life itself.

"Volodichka," Maria said, using the softest diminutive of his name, "thank you for helping me . . . for watching over me."

"I'm evil!" he confessed. "I'm horribly evil!"

And with that he fell down upon his knees, bowing his head before the last of the Imperial Family. Did she not know, did she not see what role this Volodya had played not only in her end, but in that of her entire family? Had the shock of that night wiped her memory clean?

"You don't understand, Maria Nikolaevna!" cried Volodya.

"I understand everything . . ."

"No . . . no, you don't . . . Those notes I smuggled to your family were forgeries, nothing more than an attempt to bait your father!"

"In the end this too he understood."

"With my help they were planning all along to kill him."

"Father forgave you at the time . . . and I forgive you now."

Convinced that she remembered nothing of what had happened down in that murderous cellar, he steeled himself. She had to know everything. She had to know it was he who deserved to die a thousand miserable deaths.

He blurted, "But I was down there as well—I was down in that room of death!"

"Yes, I saw you."

"I was the one assigned to kill you!"

"Perhaps, but instead the Lord God sent you to save me . . . and this you have tried with all your heart."

"No, Maria Nikolaevna! No, your Highness!" he pleaded before her, bowing his head over and over to her. "You do not understand!"

"I understand that your sin has been followed by immense suffering, and I can see with my eyes that you have repented for your sins, that you *have repented with all your soul. Likewise can I foresee that your being will be all the purer for this, which in turn will deliver you yet closer unto God."*

"No, that's impossible! Impossible!"

"I'm sure my grandfather wanted her to hate him," said Kate. "I'm sure Misha wanted her to curse him to hell. And I wonder if this was why he did it, why he killed himself—to condemn his soul for all eternity."

"Bozhe moi." My God, gasped Marina, quickly crossing herself. "He took his own life? This I did not know."

She nodded, reluctantly added, "He killed himself a few weeks after my grandmother died. I think he was determined not to be forgiven."

"But he was. She forgave him way back then. I was there. I was right next to him praying the entire time. Yes, and he knelt by her side as she faded away. He clutched at her hand. He tried to tether her to this world. But she did not want to be kept here. Maria forgave your grandfather with all of her heart, and then she—"

"But . . ."

"Just wait, my child," said Marina. "You see, their eyes met, Maria's and Volodya's, and held. He understood she was dying, and he fell upon her sobbing and begging, giving every bit of his energy to her. He inhaled her last breath . . . and then gave it back to her. You see, it was only through his strength and the power of our prayers to the Almighty Father that Volodya kept Maria tethered to this world."

"You mean, of course, that . . ."

"Yes, certainly. He saved her. Maria passed through a horrible fever, which by some miracle did not kill her. And together your grandfather and I nursed Grand Duchess Maria back to a reasonable health, at least so that we could move her. I think they hid in the woods maybe another month, even after the Whites had overtaken Yekaterinburg, and it was during this time that your grandfather, full of remorse and sentiment, snuck back into the house one night, where he retrieved a few things he'd once caught Aleksei hiding away. Before they fled the motherland, we of course turned over the suitcase of gems, and the last I saw of them was their youthful figures dashing through the woods, this young couple, Grand Duchess Maria and—"

"My grandfather, the man who was both my grandmother's executioner and her savior."

"Exactly."

So there it was: the final truth that a young princess entrusted her life to a young man who had tried to take it, and that very same young man pledged his life to the beautiful princess who had steered him from the path of evil. No wonder they had been so dedicated to one another.

"More tea, my child?"

Kate looked up at the old, shrunken face, and saw a smile that was as sweet as a spoon of honey yet as wrinkled as a dried apple. Yes, Kate herself had inherited the defective gene from her father, who'd gotten it from his own mother, May, who had in turn been passed it from her own mother, none other than . . .

No, thought Kate, you can't ever go there. Just don't. The time and place for that family is no more. You have a husband and children at home who need you, who need your protection.

"Sure, I'll have a bit," said Kate, clutching the gold bracelet on her wrist, the bracelet given to her grandmother at a time when she was young and her life so in danger.

Author's Note

While this is a work of fiction, the indented passages, secret notes, and letters attributed to the Romanovs, their captors, and Rasputin are all accurate and can be found in various archives. Taking creative license, I've made changes to only one of the documents, Empress Aleksandra's long letter, which appears midway through the book. That letter, written to Anna Vyrubova, is actually a compilation of two different letters that Aleksandra wrote and secretly smuggled out of their captivity. To see some of these documents, historical photos, and a complete bibliography, please visit www.thekitchenboy.com.